i

Dedicated as always to my two heroes, Bob and Aaron.

Liquid Velvet

Louise Furley

Liquid Velvet

Louise Furley
Copyright 2022
All Rights Reserved

ISBN: 979-8-9859963-0-2 (Paperback)
ISBN: 978-1-7378341-9-9 (eBook)

Cover art by: *Pixel Mischief Design*
Photo: *Courtesy of Shutterstock*

ALSO BY LOUISE FURLEY

Liquid Velvet

viii

Chapter One

$\mathcal{A}$nyalia Marvaux scuttled across the lawn from the main house to her grandfather's cottage. The small building was tucked way in the back yard and canopied by a shroud of maple trees.

Scant illumination in the clouded twilight shines from the windows of the two homes. Bereft of their leaves, gnarly branches reach out like black skeletons beckoning with twigged fingers to come deeper into the darkness.

Thick blades of cool dewy grass tickle her bare feet as she quickly shuffles through the soft lawn. On the cusp of spring, the air is crisp, she should have thrown on shoes and a jacket but she was in too much of a hurry to escape her parents' haranguing.

Knocking lightly before entering, Anya closed the door behind her, never seeing the dark figures skulking stealthily from tree to tree in the shadows.

Warmer inside, chemical smells mingling with the slight woody scent of the old bungalow coiled comfortably around her. The familiar aroma lessened some of the tension that pinched the back of her neck and tightened her mouth from her stepmother's continuous disapproval.

Her feet moved silently over the ancient rug, so threadbare it was like fine gossamer on her tender soles. Hurrying through the living room of mismatched, worn and lumpy furniture, she called out, "Granddad? Where are you?"

Just a few lamps were lit, leaving only dim halos of light to guide her way. Hearing a responsive grunt, she kept going, leaving the tiny living room to head to Märtin Dauphine's laboratory.

Hesitating on the wood planked threshold, Anya watched her grandfather alternate from writing notes, to toiling over copious beakers filled with a variety of liquids spread out on a metal table. Several vessels containing only vaporous gasses lined in neat rows alongside them.

The rustic cottage and the simple glass vials looked incongruous with the top-of-the-line machines anchoring the walls. Whirring sounds blending with dissonant beeps made an anomalous but familiar music to Anya's ears.

The sight of the man with short, messy grey hair, of average height, weight, and average everything else, brought an affectionate smile to Anya's tense face.

Glasses hovering on the end of his substantial but not overlarge nose, dressed in all brown with a white lab coat overlay, even with a spine of steel, Märtin Dauphine was so average he would blend into a crowd, easily becoming invisible.

"Ah, *mon chère, petite fille*, my dear granddaughter." Not looking up, he said with a slight chuckle, "I can hear your burdened sigh all the way over here."

Anya tilted her head with a soft smile. Light yellow curls woven with fine filaments of brilliant flames bounced around her shoulders and down her back. Expressing another heavy sigh, she trod over to get a better view of what he was working on.

After a few moments of silence, Märtin set down his pen and paper, rolled a stool to the table and sat down on it.

"What is it, *petite fille*?" He shoved the glasses to the top of his head causing the grey hair to spike haphazardly, and regarded Anya with the pure affection of a grandfather for his beloved granddaughter.

Pushing over a stool to the opposite side of the table, Anya plopped down with another beleaguered sigh. "Oh Granddad, stepmother and papa cornered me earlier, ganging up on me with the same, sorry old lecture." Her tiny yet full lips turned down.

Märtin crossed his arms. One grey brow arched, he asked, "They still want you to go make up with Raoul?" His aged voice held a tsk of annoyance.

She nodded, fiery blonde curls sprung over the front of her blouse. Anya crossed her legs and looked down with chagrin at

2

the damp hems of her jeans. Great. Her stepmother, Maisa, would know she had been here.

"Yes," she sighed, then her soft features hardened. "They don't know what happened, *Grand-père*, I never told them. I just said we broke up and of course they blamed me. Said I was too young at seventeen to know what I wanted. Huh," she snorted, "at least I know what I don't want."

"It's been what, over two years now since you refused his calls, although he still perseveres. I would think your parents would give it up, especially considering your father's chronic absent-mindedness. But-" he said abruptly as Anya made a face.

"I know, it is undoubtedly Maisa's tenacious stringency that keeps that tact open. It has always been clear that she is perversely jealous of you. She thinks you steal her light, and wants you married off and stuffed fat with a baby."

His voice went from slight exasperation to gruff. "You never told me what happened with Raoul either." One eye squinted in accusation at her.

Nodding, Anya didn't meet his gaze. "No, and I'm not going to. I know if you knew what he did to me-" she broke off at the lowering of his grey brows. "Never mind. I never told you because I knew you would have gone after him-" she broke off again at the darkening of the older man's face.

"Anyway," she exhaled hard, "as usual, Maisa wants me to quit my new job at the museum on weekends, and stop my studies at university, and I've only just gotten started. She thinks the museum is too lofty and pretentious, and school is a waste of money even though I'm on scholarship. And, as you said, Maisa says I should be married, barefoot and pregnant and chained to Raoul's kitchen sink."

She didn't dare tell him she believes Raoul even paid Maisa big money to talk Anya, *push* her, into marrying him.

Märtin's lip curled up at her account of things, then his eyes lowered to her feet. He said with a fond grin, "Ah, you have the bare feet part down pat."

3

Scraping a few fingers over his grey evening bristles, Märtin shrugged. "As I said, I don't know what happened between you and Raoul, but, you are a young woman, don't you want a husband and children, a family of your own?"

Anya set her elbows on the table and dropped her chin on her fists. "No. I want nothing to do with the male species. Except of course you, *mon grand-père*, my granddad. My experiences so far have not been positive."

At the inverting of his brows, her mouth twisted before she explained.

"When I was 12, as you know, we left the isolation of the sheltered consulate in Mingronue, such a tiny country no one ever even heard of, to come here to Washington. Maisa and Papa thought we should join civilization in Shrivesport.

"The first moment I was alone, Mr. Fridely, our neighbor, pounced on me, and if Mrs. Johansson from down the street hadn't chased him with a broom, well, I don't know what would have happened." If not for the content, the picture would have been comical.

Grooves around Märtin's mouth and eyes deepened in anger, his lips thinned. Rolling his hands into tight fists, he said, "Then your parents moved to this rural area in Wildhaven where I've lived for years. I wasn't present at Shrivesport, or I would have seen that Mr. Fridely never inappropriately touched another woman again."

The corner of Anya's lip ticked up with a slight grin. "Yes, and that is why I won't tell you about Raoul. Anyway, being home-schooled by an elderly tutor kept me away from other kids my own age, ensuring I was even more secluded and naïve so that day at church when Giles Smart asked me to go get ice cream with him, I was so excited. Then," she paused, one shoulder rose and fell in despondence.

"He attacked me too. And, yet again with Raoul. So, you see, I want nothing to do with men. Ever. They don't look at me as a person, just a thing to- to appease their...uh, animal needs. I am but a body to them, they care not about my mind or my personality." She sniffed with her tiny nose tilted up.

His grey head nodding, he replied, "I know, my Anyalia, you have this, ah, how do I describe it, ethereal, exotic beauty you inherited from my daughter, your dear sweet mother, that men lose their minds around you. And, it's not likely to end.

"It was dreadfully unfortunate your poor mama died when you were only two, you never got to meet her. You keep up with your French in her honor." He shook his head, then smiled away the bemusement from his memories of his beloved daughter.

"You need to find a man you can tame, like your *grand-mère*, your grandmother, my precious Emmaline did to me. I was on the edge of drowning in delinquency when she molded me with her soft, sweet, gentleness." His hazel eyes blanked as his mind reverted to a world from a long time ago.

"Uh huh." Anya picked at a button on her shirt. "But you, Granddad, are one in a million. There are no other men out there with your honor, integrity, bravery. I mean, you chased that bear away that day at Montagne de Céüse, in the Alps, remember?" Her lips bowed up in an affectionate smile.

The far-away look tunneled from Märtin's eyes, leaving a fissure of emptiness, a dull aching, a longing that nothing would ever fill again.

"Papa is a good man, don't get me wrong," Anya said. "But he's so vague and absentminded. If it weren't for his pension and Maisa's iron-handed overseeing, his bills would never get paid."

"Anyway," her sigh gloomy she went on, "it's kind of you always trying to build up my confidence. But, Maisa and papa have always told me how homely I am."

She mimicked her stepmother's cool unpleasant voice, "It's unfortunate, *Ahn-yah-lee-ya*, that you are too plain and dull. Much too thin, too small and delicate to be of any use other than as a wife and mother."

Anya held a dainty hand up to hold off her grandfather's angry retort. "No, don't say anything, I have a mirror, I know what she says is true. But Granddad, it doesn't bother me, truly. All I desire is to work with you on your subcontracting projects with the military, and do my bio-chemistry studies.

"I've only had a couple of semesters and already I can see that due to your mentoring I am light-years ahead of the other students. Besides," she smiled, "you are the only family I need."

Leaning back on her stool, she said, "Can I stay with you a while right now? I can help, and you can tell me about you and grandmother."

Märtin regarded his granddaughter sadly. Maisa had always been jealous of her extraordinarily beautiful stepdaughter and thus had treated her coldly, and often, cruelly, disparaging Anya's looks and intelligence at every opportunity.

Maisa has kept her secluded in this rural countryside because she goes crazy with jealousy whenever any men young or old, pay attention to Anya.

If she could have drowned her like a kitten and gotten away with it when Maisa had maneuvered Eduard into marrying her, she absolutely would have. Now, Maisa's hope was for Anya to become swollen with Raoul Lombardo's child and then maybe the men would not eye her like she was a precious jewel they desired to own.

A sardonic snort groused from Märtin. Even heavy with a baby, Anya would still always be dazzling, like his wife. Even while pregnant, Emmaline had shone like a diaphanous gem.

And Eduard, Anya's papa, being a weak and often confused man, did as his wife told him, mostly just parroting the things she said.

So, when Maisa drilled it into Anya's head that her looks lacked, when in fact she had a luminous beauty that drew men like mindless fish to an exquisite hook, Eduard babbled the nonsense right along with her.

Märtin smiled, fond and proud of his intelligent, sweet granddaughter. "Of course you can stay with me. Come, I will show you where I was at when you came in." He tipped his glasses back down on his nose.

While they worked, Märtin told her stories of his deceased wife. "Ah, one day we were invited to a grand party at the Fondateur Hotel and Ballroom. We ate, danced, drank, then slipped away for some, you know," he winked, "private time. So we snuck out the back of the dining room through a servant's door and scurried down a hall to the end." His lips curved in mischief at the widening of Anya's already large eyes.

"The Fondateur is listed on a historic registry and the family resides there as well. The familial portion of the estate is forbidden to outsiders, but," he grinned with a conspiratorial wink, "we did sneak in." He chuckled at her surprised look.

"Darling granddaughter, I wasn't always just a grey-haired staid old scientist, I did once have a wild side. A few times I managed to corral your sweet grandmother into a not quite lawful adventure."

"Grandad!" Anya's outburst was half appalled, half enthused.

"Anyway," Märtin went on, "there were these ornate glass, double doors with flamboyant peacocks engraved in them, we opened them and found ourselves in the most opulent, magnificent room I've ever been in.

"Cathedral ceilings with stained-glass windows from floor to ceiling. All white luxurious furniture and rugs, drapes of satiny gold, immense stone fireplace. Everything, paintings, mirrors, were all gilded in gold. But, there was one thing that I'll never forget."

Getting up to go around the table to stand beside him, brilliant green eyes huge with wonder, she asked, "What? What was that, Granddad?"

"Ah, honey, it was a huge painting of Romeo and Juliet on Roman velvet. All deep reds, burgundies and forest greens. The look of love on the couple's faces was extraordinary, they veritably beamed at each other. Your grandmother and I kissed under the painting, and then, uh," he cleared his throat.

"Well, never you mind missy what happened next. Anyway, I was just there last week for that conference and it brought all

7

those memories of that night with Emmaline flooding back. I miss her so…" he stuck a finger under a lens and dabbed at an eye.

"It was a remarkable night for us, and I want you to remember the story, keep Emmaline and me alive in your heart even after I'm gone."

He took a breath, mouth firmed, lids levered over his serious hazel eyes, he said oddly, "And in your brain. Okay?"

Anya moved closer to her grandfather and gave him a huge hug. "Of course, Granddad." She rebuked him, "Now, no more of this morbid talk of you…leaving. Can we keep working?"

Märtin rolled a thin arm around her slim shoulders and hugged her close. "Yes, yes, we can continue. Just never forget the stories I tell you. Especially that one."

They worked quietly for an hour then Anya could hear her stepmother calling for her.

Reluctantly setting down a glass cylinder on the table, she peeled off her plastic gloves, removed the protective goggles and sighed. "I have to go, Granddad."

"Of course. I will see you at lunch tomorrow, eh? We'll review the notes for the next steps."

Anya smiled wanly, kissing his proffered cheek. "Yeah, okay. Night, Granddad." Leaving the cottage, she locked and closed the door behind her.

Anya came looking for her grandad the next day when he didn't show for lunch. When she reached the cottage, Anya froze and then screamed, and screamed, and screamed.

His front door was broken in, and there was blood on the stoop.

Chapter Two

Between them, the two strapping males dragged the bloody, moaning man to a chair and pushed him down on it. They tied his wrists to the chair arms and his ankles to the chair legs.

Barely able to draw a breath from the beating the two had given him, the man begged with gasping wheezes, "Please, please, no more, please."

Déisi Zukov wiped the blood on his hands on his black jeans and shoved his raven's hair out of his eyes, pushing it back off his forehead. Hooded lids concealed most of the eyes as black and dead as burnt coals.

He said to the man in heavily accented English, "Rankin, you know the only thing we want to hear out of you is where the funds are that you stole from Anton de Vos." Like a snake's sudden strike, Déisi lashed his hand out and gripped Rankin's neck, squeezing his windpipe with fingers as thick and strong as iron pegs.

Rankin's eyes bulged, veins in his sallow skin enflamed and enlarged. Déisi clinched his throat so tightly he couldn't even gag.

"Bro, dude," Kaloyan said calmly without moving. "He can't tell us anything with that death grip you have on his throat. Actually," crossing his arms over a harshly muscular chest, he perused their prisoner, "I'm surprised he can speak at all after you knocked out most of his teeth."

10

Ignoring his brother, Déisi's fingers dug deeper into Rankin's throat. The man's skin lost all color and his eyes started rolling as he was losing consciousness.

Déisi abruptly released him. Rankin's head flung forward as he choked and hacked, chest heaving. Blood from his wounds streamed down and off his face, spilling and mixing with buckets of sweat that splattered into pink puddles on the floor.

Sucking in a beleaguered painful breath, Rankin whined hoarsely, "All right, all right, I'll tell you, then you'll let me live?"

Kalo shrugged one shoulder. "*Da*, sure, I'll let you live. Tell us."

Rankin stared up at the brothers with their strange accents, identical brawny chests and shoulders bulky with muscles, biceps bulging, and the sheer lack of compassion in either of their eyes. Kalo's dark blues, or Déisi's fathomless black tunnels.

"Okay," he exhaled, then spat out blood and a tooth, the tooth clicked across the floor. "It's stashed in my cabin. I got a cabin near Loon Lake."

He let out a heavy aggrieved breath. "In the rafters. 1212 Terrace Lane." Rankin peered up at the brothers with hope through stringy sweaty hair. He knew better than to lie, he would only suffer worse beatings.

"*Bună*, good," his voice deep and dark, Déisi suddenly lunged and sliced across Rankin's upper arm with a knife. Not even blinking at the man's shriek, Déisi dragged the blade across Rankin's jeans cleaning the blood off it.

Rankin cried, "Wha- wha- you said you'd let me live!"

"Huh," Kalo snorted. "*I* said *I* wouldn't kill you, I didn't say anything about my brother here. When you took what was Mr. de Vos' you knew what the repercussions would be. We might have let you live with maybe a broken back and mutilated limbs, a punctured kidney, but, alas," Kalo glanced at his stone-faced brother.

"There was that little matter of when you stole the funds, you set fire to the manager's house to eliminate him as a witness. He didn't live there alone; you knew he had a wife and three kids under the age of five. According to the neighbors, their screams could be heard for quite some time. They say it was a pitch black night except for the blazing flames that lit up the sky around the house.

"Unfortunately, the fire was so intense the responders couldn't get to the family and were forced to just stand there until there was nothing but burning embers, and eventual silence."

Kalo sighed with a wan smile. "You see, your actions brought undue attention to Mr. de Vos."

"Uh, but- but, I- I-" Rankin whimpered, watching the blood ooze out of his arm making a wide scarlet trail from his bicep to his forearm. "Someone's pissed about a little collateral damage? Shit-" Choking on the blood that slid down his throat, he coughed, expelling even more of the viscous red fluid.

Déisi slammed his fist into the side of Rankin's head. More blood sprayed the wall as his head snapped to the right.

Rolling his eyes at his brother, Kalo said to Rankin as his head bobbed and his eyes wobbled, "*Yah.*" Kalo nodded. "So we decided to make sure you suffer like those people did, as well as a few others you tortured before slaughtering."

He smiled brightly at the injured thug. "And you are! See, all's well that ends well, right, Déisi?" He nudged his brother who didn't move, or lower his blank gaze lanced straight at Rankin.

"Who- who the hell are you fucking foreign bastards anyway?" Rankin cried, his eyes glued to his lifeblood seeping away.

Smiling amicably, Kalo told him, "We are Kalo and Déisi Zukov. We're from a tiny obscure country you've never heard of near Romania. *Mi bréthaïdne*, ah, I mean my brother here is actually the one Anton de Vos hires, I'm just additional muscle for this mission.

"Déisi is Mr. de Vos' jαύdraç. In America he would be like, oh, I guess he'd be like an enforcer. Mr. de Vos has business internationally, from China to Russia, Algeria to Ireland, Brazil to the States. And boy, I'll tell ya, that means a lot of enforcing is needed. You'd be surprised how many people welch on deals, rob Mr. de Vos, attempt take-overs, deliberately deflate his stock.

Déisi remained a silent rock.

"*Yah*," Kalo nodded, dark blond hair flopping with his movements, "you'd be surprised at how many shysters there are out there."

Grinning amiably at Rankin, he said, "*Na* offense, dude." He snapped his fingers. "Oh, did I mention what they call my brother?"

When Rankin made no response, Kalo cheerfully told him, "They call him, *a čelu vlad.* I'm sure you've heard of him. In English it means Death Comes."

Already ashen, Rankin's face paled until not a drop of color touched his skin. He looked from one man to the other, at Déisi's black pits of emptiness then back to Kalo with his plea. "Listen, please-"

"Ah, sorry, my friend. So," Kalo smiled jauntily. "I'm off to get the money. If tis not there I will call *mi bréthaïdne* and I'm sure you can imagine what he will do to you. Because, for now, he's only going to sit and watch you bleed out."

Before Rankin could speak, Kalo turned to Déisi. "All right, bro, I'm outta here. After I return the money I'll be joining our other brothers in Katmandu."

Aware his brother repelled most physical contact, Kalo nonetheless gave him a fist bump to the arm. "I'll call you when I get the bucks."

"*Bună*," Déisi grunted with a brief nod. He grabbed a chair and dropped it in front of Rankin, and sat down.

"Mister, wait-" Rankin's rasped shout was barely audible at Kalo as he saluted them and left the room.

Rankin's terrified, bloodshot eyes shifted slowly to Déisi. "Uh," he swallowed hard, "you gonna just sit there and stare at me?"

Another short nod, face like sculpted iron, hooded lids so low only a glitter of dark light shone under black lashes, Déisi scratched at the dark scruff on his hard jaw and crossed his arms over the big chest.

Settling back in the chair, the dim light from the window a pale stripe across his sharp, angular cheekbones, he muttered, "*Da*. Until you bleed out. Then I dispose of your body."

Chapter Three

The blast of frigid air smacking red into her cheeks reminded Anya that she had forgotten her jacket.

The bitter wind cut right through her thin, ivory blouse ruffling the collar along with her long hair, and the pale blue jeans weren't much more protection from the cold.

"Darn it all, it's been so long since I've been at work, and I need the money so badly." Turning back to her car to grab her jacket, she mumbled weakly, "I hope there are donuts or something, I had to flee so quickly I couldn't get anything into my stomach."

With her head down as she rifled around inside her purse looking for her keys, she didn't see the black bus pulling up on the side street.

A cold hard hand suddenly clamped over her mouth, and an iron band of muscle roped around her arms, pinning them to her body and lifted her off her feet.

She was too surprised to scream even if the huge hand wasn't covering half her face. A door to the bus stood open and Anya was only able to give a few futile kicks of her legs before she was rustled into the car.

As soon as she, and the monster that held her cleared the door, a man reached over, closed the door and the bus took off.

The man crushing her to his body carried her to the right side of the vehicle. He removed his hand from her mouth and set her on her butt on the bench seat then dropped down beside her.

Gulping rapid shallow breaths, Anya shoved her long curls out of her face and opened her mouth to scream or protest or question, but her eyes widened into shocked green plates, her lips stayed parted but no words came out.

The extra-wide bus was set up like a huge party bus. Long, beige leather bench seats stretched along the sides, the windows were dark tinted, and a small refrigerator door was open revealing a variety of alcoholic beverages and sodas.

Blinking back her astounded panic, Anya observed the group of people seated in the bus.

The men looked unsavory, unshaven with mean eyes, and the women looked, well, bawdy. They were all staring avidly at her with avaricious interest.

Her head whipped to the man beside her who had abducted her off the street. Again she opened her mouth to demand an explanation then froze when her shocked eyes collided with his black discs of chilling emptiness.

His mere presence raced alarming fingers of fright up her spine. He was tall, maybe over 6'5. Dark hair tousled from the wind outside flopped over an ebony eye, he shoved it back with annoyed impatience.

Her trembling gaze shuffled around his face looking for a trace of kindness or compassion, but his harsh, hard-carved features were only grim and forbidding.

Oddly, Anya thought, for a thug, he wore an expensive looking grey suit, and a thin black silk tie, he ran his large hand down neatening it. The slacks were sharply creased; his dress boots masculine and polished.

But the swank suit did nothing to hide the massive shoulders and bulging arms. The dark eyes regarding her were hooded, hiding his thoughts. To Anya he had a callous look, such a tough exterior. A scar jagged from the end of his temple to the beginning of his cheek, made her think of gangster musclemen she'd seen on TV that hurt people.

One of the men sitting opposite of them, stood up. The man started over towards Anya, the greedy leer on his face clearly indicating his intent.

"Yeah, nice, fucking nice, Zukov, let's get this party started." As the man moved closer to her, he rubbed his palms together. This man was tall and muscular as well, with thin, straight, light brown hair parted on the side. His face was pocked and his brown eyes bared his unmistakable malice.

Zukov, the man next to her spoke in low, brusque, heavily accented words, "*Na.* No party, sit down."

"Huh?" The approaching man's head snapped from Anya to the man beside to her. "The hell you say. Bitch is steaming hot, man, young and fucking tender. De Vos don't give a shit what shape she's in when you get her there, as long as she's alive."

His nasty gaze swung back to Anya. Smarmy eyes dropped to her breasts, his tongue swirled around his thin lips. "Yeah, and damned stacked too. Time to fuck, baby, come to daddy-" he took another step.

Her arms rigid, hands gripping the seat, Anya pressed her jean-clad legs together, and rounded her shoulders in front of her as if she could stop him from touching her.

The man next to Anya leaned forward. "I said *na.*" Zukov's voice deep and dark as the night, he spoke in a low tone but the menace carried. "Go back to your seat, Dassey."

Darryl Dassey's forehead furrowed. "What the fuck? Come on, man. Okay fine, you go first then I got seconds. The others can draw straws for their turn-"

"Sit. Down." The words hard clipped came with black brows drawn like rapiers over dark ominous eyes.

Dassey hesitated, then scowled. "Fine, you foreign asshole. At least let me strip her so I can have those bitchin' tits and her pussy to look at during the drive. You can hold her legs apart so I can get a bird's eye view." His leer shifted to Anya. "I bet she's all pink and pretty down there, eh?"

18

Wrapping her arms around her body, Anya's head was roiling so crazed with fear, she could hardly think. Her petrified eyes darted from Dassey to Zukov sitting like a big bull beside her.

Zukov sat back in a relaxed pose. Strong hands, the backs sprinkled with black hair and tattoos splayed on his thighs, but Anya could feel the strength radiating from him coiled and ready to spring.

Behind Dassey the other people watched with wicked interest.

Dassey moved within a couple of feet and reached out for the buttons on Anya's blouse- Zukov stood up and backhanded Dassey so hard the man stumbled backwards slamming down awkwardly back on his seat.

Anya jumped up behind Zukov and made for the door.

She had her hand on the handle when Zukov snapped his arm around her, jerking her away from the door and moved with her back to their seats.

He sat down, spread his long legs and pulled her to sit on the bench seat in front of him. His angry breath rough in her ear, his body strung around her felt like a thick, grey-suited iron fence. "Stupid bitch," he snarled.

His hand on his red cheek, Dassey cawed from across the bus, "Yeah, dumb as dirt. We gotta be goin' 70, you woulda been splattered all over the fucking highway!"

"Let go of me!" Anya pealed, struggling to get loose of Zukov's hard fingers wound around her upper arms.

Tightening his knees around her legs to hold her immobile, he grasped one of her hands, pulling it behind her back and snapped a handcuff on her thin wrist. Then he jerked her other hand back and clamped them together.

Gasping, appalled and terrified, turning her head without looking at him, Anya whispered desperately, "Why? Why are you doing this?"

Not answering her, he put his hands on her waist and lifted her to sit beside him, then he pulled her to lean back against the wall in a corner. Smoothing his tie back down over his abdomen, he maneuvered his big body so he was blocking her in.

Anya pulled her legs up with her knees protectively pressed against her chest and huddled as tightly to the side wall, and as far away from Zukov as she could get. Hearing snickering, she peeped over at the other people sitting around the bus.

The group of men and women were staring at her and making lewd comments.

One man snickered, "Can't wait to see the little girl buck naked and legs spread wide for me."

The others laughed crassly.

The man that Zukov had hit, Darryl, pulled one of the women from her seat and shoved her down on his lap.

The woman faced out, her legs lifted and straddled his legs. Her Marilyn Monroe styled golden blonde hair, fuller on one side than the other waved around her face, and dark brown eyes smirked at Anya.

Audaciously voluptuous, she wore skin tight slacks, and unfortunately her blouse was body clinging too, because Anya could see the man had his hands up under it and was fondling her huge breasts. Blushing, Anya quickly averted her eyes.

Two of the other men turned their attention to another woman. A brunette with a round face, hair that wisped down her back, her amber eyes were cat shaped with thick liner. She was slightly plump but didn't have the big curves the other woman had.

The brunette's giggles vibrated around the room as she was pushed to her back on the bench, and one of the men sat with one leg between hers and the other on the floor. As his hands skimmed up the woman's body, Anya closed her eyes and turned her head to face the wall.

But, she popped them right back open, she didn't dare close them to the danger that was in the car with her, she stared at the wall. Unfortunately, looking away didn't shut out the moans and groans, gasps, squeals and ribald laughter that reverberated in the bus.

Liquid Velvet

Every time Anya took a chance and peeked out, all she saw was erotic movements, a naked orgy of body limbs and parts thrusting and squirming, and Dassey, with his hands now down the front of the blonde's open pants was staring straight at Anya. Beside her, Zukov remained silent. He crossed his arms over his chest, tilted his head back, and appeared to be sleeping. Feeling his heat and intensity practically vibrating next to her, Anya highly doubted the man ever slept.

The ride was long, taking most of the day, the sun was setting. The bus droned, bursts of laughter rang out with loud conversations. After a while it grew quiet as people nodded off.

Anya struggled to keep her eyes open, fearing the second she closed them one of the men would be on top of her. However, she must have dozed, because the movement of the bus changed, it was slowing.

Slumped in the corner, she cracked her lids open. When she did, she saw most everyone was still asleep, but Zukov was staring unblinking at her. His gaze was so formidable and cold, it made her heart pound. She struggled to sit up with her hands still bound behind her.

The voluptuous blonde woman moved across the bus and knelt on the floor between Zukov's legs. Her grin slyly beguiling, she stroked her hands up his thighs. "Déisi Zukov, my hunka brooding stud, why doncha give the little girl to Darryl. Get her out of the way and I'll show you what I can do for you."

Her fingers spread over his thighs as she stroked them up towards his groin. Zukov moved his gaze from Anya to the blonde who now brazenly cupped his man's package. "Ahh," she cooed, "yeah, so big. Come on honey-"

Zukov snagged her wrist and pushed her hard enough she fell back, plopping on her ass.

"Hey," she protested shoving blonde hair out of her eyes. Her legs landed spread straight out, breasts about bounced almost

21

clean out of the low-cut top. "Déisi, I give fantastic head. They call me the Vacuum. I can do you-"

"Not interested." His deep growl guttural in his accent, he told her, "Go back to your seat."

She rolled over to all fours, the blouse dipped so low it revealed she wasn't wearing a bra and her nipples were a pinkish-brown.

Anya gasped and quickly turned away.

The woman sneered at her then started to crawl back between Zukov's legs.

He stared down at her. His voice cold, he said flatly, "Do not make me tell you again, Paulina."

Paulina's long fake lashes flapped surprised at him that he would turn her down, again. Every time before she had flirted with him, he gave her the cold shoulder. So this time she tried the direct approach, which didn't get her anywhere either.

Standing up, Paulina swallowed hard at his dark, glittering gaze. "Uh, okay then, maybe later." Turning to go back to her seat she shot Zukov a coy smile, invited, "Whenever you're ready, pet," gave him a saucy wink and parked her hugely rounded derrière down.

Zukov sat as a statue, staring blankly out the window across the bus.

Anya could not believe what was happening. She was in a mobile den of lusting iniquity, and she didn't know why she was there, or where they were going. And worse, what would happen to her when they reached their destination.

In confusion and abject terror, her knees still up against her chest, she turned her head to gaze out the side window while she silently said prayers.

Chapter Four

The noise outside the bus grew louder, harsher.

Anya could hear the roar of jet engines. A fresh flush of fear and bewilderment rushed up her neck to her face. Out the window she could see they were winding around a small private airport.

The other occupants were chattering, gathering their personal belongings like jackets and purses they'd scattered around the bus.

Dawn was breaking when the vehicle came to a halt and the motor shut off. Her eyes wide, Anya craned her head to see as much of the outside as she could.

They were on the tarmac, a series of planes of all different sizes scattered over the blacktop. Two had just taken off and a third appeared to be about to go.

The bus parked well away from a one-story building that a few people were buzzing around. A cluster of hangers, some closed, others had their doors swung wide open, semi-circled the lot.

Anya's head jerked when the door sprang open. She burrowed herself into the back of the seat as the other occupants started exiting the bus.

Darryl smacked Paulina on her vast rump and said with a chuckle, "Now don't you go running off hon. Remember, you and Tammi were bad girls, and we're bringing you back to face the music with Mr. de Vos."

Giggling, Paulina shook her ample bootie. "Come on, Darryl, where would I run to? You would only catch me again. Besides," she wound a curl of hair around a finger tilting her head coyly at him. "Anton won't hurt me, we've had some…" she wriggled her bust, "good times. He can be quite exceptional in the sack you know."

Darryl's brows hopped. "Oh yeah? Well," he patted her butt then squeezed it. "We'll see what you think about exceptional once we're airborne and can lie down flat, eh?" The pair chortled together out of the bus.

Anya saw now that two of the men were being handcuffed before being escorted from the vehicle. Everyone except Zukov and Anya left the bus.

Anya stayed unmoving and quiet, hoping the big man would forget about her and just leave the bus. And pigs fly.

Zukov grasped her upper arm and pulled her with him to the door. He stepped down first then reached in, gripped her tiny waist and lifted her out and down to her feet.

With her hands cuffed behind her, she stumbled awkwardly. Zukov moved his tight grip to her upper arm to hold her steady.

The bus had parked right next to several small brick buildings that the passengers were all hurrying in and out of.

Without a word, Zukov pulled Anya away from the other people. He un-cuffed her then opened the door to one of the rooms. Giving her a little push inside, he said, "Make it quick," and closed the door.

It was a cold, dank, dark bathroom. But she had to go so badly she bucked up and did her business quickly. There was a dim overhead light and no window.

When she opened the door, Zukov was braced in front of it, waiting for her.

Seeing her chance to escape, Anya opened her mouth to scream- Zukov quickly slapped his hand over it.

Bending over, putting his face right in hers, he held one slender arm keeping his hand over her mouth and said, "Miss Marvaux, you behave yourself, no screaming, and come with me peacefully, I will release my hand. If you don't, then I will gag you and throw you over my shoulder. What do you say?" His hard eyes bored into her wide green saucers.

He waited a few beats, then moved his hand.

Immediately Anya opened her mouth to scream at the same time she jerked her arm from his grasp to run. She got half a squeal out and one step before he roped his arm around the front of her, and clamped his hand back over her lips.

Muttering, "Ah, *Engleză ilgáně*, English brat." Keeping his hand over her mouth, Zukov clutched her face tightly. He reached in his pocket, pulled out a handkerchief and quickly tied it over her mouth. He slapped the cuffs back on her wrists, then before she could move, he bent and swung her up over his shoulder.

Shocked, Anya's screams muffled, her wrists were bound behind her back, but her legs were free and she kicked the hell out of them- Zukov smacked his hand on her butt. It wasn't hard but it stunned her, for a second, then she started kicking again.

He smacked her again, harder.

A cry squeaked from her.

He said quietly, gruffly, "No one will think twice about a man carrying his bride into the plane, they will think we are playing. But, you keep kicking, attracting attention, and the next swats will be on your bare ass."

Anya paused, he wouldn't dare- she gave a little kick. He reached up, slid his hand under her hips and yanked at her belt, muttering, "I don't make empty threats, *ilgáně,* one more kick and every person here will see that naked, round little ass of yours meeting my hand."

Realizing she was profoundly helpless, the agitated energy left her. Anya hung limp and hopeless over the man's warm brick wall of shoulders, her long fiery curls draping down his back. Her cheek brushed against his suit coat, it was surprisingly silky, verifying as she had thought, it was an expensive suit.

With long-legged strides, he carried her effortlessly across the tarmac to a waiting private jet.

A few people gathered to board other small planes pointed and chuckled commenting as he'd said, either they were a couple playing or she was drunk.

One hand around her legs, Zukov spread the other on her back to hold her tighter against his back as he smoothly made his way up the steps of the plane carrying her easily as if she were a doll.

White captain chairs interlaced with bench seats lined both sides of the private jet.

Ignoring the other occupants, Zukov carried Anya to an unoccupied section of leather cushioned bench. His hand still spread over her back for support, he lowered her and set her on her feet.

She swayed backwards, he held her taut. His voice low, he instructed her, "*Na foi*, ah, that tis, no one here is your friend. No one is going help you. I will remove the gag. One scream and I will put it back for the duration, you understand what I say?"

His inscrutable eyes scanned her pale face streaked with tears, the big green eyes shrieking her terror. "Well?" he growled.

Her tremulous nod was slight.

"*Bună*, good," he grunted and untied the gag. Dragging it lightly across her eyes and cheeks, he wiped the tears before tucking it back in his pocket.

Her voice tiny with tremors, half-turning her back, Anya asked, "The cuffs too, please?"

"*Na*," he said bluntly. "Sit down," he ordered, pointing to the bench seat.

Anya stared at him for a second until his eyes narrowed, then she sat down.

When he reached around her, she jumped and went to get up.

"Calm down, *Engleză*, I need to buckle you in."

Her body rigid and shaking, Anya held still while he buckled her seatbelt, then he sat back without doing his own.

A flight attendant started towards them with a flirtatious smile aimed at Zukov. He was big, tough, scarred and harshly rugged, yet somewhat handsome in a violently menacing way. The flight attendant regarded him with admiring interest.

Zukov shook his head with a short jerk. She frowned, shrugged, then went to offer someone else a cocktail.

Trapped on a plane going to God knows where, Anya murmured in a small voice, "I am not English." Maybe if he thought he'd taken the wrong person he would let her go.

But, he'd said her name. He knew who she was. What on earth was going on here? Why would someone abduct her? Her family wasn't ridiculously rich that she would bring in a fine ransom.

He turned to face her. Licorice eyes scanned her heart-shaped face then traveled slowly down her body, so slowly Anya felt as if he was literally touching her. Her skin burned and tingled everywhere his eyes scrolled.

His gaze so harsh yet weirdly intimate, Anya shivered from the intensity of it.

The doors closed and the jet engines started up. The rest of the people sat down, still chatting, many held drinks. The volume of conversation and laughter rose over the discordant noise of the engines.

The jet rolled slowly then picked up speed until it flew off the runaway and streaked up and up, slicing through hunks of blue sky as it swiftly rose. In moments only a stream of slick white vapor was left behind.

When the jet leveled off, people unbuckled their seatbelts. Many got up to roam around. Eyeballs bounced around the room, constantly landing on Anya. Her cheeks heated pink at the attention.

The two men that had been handcuffed were both released.

Anya was the only one that was still bound with a watchdog at her side. More scared and mortified than she had ever been in her life, she figured the creep cuffed her and stayed with her because she was the only one who had tried to run.

Paulina the blowsy blonde, and Tammi, the brunette that allowed two men to bang her at the same time sneered at her from across the jet.

Paulina cupped her hand to Tammi's ear whispering something. They both laughed, smirking at Anya.

Her cheeks flaming, Anya lowered her eyes.

Darryl jumped to his feet, drawing his jeans up like he was an important man. Starting, "Okay, then," he glanced over at Déisi with a nod, then said to the crowd, "a few of you are being brought to Anton de Vos to face some music. It is procedure for us to strip search and frisk each of you for everyone's safety."

Crossing his arms, he looked at the people. "We did a cursory frisk after hauling you onto the bus, but now we will conduct a very thorough search."

His gaze slid over to Anya, boldly raping her with his light brown eyes.

Déisi casually stood up, his hands on his trim hips, jacket pushed back behind his wrists, and placed himself in a calm stance in front of Anya.

Scowling, Darryl sighed, then smiled. He said to the big blonde woman, "Okay, Paulina, you first."

A wide mouth stretched wider across her face, Paulina got up and moved to Darryl with her arms straight out at her sides, offering, "I'm all yours, sugar, see if I have any weapons hidden on me."

Laughter rang around the room, her clothes were so tight, blouse so low, it was obvious if she had a weapon it would be visible.

First, Darryl ran his palms over her arms, her neck, her shoulders, down her back then lower to cup her ample ass. As if he was tickling her, Paulina wriggled and giggled.

The corner of his mouth tucked up, Darryl crouched and ran his hands down her legs. As he stood back up, he dragged his palms up the insides of her thighs, deliberately stroking them over her sex, bringing a lusty giggle from Paulina, who never even flinched from his touch.

Darryl shoved his hands up the front of her to grab her big breasts, and squeezed them, hard, inducing only tart laughter from Paulina.

Her face white with shock at the behavior, Anya stayed still behind Zukov's solid body praying everyone would forget about her.

Darryl moved to stand behind Paulina. Reaching around her, he pushed her blouse up to her armpits exposing her bare breasts. Kneading them briefly, he pinched her nipples, a laughing squeal came from Paulina with a wiggle of delight.

"Ah," he grinned, "no weapons here, at least no lethal ones!" he joked. Darryl grasped her tight pants and drew them down to the floor revealing the black thong that did nothing to cover the thin shaved Mohawk strip of dark hair over her sex.

Undoing his pants and shoving them down his hips, he put his hand on her back pushing her to bend over placing her palms on a chair. She obliged with a lusty laugh stepping out of her pants.

He said, "Let's see if you have any contraband stashed in any of your holes, shall we?"

Some people conversed as if there wasn't a porn show going on right in front of them. The rest, mostly males, hovered with their hands on their boners watching Darryl shove the thong to the side, spread Paulina's butt cheeks apart and try to enter her.

Bent over, her huge naked melons flopping, Paulina stared straight at Déisi. Her full lips widened into a lush grin, tongue slicking around those big lips indicating she would take him next if he desired.

But Déisi wasn't looking at her, he was staring impassively at the floor.

As Darryl gave up trying to impale Paulina standing up, he pushed her to the carpet on her hands and knees and dropped down on all fours behind her.

Another man lunged for Tammi. She squealed with glee and pretended to run. He caught her as a second man came behind her, the two men sandwiched Tammi, their hands raking all over her plump body. She squealed louder, like a hog getting greased.

30

Other women apparently being taken to the man, de Vos, remained unmolested. But maybe not for long, they were rapidly making friends with the males on board.

The rest of the men eyed Anya like she was candy waiting to be licked.

Her throat closed with fear, Anya couldn't swallow, her body shook so hard her teeth chattered. Twisting and scraping, jerking her wrists, she futilely strained to get free of the cuffs. Feeling vulnerable as male eyes loitered over her bosom pressing against her blouse that she was helpless to cover, she shifted her head so her hair would curtain the front of her.

Zukov turned and gripped her arm, pulling her to her feet. Without a word, he started walking down the aisle towards a door at the back of the jet. He opened the door, moved his hand to her back and prodded her inside.

"Hey Zukov," Darryl called out. His light brown hair hanging straight over glazed eyes, not even pausing while he thrust in and out of Paulina, his balls slapping her abundant thighs. "I get her when you're done, amigo!"

Déisi stepped into the room closing, and then locking the door behind him.

The small, white room was empty of furniture, but luggage and boxes were stacked along a side wall.

Her wrists restrained, Anya backed away from the imposing brutish man.

He removed his suit coat and laid it on a box. As he moved, his chest and shoulders huge with cordons of muscles strained against the long-sleeved shirt.

Tugging at the knot in his tie, loosening it slightly, his gaze never wavered from Anya as she continued backing away like captured prey until she hit up against a wall. Déisi prowled slowly to her like a powerful wild beast.

"D- don't touch me, don't you dare touch me, you- you gangster!" Her breathy voice rasped through a tight throat closing with fear. One shoulder curled in over her face in useless protection from the aggressive man, long light hair veiled over half her face and over her shoulder and arm. She curved into the wall trying to meld into it.

One black brow arched, the corner of his full, harsh lips quirked. "Gangster?" He unbuttoned his cuffs, and rolled the long sleeves up his burly forearms while moving towards her until he was standing right in front of her.

Her back against the wall, Anya had nowhere to go. Her quivering eyes rose to his, the plea withered on her lips. His lids hooded, the seams of his dark orbs that she could see were bone cold and pitiless, and determined.

Zukov raised his hands and set them on her shoulders turning her to fully face him. The slender blades shook under his strong grip. He lightly stroked his weighty palms over her shoulders and down her arms like Darryl had done to Paulina.

Then he brought them back up to slide behind her neck. Lifting her hair, he drew his fingers lightly over her nape, a shiver at the faint touch shook her entire body.

At her shiver, the hooded lids lifted to her eyes, exposing his flaring pupils. When she lowered her gaze to stare anxiously at his chest, his lids dropped back covering his enigmatic eyes.

His face a veneer of implacable bronze, he sifted his fingers through her hair. It seemed to take a long time for him to slide his fingers through the thick, silky curls. His eyes flickered from the locks he stroked to her face and back to the locks.

Holding her breath, Anya prayed that was all he was going to do. Her breath caught when he stopped stroking her hair and reached for the top button on her blouse.

"No!" She jerked from him, pleading, "Please don't!"

Her plea was to no avail, Déisi nudged his hip to hers pressing her securely against the wall and continued undoing the rest of the buttons.

His voice rumbled quietly without inflection, "What Darryl said was true, procedure is necessary. People hide weapons every...where."

As his thick knuckles grazed her soft breasts, Anya dropped her head with a sharp inhale then snapped it up. Appealing to those blank eyes, she begged, "Please, mister, don't," biting her tongue to ward off the tears.

His gaze lowered from her terrified face to her blouse. Moving his hip back, he put a hand on her hip holding her and set his other palm lightly on the swell of her breast.

Ignoring her sharp inhale and hitching breath, he slowly moved his hand inside her bra, his hard palm just barely skimming the top of her soft flesh.

She tried to shift her body away from his grasp, but he was like a steel cage. He was so strong he didn't budge a hair when she pushed against him.

Anya's chest quaked with the strain of holding her sobs in, she turned her head from him. Tight short breaths scraped through her throat. His strength was immeasurable, but his handling of her was surprisingly gentle, if agonizingly violating.

Although he kept his body slightly from her, she still felt the hardness of his broad chest beating at her. The big shoulders looming over her, huge biceps flexing with his movements. His virile heat enveloped her, the masculine scent of mild aftershave mixed with a whiff of cigar smoke rolled around her senses

Staring hard at her full breasts molding over the pale peach bra, Déisi's pupils expanded wider. His cold hand palmed lightly over the other warm breast, he shifted a few fingers between her cleavage, then he ran a finger under the bottom of her bra.

She lowered her head as helpless tears gathered, then she suddenly pushed from the wall trying to knock him off balance. It was like shoving a tank. He didn't even twitch.

Pushing her back against the wall, his voice rugged and chilled, without emotion, he said, "I am not going to fuck you, Anya-lia," he broke her name into parts trying to pronounce it in his heavy accent. "Skinny little girls don't make me hard."

A vein beat at the temple with the scar drawing her gaze. His jaw worked, tanned skin darkened. If she looked down, she would see his lie.

The wall behind her hard on her thin shoulder blades, Anya's eyes flit over his rough face. "Oh," her voice small and tight, relieved she said, "you go for- for big blondes like that girl Paulina with giant um," her cheeks reddened, curly lashes lowered over her embarrassed eyes. *Why was she talking to the beast for heaven's sake?*

"Tits," he filled in for her.

"Please," she pleaded, "just let me go and you can go and have…uh…relations with Paulina. I can't escape anywhere."

Silently, he reached behind her and under her shirt, to run his calloused palms up her back. In doing so, he pulled her from the wall forcing her half exposed breasts to press against his chest.

His gaze dropped to her supple flesh wedged against his starched shirt, his thin tie lying like a black silk viper between the valley of her cleavage. His quickening breath forced his chest to press harder against her.

Seeing him look down, Anya watched him.

When he just stared and didn't move, she squirmed in his arms. Her soft body wriggling against his brought streaks of color to his angled cheeks, and he let go of her, pushing her back to lean against the wall.

Thinking he was done, a deep sigh of relief oozed from her loosening some of the tension in her shoulders. Then he reached for her belt.

"No!" she screamed. Violently twisting her body, she tried to shove to the side of him. He grasped her arms and flung her back against the wall so hard she cried out.

His low, hard brow rigid, Déisi's chest pumped with heavy breaths, he wiped at the sweat beading across his forehead with the back of his wrist.

Hesitating, he studied her as if apprising if he'd hurt her. Then, her breasts heaving in her distress drew his attention. When he looked down, Anya bent and bucked at his chest with her head. Déisi blocked her hit and she tried to bite his arm.

Swinging her around, he snapped her spine hard against his chest and lassoed his arms around her. Irritation thickening his accent, he growled, "Your wrists are cuffed you little fool, even if they weren't, what on earth do you think you can possibly do to get away from me?"

Struggling, she screamed under her breath.

He shook her, rebuking, "You keep fighting me and you're going to get hurt. You are too small and delicate; I will harm you without meaning to. This is supposed to be a full, invasive, nude strip search, I am trying to leave you a shred of dignity."

The word, strip, only fueled her fear, upping her writhing struggles. His muscled arms tight around the front of her, he squeezed her against him.

His breath in her ear, he whispered, "Anya-lia, would you rather I let the others do this? Darryl perhaps? Trust me, wee *ilgáně,* brat, he would have taken you in a heartbeat, way before the whore with the big tits. And he would have had you naked on your back on the floor with his dick rammed up your cunt ten minutes ago."

Anya gasped at his vulgarity.

He said, "So hold still and let me finish or I'll let him in. Keep in mind, when he's done, the rest of the men out there will come and have their turn at you."

Tears rolled out and down her cheeks. His embrace too tight for her to even wriggle, Anya stopped fighting him. Her deep, gulping exhale signaled her surrender.

His strong warm arms holding her against the hard chest, Anya could feel his breath fluttering wisps of hair against the sides of her face.

At her submission, he turned her around and leaned her back against the wall. He pushed his boot between her feet, nudging her legs slightly apart. Keeping her legs secure so she couldn't kick or move, he unbuckled her belt, unbuttoned, then pulled the zipper down on her jeans.

His big palm now warm from their struggles, set on her flat belly, then, he slid his fingers around the top inside of her panties.

Forcing herself to not move, Anya couldn't help her hips twitching at the invasion of his rough hands on her innocent body, small frantic sounds eked out.

Ignoring her whimpers, Déisi moved his hands behind her and skimmed them down outside the back of her panties. Just barely palming her butt, he kept his hips turned from hers so she couldn't feel the lie that he didn't desire her pressing like a thick iron rod into her belly.

Anya inhaled hoarsely, but said nothing, she held her breath.

Moving his hands to her front, he quickly, lightly, cupped her mound over her panties. Startled, Anya jumped and a strangling sound gouged deep in her throat.

Déisi crouched, running his hands down her legs along the denim. Anya was gasping so hard in panic she couldn't catch her breath and started to pass out.

Her knees buckled and she crumpled.

Chapter Five

Cursing, Déisi threw his arms around Anya.

Holding her, he gently lowered her to the floor. Sitting down cross-legged, he tucked her half in his lap and cradled in his arm. Her head fell back over his arm, the long curls swiping the floor. He scanned her pale face.

Long blonde lashes with hints of fire in them curled on cheeks round with youth. Fat curls swirled messily around her small slightly pointed chin and slender shoulders. Her lips were tiny yet full and plush, agitated breaths still puffed from them with the rapid rise and fall of her chest.

His gaze heated as he stared at her lips, his neck bent and he lowered his mouth to hers before he was aware of it.

Then her breathing slowed, and the long lashes fluttered. His mouth hovering a bare inch over hers, Déisi leaned back.

Making soft mewing sounds, Anya's lids pushed up. Bleary eyes blinked in confusion at him. Slowly she became aware of the big brute of a man holding her, then realized her shirt was hanging off her back, and his eyes had drifted down to her half-bared breasts. Panic struck and her lips opened as she started to scream.

Déisi gently settled a hand over her mouth to stifle it. Her arms trapped behind her, she lay across this strange man's lap, blouse more off than on, pants undone, the green irises twittered with horror.

"Calm down, little girl. I'm done. You don't want those people out there to imagine what I'm doing to make you scream, do you? They will think I am breeching that tiny hole in your plum of an ass." Holding her, he stood up with her in his arms, moved to the wall and set her down on her feet to brace her body against it.

Her pants were slipping down her slim hips, her blouse shifting off her back. His gaze lingered on her chest heaving in fright. Creamy plump breasts jiggled, mounding over the tiny bra.

The plane suddenly dipped, Anya yelped stumbling. Déisi caught her and propped her back against the wall to support her.

Seeing her steady, he said, "I'll be right back," then stalked to the door, unlocked and opened it and left the room closing the door behind him.

Déisi passed through the short hall into the body of the jet.

The vessel, like the bus had, looked like an orgy gone wild, half the plane's occupants were fucking. Motorcycle clubs had nothing on the debauchery going on here.

As Déisi strode through, Darryl lifted his head. He was panting hard, lying on his back. Paulina lay stretched across his chest while another man curled beside her with his hand clutching her bare tit. Darryl muttered to Déisi, "You done?"

Then he saw Déisi's thick wood straining at his pants. He snorted, a crude vulgar sound. "You can't get off? You're still hard." He pushed Paulina away and went to get up. "I got it covered. I'll take care of the little one."

Paulina squawked being shoved aside. Darryl grunted as he rolled to his knees. Déisi put his boot to Darryl's shoulder and shoved him back down.

"Hey-" Darryl yipped, falling back on his rump.

"Stay here, you don't fucking move," Déisi commanded, eyes narrowed at him. Satisfied that Darryl sitting on his butt with his pants wrapped around his ankles scowling up at him wasn't going to try to get to the back room, Déisi trod off down the aisle to the front of the plane.

He knocked twice on the small door to the cockpit then opened it and went in.

The pilot glanced over at him with a quick smile. "Hey, Zukov, what's up? Good to see you."

Without preamble, Déisi asked, "The plane took a steep dip, is there trouble?"

The corners of his mouth nicked in, the pilot shrugged. "No biggie, nothing to worry about. Just heavy turbulence, everyone should buckle in for safety. I'll try to fly over it."

Déisi watched out the window for a minute seeing nothing but vast blue and puffy clouds.

The pilot chuckled. "The attendants tell me there's quite some activity going on back there, Zukov. I hear the liquor's flowing and the clothes are going."

Pushing a button, he glanced at Déisi quickly then back out the window, the auto-pilot was on but due to the rough air currents he kept watch.

"You getting any action, Zukov?" His mouth curved up in an envious grin. "Big strapping guy like you must be sowing oats clear through the entire damned jet, huh?"

Déisi's mouth turned down in a serious frown. "*Na.* I am working."

Cranking his head at him, the pilot's eyes roved down and back up Déisi's muscled body. "Shit, right, bro. I saw you carry in that little honey all caveman like, hauling her off to your lair. In handcuffs no less, that's fucking hot.

"Gorgeous babe restrained for you to do whatever you like to her? Whew," he swiped a palm across his brow with a grin. "Yeah, there's no way you passed on that sweet sugar, yo?"

Piercing the pilot with a stiff glare, Déisi grunted. "I said I am working." His hand on the door, he said, "I want to know immediately if there is anything to be concerned about, Griffin." He nodded shortly at the man then stepped back out into the cabin.

Making sure everyone, especially Darryl was accounted for, he strode quickly back to the room and opened the door.

Moving inside, he saw Anya sitting huddled on the floor against the wall, fresh terror darkened the green. The bit of color that had returned to her cheeks fled at the sight of him. Her small body was shaking like a leaf, she grit her teeth to stop their chattering.

"All right, come on," Déisi said, bending to grasp her arms. He pulled her to her feet, turned her around and unlocked the cuffs. Removing them, he stuck them over the back of his belt and ordered, "Fix your clothes."

He stood a few feet from her, face blank, watching her sniffle. She moved her arms but cried out with a wince. Her arms were numb and sore from being pulled back with the cuffs.

Muttering a curse, he stepped close to her again. Ignoring her cringe, he wrapped his big hands around her thin arms and rubbed them.

He stroked his palms up and down her arms, gently squeezing them and her shoulders while he carefully drew her arms forward. When he saw the pain clear from her pretty face, he released her and again stepped back.

At his sharp nod, fingers shaking, Anya buttoned her blouse, fixed her jeans and buckled her belt all under his unwavering scrutiny.

"I will allow you to keep the clothes for now, but they will be burnt as soon as we get off this jet." His eyes slit at her shocked gasp.

She wrapped her arms around her body as if she could stop him from removing her clothes. Teeth chattering like crazy, her body trembled all over.

Sighing, Déisi picked up his jacket. "I said I wasn't taking them now for fucks sake. Be happy I didn't conduct a full exam as Darryl was doing with Paulina. He inspected her entire body, inside and out, checked all of her holes. And not gently." Turning aside he muttered, "Not that Paulina wouldn't be happy with as rough as possible."

His mouth curled in a sneer as his gaze roamed her body.

41

"Clearly you are one of those innocents that it would never enter your mind to shove a tiny sheathed knife or whatnot up your twat. Plus, you had no clue you were going to be snatched."

Glaring her fear, mortification, and anger at him, pointing her finger, the words barreling out of her mouth, Anya scourged, "You- you are a horrible man, a despicable pig. You should be ashamed of yourself abducting women off the street, mo-molesting them and running a- a filthy perverted sex den! What are you- one of those…what are they called?"

The word popped into her brain. "A- a pimp, that's what you are. You are a disgrace. Your mama will not be proud of you," she reproached, struggling to still her frightened shakes and shivers.

His brows arched half amused, half angry. He muttered, "Then tis a good thing I never really had a mother," and dropped his jacket over her. Ignoring her fighting him, he helped her put it on. She wrapped her arms around herself.

"Back out front, let's go." He took ahold of her upper arm and brought her back out to the main cabin.

Thankfully, the orgy had burnt itself out and the people were quietly resting, or passed out. Some were still drinking and semi-carousing, but more doing so slowly and quietly.

Déisi brought Anya back to her seat and helped her to sit down.

"I'm going to the facilities," he nodded towards the lavatory at her puzzled look. "Do not move, I will be right back."

When she scooted back in the seat and leaned back against the cushion, he headed towards the loo.

Déisi hadn't even unzipped his pants when he heard a scream. Throwing the door open, he raced out in time to see Darryl slap Anya so hard her neck snapped.

Reaching for her, Darryl barked, "Now, no more fucking screaming, you'll be compliant you little bitch-"

Déisi punched Darryl in such fury the man flew back crashing into the far wall. Smashing his head, Darryl slowly slumped to the floor knocked out cold.

Déisi turned to Anya who had her hands covered over her mouth in shock. The grass-green orbs over them swelled and shimmered with welling tears.

Sitting down, he pushed her hands aside and cupped her chin to look at her face. A red print was there, but Darryl hadn't bruised her. "Come, let's splash some cool water on your face." He helped her up and walked her to the bathroom.

Opening the door, he kept his hand on the top of it as she moved warily under his arm passing into the lavatory.

He waited outside the door while she was inside. When the door slowly opened and she peered out, he held the door and motioned for her to come out.

When she did, he put a foot inside and said, "I'd bring you in to keep the fuckwads off you, but we wouldn't both fit." Half his lip curled at her look of disgust of sharing the small space with him.

As he closed the door, he said, "You stay right here. Anyone comes within 10 feet of you, you holler."

When he emerged, she was standing just behind the door, her eyes bouncing around the room as if waiting for the next animal to pounce on her and tear her to shreds.

Her body jerked at the door opening and she stepped back. Her nervous gaze bounced from the room to him.

His face was damp as was his hair. He'd combed it straight back. Without a word, he took her arm and brought her back to the seat.

When she got situated, he left for a moment then returned with a couple of sandwiches and bottles of water and flopped down beside her. He handed her a sandwich and a bottle.

She set the sandwich on the seat next to her and opened the water, quickly gulping down a quarter of it. With her stomach tied up in knots and her heart palpitating wildly waiting for the next indignity to occur, she had no appetite.

Softly, Anya said, "Mister...um, please, tell me why you are doing this, why have you taken me? What did I do?"

When he didn't answer, she drank more of her water, but didn't touch the sandwich.

Déisi gobbled down his sandwich in four big bites and drained his water. Sighing, he leaned back in his seat and looked over at Anya, and frowned seeing the uneaten sandwich.

Around the cabin, people wandered, eating, drinking, a few played cards. The volume of conversation was a steady drone along with the engines.

"You have had nothing to eat all day and half into the night, Anyalia." His deep voice low, he said quietly, "You need to keep your strength up."

Seeing the new fright strike her already pale face at his inference there was something more horrible ahead of her, he sighed with annoyance. "I didn't say anything was going to happen, I just said you need to eat."

With him glaring at her, she certainly wasn't about to start shoveling food into her mouth. Her head lowered, she lightly rubbed at the red rings around her wrists made from the cuffs.

A prick of guilt, a totally alien feeling, stabbed his gut at the sight of the rings. Damn the bitch was delicate. His sigh roughened. He said, "Anyalia," to get her attention.

When she ignored him, his face darkened. He caught her jaw carefully, his fingertips barely denting her skin, and turned her to face him.

Feeling her stiffen under his grasp, his accent thickened. He became harder to understand, but his threatening, commanding tone was clear. "We will have a length of time together, it will be easier," he took a breath, "on both of us if you just obey me."

His lip twitched at the defiant drawing down of her brows. It made him think of a few minutes ago when she'd dressed him down. This tiny, fine-boned female half his size chewing him out, pointing her finger at him. He bit back a grin, she was cute and glorious in her righteous rage.

But, he sobered, he was in charge. This was his mission, and she was his prisoner. She would follow his dictates regardless of her feelings.

Her lips pushed out. The yellowy brows drew down further over green eyes flashing her ire, dainty hands plopped furiously on round yet slim hips. "You can't tell me what to do, you- you pimp."

He frowned at her disparaging portrayal of him. His grip on her jaw tightened. "First of all *svini ilgáně*, little brat, you fucking stop calling me that. And second," he lifted her chin so their eyes connected, "you will do exactly what I say and when, without hesitation or further argument."

"Huh." Shifting her jaw out of his grip, she snorted. Crossing her arms over her chest, her fear forgotten in her pique. "Or what? You've already abducted me, humiliated me, molested me. I would think starving me would be on your list, right up your abusive alley."

At his silent scowl, she went on, "When will the beatings commence? Besides," her lids narrowed, shoulders bunched, "you keep calling me a brat. So," she tossed her hair back with a harrumph. "I guess we're even, Mr. Pimp."

Her defiance sharpened the planes on his hard face. His expression became stony and unreadable. Lids lowered, making his irises almost invisible. His coarse lips firmed into a severe line. He looked so coldly fierce, Anya squirmed a few inches away from him.

He leaned into her, bringing his face a scant inch from hers, so close, his breath stirred the hair near her jaw. So close he could see the gold in her green eyes spark with fear.

Déisi had never dealt with this kind of woman before. He was used to women that were as tough and cold as he was, not a dainty, feminine, *innocent* female like Anyalia.

He was also used to everyone following his orders. They knew his violent reputation. No one balked or argued, except, his eyes narrowed further, this slip of a girl with more bravery than brains. But she will learn. Quickly.

"*Svini ilgáně*," he smothered an angry, taunting grin at her frown. "The things that I have done to you are infant's play considering what I can, and will do to you, if you do not do as I say."

Black threat stabbed so fiercely from under the hooded lids, Anya leaned back as if the force of it physically pierced her, staking her down.

He said, "I answer to no one but myself. There is no one to stop how I treat you. There is no one for you to complain to, or garner help from."

Her swallow was audible. He glared at her silently, relentlessly, until her gaze wavered, then fell.

They sat in silence. Under his low lids, Déisi watched her swallow her fear, choke back the tears that threatened to spill, and, he felt the oddest feeling…a twinge in his gut.

It was unfamiliar and uncomfortable. His gaze flicked from her lowered head to the bottle she squeezed fretfully in her small hands. "Well?"

Her eyes rose gingerly to his, brows up in question.

His sigh terse, he snapped, "The sandwich, girl, are you dense? Eat the fucking sandwich." He couldn't believe he was sitting there on a jet plane brow-beating a young woman into eating.

All his gruff threats would undoubtedly only make her stomach tie up in more knots, making eating, swallowing, or keeping the food down impossible. But she was already too thin, and was going to need strength and stamina to face what he was bringing her to. *Uhn*, there was that weird twinge again.

Her lips pulled in then bunched. She turned her body completely from him and picked up half the sandwich. Staring off into space, she nibbled at the end of it.

Déisi leaned over, rested his forearms on his legs and folded his hands together, staring at the back of her head, watching her trying to force the food down her constricted throat.

"Ah, fuck," he cursed and got up. He knew she was aware he stood up by the further stiffening of her shoulders as if she was preparing for him to strike her.

Liquid Velvet

He stomped off towards the back of the plane and pulled out a pack of European cigars. A few people glanced askance at him. Ignoring them, he lit up and sucked hard on the cigar. No one there would have the balls to tell him smoking was not allowed.

Hanging a bit around the corner of a wall, he surreptitiously watched Anya pause, look around, not seeing him, she got up and dropped the uneaten sandwich in the trash then hurried and sat back down.

Against his will, a grin at her mutinous behavior tugged at the side of his mouth. His gaze flit to locate Darryl. The man was off in a corner making out with one of the women de Vos was hiring, not one that was being transported to him for discipline.

He fished his phone out and pushed a button. Again, a few people gave him a look, he shrugged. It was a private jet, owned by de Vos, Déisi could do whatever the fuck he wanted. He tucked the cigar in his palm when his brother answered.

"*Yah*? Dez?" Kalo said.

"*Da*, I got the girl." Déisi nodded as Kalo acknowledged the mission.

"So? She hot, or fat and ugly? Big tits or just a mouthful? How's the ass on her?"

Déisi snapped, "What's the difference? The job was to snatch her and bring her to de Vos, it doesn't matter what she looks like." He switched to their language as people in his vicinity blatantly listened in. "When we get to the train station, I need to take her clothes and burn them."

"Ah, Dez, you go overboard with wariness. Why would someone have sewn tracers into her clothes? No one had any idea we were going to take her."

"I take precautions, Kalo, that's why I'm still alive. Anyway, you're going to have to get her some clothes when you meet us at the station. I only thought about burning her shit, I didn't think about her not having anything to wear."

But now the thought of Anya sitting beside him buck-naked rolled into his vision, shit, he was as bad as that horny fucker Dassey. He blinked rapidly to dispel the picture.

47

"What the hell, Dez," Kalo sneered. "I'm a personal shopper now going out to buy girls' clothing? What the hell do I know about women's clothes other than taking them off?" His grin came through the wire.

"*Yah*, whatever. You need to get everything, blouse, pants, shoes, socks, jacket, and," he hesitated, "you know, underwear stuff."

"What? No way, Dez, I am not going to buy some strange girl panties and bras. Unless I'm fucking her I won't-" he broke off. "On the other hand, you didn't confirm or deny her looks. Maybe I do want to fuck her. What size is she?"

Déisi sucked hard on the cigar, blew the smoke out and up. "No one is fucking her, Kalo, knock it off, she is our job. Anyalia is small and thin, like Jordy's little sister, the youngest one, ah, Katie is it? Except she's got tits that don't fucking stop and an ass that King David would toss Bathsheba aside for."

"Yo, what?" Kalo laughed. "I guess that answers my question about her looks. Well, her body anyway." He was thoughtful, then said, "So, you've gotten her this far, why don't I take over when we meet at the train? Luc will meet us there."

"Fuck you, bro, she's in my charge until tis done, back off. And don't get any really sexy shit, I already have to fight off the goddamned wolves here as it is. She doesn't need to show what she's got on a fuckin' silver platter. Get shit that will hide her figure."

"Whoa, *bréthaïdne,* it sounds like the little honey already has your unheard of 'possessive' balls clinched in her tiny little hand. You've already done her? Not like you, Dez, to mix business with pleasure. She must have one sizzling pussy-"

"Enough, Kalo, shut the fuck up. She is not my type. Too dainty, too ladylike."

Knowing his mocking laughter was irritating Déisi's ears, Kalo chuckled. "*Da*, sure. She's going to need shoes, what size?"

Silent while he thought, then Déisi said, "Ah, I think around the little sister's size, the girl is what thirteen or something?"

"Yeah, teeny feet, huh? Little bitty suckable toes?"

"For fucks sake, Kalo, focus." But Déisi pictured himself on his knees in front of her, licking a toe and her sexy giggles-

Kalo laughed, breaking up the image. "Okay, her tits. Katie's have barely sprouted yet, your girlfriend flat? That's no Bathsheba my son."

An impatient growl of annoyance reverberated from Déisi. Stuffing the cigar between his teeth, he dragged his hand through his hair. "She is not my girlfriend, you asshole. Her size, she's like, ah, delicate, small like Katie, but has tits like," he thought for a second. "Jordy's cousin, Cynthia, but not big all over like Cynthia, just the breast size."

His mouth ticked up at the corner. "And a shitload finer, but the chest size is close. *Gah,*" he cursed a few choice words as the image of Anya with her hands bound behind her, blouse falling off her back, and her rack just tumbling out of that silk bra was making him hard.

While frisking her, he'd tried not to *feel* her flesh, just check for weapons. But *mi Dios* she was lush. Then he remembered her frightened, mortified tears and he dug in a heavy breath.

Speaking through teeth clenched around the cigar, he said, "Just get the fucking clothes, a few days' worth and toiletries, whatever girls need. Don't even fucking ask me about that shit, get a clerk to help. Use my credit card number and meet us at the station." He clicked off the phone as his brother kept talking.

Déisi dropped the cigar in a cup of water, stopped off at the attendant's stand, grabbed a beer and a cup of ice cream and headed back to Anya.

Of course, as he neared her, he could see a man was sitting next to her. A smile nicked the side of his mouth seeing her shuffle away from him, and looking around like she was searching for Déisi to protect her.

"Come on, sweetness, loosen up. Let me get you a cocktail. My name is Eddie, what's yours?" As he spoke, he pushed Déisi's jacket off her and settled a hand on her shoulder. Anya jerked away.

When he didn't let go, she tried to brush his hand off. "Mister, please leave me alone. I don't want anything to drink, please go away."

Instead of leaving, he leaned closer to her and rolled his arm around her shoulder. His other hand cupped the side of her head pulling it towards him. "Aw, a kiss then, come on, I'm not asking ya to shag, not yet anyway. Let's just get acquainted."

He pulled harder at her resistance, and gripped the side of her face with his hand trying to latch his lips on hers.

"Stop, stop it," Anya whispered loudly. She didn't dare raise her voice and draw more attention, more disgusting men might come.

Insisting, "Babydoll, come on," he forced her mouth to his with a tight grip and then moved a hand to clutch her waist, sliding it up to just under her breast.

Anya gripped his arms trying to push him off her, but he was too strong.

"You don't get your hands off her and get lost in one second, I will open that door, hurl you out and see if you can fucking fly, asshole."

Anya gasped.

Eddie froze. He leaned back and looked up. All 6'5 plus muscular feet of Déisi was braced in front of him, with the enraged bestial look of Lucifer brazing his face. A vein beat at his temple against the scar. Charred eyes guaranteed he would follow through with his threat of death.

"Uh…" His Adam's apple bobbing with a nervous swallow, Eddie slowly lowered his hand from Anya's face and smiled sheepishly at Déisi. "Shit, Boss, no harm done. A beautiful girl sitting alone, you know. I thought you'd gone off to shag some other bitch. She looked like free game."

Déisi's furious ebonized eyes narrowed down pointedly at the hand Eddie still had clasping Anya's midriff. "Your second is up. First I'll rip that hand off your wrist before I toss you out the fucking plane."

Face white as a sheet, Eddie jumped up and took off without looking back.

Déisi stood glowering down at Anya. "What the fuck, woman, I leave you alone for a minute and you just open your legs for any man that comes by?"

Her offended gasp burned his ears. Even to his jaded eyes, she was clearly a virgin and had been fighting the jerk off. It was just that he'd seen red when he saw that fucker with his hands all over her. For the time being she was his property, he owned her, and a possessive knife twisted in his gullet every time another man was near her much less touching her.

He sat down. Without looking at the embarrassed, pained distress in her eyes at his vile insult, he handed her the ice cream. "Here, this might be easier on your stomach than the sandwich."

She stared down at the cup of vanilla ice cream without moving. Around them, conversation hummed with the drone and slight vibration of the jet as people visited, some napped.

"Go on," he thrust it into her hands, "it'll be soothing, won't upset your stomach."

She had to take it or it would fall.

He sat back, rested an ankle over a knee, stared off blankly, sucking on his beer. He didn't look at her, but peripherally he could see her scoop a spoonful of ice cream, and then the slightest, barest, moan of delight as she tasted it. The sound went right to his dick.

Déisi turned to her, grasped the jacket and pulled it back over her to cover her. Disregarding her twitching at his nearness, his knuckles brushed her breasts as he tugged the lapels closed in front of her. Her body was pure sin tempting every man on board, and de Vos would not be pleased if Déisi slaughtered a dozen or more of his horndog men.

He finished the beer and she finished the ice cream. Déisi took the bottle and cup and tossed them in the trash then had her move to a couple of captain chairs.

He hadn't slept for over 48 hours. Between tracking Anya, snatching her, and keeping an eye on her in the bus, he hadn't been able to close his eyes for a second.

When she was settled in her chair, he lifted the lever pushing the seat back at an incline and the footrest popped up. Her little yelp of surprise at falling back tugged at the side of his mouth.

"I gotta get some winks, *svini ilgánĕ*," he growled at her as he shifted his own seat back. "You need to use the bathroom or need something, wake me. Do not get up. You hear me?"

He lay on his back, his head turned to face her.

She was lying facing him. Long, light lashes fluttered like butterfly wings on rosy round cheeks. Fiery hair swirled around her, a few tendrils spindled against her soft face.

She nodded faintly, then her lips puckered in a moue. "I am not a brat."

Regarding her under low lids, he said mildly, "But you are small." At her confused look, he smiled with an amused tease. "*Svini,* it means small."

Rolling her eyes, she turned on her back with a groan. Her voice weary, she complained, "You are not only horrible, you are also rude and belittling to me."

A smug smirk softened his face. "*Yah*, see, as I said, little."

Slapping her hands on the chair arms, she groaned louder.

His voice roughened, "Just do as I say, you understand me?" He waited. A long time.

She finally whispered, "Yes."

"*Bună*- good," he grunted. Déisi shoved his own black locks out of his eyes, then reached over and laid his arm across the front of Anya like a steel seatbelt.

She flinched at his touch, but didn't fight him. Closing his eyes, he almost smiled, she wasn't going anywhere without him knowing, and no one was getting past him to her, he could finally relax.

He felt it the second she slipped out from under his arm. Annoyed that she just refused to listen to him and risked her safety, Déisi sat up to look for her. He saw her right away. Hell, with that remarkable hair she was hard to miss.

At least he had gotten a few good winks before abruptly wakening. His forehead creased watching her as he slid to the edge of the seat to get up.

She was crouched beside a woman's chair, her hand patting the woman's knee, and murmuring quietly to her.

Unaware that Déisi was standing behind her, Anya said softly to the woman, "Of course you're scared, Leila, but I'm sure as you only owe this man a monetary debt and you said you have the money to repay him, it will all go quite smoothly. You pay him off and you will be home before you know it."

Anya spoke soothing words while the woman cried into a wad of tissues. As Anya talked, the woman calmed, sniffed, wiped at her eyes and gave Anya a wan wobbly smile.

"Thank you, Miss. You are so nice, nothing like the bitchy slut Paulina said you were. You were so kind to take the time to comfort me, listen to me whine."

"And now that all is well, Anyalia will return to her seat." Déisi saw her slight shoulders stiffen at his voice. He was already bending over, winding his fingers around her arm and pulling her to her feet.

Ignoring him, Anya said to the woman, "Are you sure you're all right now? I can stay and-" she tried to dig her feet in as Déisi pulled her away.

Leila looked up at the fierce man dragging Anya away and gave her a genial smile. She said with reassurance, "I'm fine, really. Thank you for helping me."

When they reached their chairs, Déisi had to hold himself back from roughly shoving Anya into hers in his anger and frustration at her disobedience.

Instead, he waited silently until she sat down and buckled herself back in before he settled back down into his seat, and again, laid his arm across her.

"Mister," Anya said softly. "She was crying, scared, very upset, everyone was staring at her but no one was helping her. I couldn't just sit here and watch her suffer."

Lying on his back, his eyes closed, Déisi said, "I don't care if someone is on fire, you leave that seat again and I will wail on your ass so hard you will have to stand for a month."

Chapter Six

After traveling the rest of the night, the sound of the jet changed as it made its descent.

Feeling something on her shoulder, Anya's eyes popped open.

A man put a finger to his mouth in a shh motion. He sat on the arm of her chair, his hand kneading her shoulder. He whispered, "Come with me, honey, I'll take care of you." He stroked his other hand down her arm while unbuckling her seatbelt and pulling her forward out of the chair.

"I will kill you where you stand if you don't get away from her. Now." Déisi's arm lay across the front of Anya like an iron bar.

Stammering, "Uh, she," the man stood up, but his hand was still on her arm.

Déisi shoved his foot rest down with a bang. The man jumped in alarm then hurried away. *Fuck*, Déisi thought, *this will be the last goddamned female abduction I do.*

Drowsy, drunk people slowly stretched and yawned as the plane landed efficiently and came to a smooth stop. Déisi spoke quietly on his cell while everyone disembarked.

Anya was sitting forward, back rigid, wringing the hell out of her fingers, watching everyone leave. She shifted her head to look out the window. People from the jet were climbing into another bus.

Turning back to Déisi, her fingers moved to clutch the ends of the chair arms. "Mister...um, Zu...uh, kov...please, where are we? Where are we going? What is going to happen to me?"

Stuffing his phone back in his pocket, Déisi said coldly, "You don't need to know what is going on. You only need to follow my orders."

He watched the fear war with the defiance and the uncertainty wash over her face. Relenting somewhat, he said, "We are going to the train station."

"But what train sta-"

Interrupting her, his voice hardened along with the clear threat in his dark eyes, he said, "You will keep your mouth shut. You will not scream or try to flee, you will do exactly as I say. If not, I will knock you out and take you on the train the same way I brought you on the jet. Do you understand?"

He followed the emotions traveling her pretty face; the plan to run at the first available opportunity was present in the way she didn't make eye contact with him.

"You scream, Anyalia," tough voice gruff with his cold expression, he threatened, "and I will strike you and knock you out." The lids hooded low as he held his breath to see if she would call his bluff. Cripes, one punch from him and he could kill her.

"Tell me you will behave and we will leave." He stared at her.

Anya looked out the window, obviously contemplating how she could get away from him. She turned to him, her gaze traveled the broad shoulders that completely filled the big captain's chair. Powerful chest, biceps that pumped at his shirt, large, tough hands, and the harshest, coldest, most ruthless face she'd ever seen, and her skin paled.

Seeing his reflection in her eyes, Déisi saw his own enigmatic eyes hard and unforgiving, reflecting nothing kind, only simmering danger.

He imagined she was remembering him carrying her as if she was a feather across the tarmac and up the steps of the plane. Then later when he easily restrained her while he undid her clothes and ran his big hands all over her body.

A shiver rattled her teeth, she had zero chance of getting away from this brute of a man.

"I, uh," her voice and hands trembled. "I will not scream or try to run until we're on the train." Maybe she could get off when the train made stops, climb out a window, find a stranger to help her, call the police for her. She didn't even know what country she was in.

His lips twitched at her specific wording that she would behave only until they got on the train.

Studying her, his stony face hardened, eyes narrowed as he mused, *she believes she'll be able to get away from me and off the train. That this dainty little female thinks she could get away from me, a soldier practically from birth, a trained assassin, mercenary, an enforcer for Anton de Vos, was laughable.* It was laughable, but his lips did not curve in humor.

Stating, "Okay," he stood up. "Let's go." Déisi waited for her to slide out of the chair.

Setting a heavy hand on her shoulder, he put her in front of him and he ushered her through the cabin and down the steps to the asphalt, ignoring the pilot, Griffin's lascivious wink.

He walked her to a Lincoln Town car, opened the back door and motioned for her to get in. "Slide over," he instructed then trod to where the driver stood and took out his wallet.

From where she sat, Anya could see him peel out hundred dollar bills and hand them to the driver, then he walked back to the open door and shoved in beside her.

The driver closed the door and slid in behind the wheel. The car swung out of the lot and to the road.

Anya craned her neck looking out the window. Ahead down the road she could see the bus the others had boarded. "Why are we not taking the bus?"

Déisi sat back comfortably and crossed his arms. His spread legs took up more than his share of the back seat. When his knee touched her leg, she recoiled as if he'd burnt her and she quickly shuffled closer to the door.

It shouldn't have, but her action annoyed him. He was used to having to fight off women that constantly threw themselves at him. Intrigued by his hard looks, they figured he was a rough aggressive ride, which was true. Brazen, hardcore females pursued him relentlessly.

But he was choosey. And he never went with the same woman twice. He didn't need the complications of a relationship, ha, make that didn't *want* the complications of a relationship. Women had one job. He had a cook, housekeeper, secretaries, he only needed a woman for one thing.

Under low lids he canted his eyes at Anya.

She was soft and sweet, and terrified. Curled against the door, her gaze was trained at the scenery out the window. Yet, although scared herself, she had gone to comfort a strange woman who was just as afraid.

Déisi noticed Anya discreetly try the door handle, and then look for the lock when she realized the door was locked.

He smiled to himself, the driver controlled the locks. After the episode in the bus with her insanely trying to open the door and jump out, he shook his head, stupid wench, he was taking no more chances.

He wasn't often taken unaware, but her trying to jump from the moving bus shocked the shit out of him.

He hadn't realized how scared she was that she would take that chance with her life. But then, he hadn't put himself in her position. A young, abducted, terrified, bewildered woman that saw the men in the bus, Darryl Dassey especially, were eager to throw her down right then and there and rape her.

All around her, wanton strangers had a sexual free-for-all in the bus. Nudity, cursing, moaning, screams of arousal were so rampant the girl had hovered in her corner with her eyes closed and hands covering her ears. To say she was a sheltered virgin was almost an understatement judging by her aghast horror at the lewd activity.

And, then there's Déisi himself. Mean and tough, he snatched her right off the street. Handcuffed and gagged her, carrying her like a primate with his dinner over his shoulder into a plane, then half stripping her and feeling her up. His lips thinned. *Yah*, if he were her, he'd be out of his mind with terror too.

Remembering her question as to why they weren't on the bus too, Déisi answered, "I grew tired of watching those fucking men pawing you."

Anya's eyes rounded at his statement. It sounded as if he cared about her wellbeing, but he couldn't possible give a damn as he was the one who had abducted and molested her. She kept her head lowered as she looked up at him and said with a shade of sarcasm, "Does that include you?"

Not responding, Déisi handed her a baseball hat. "Here, put this on, tuck your hair up."

Anya looked at it in confusion, but took it and did as he said. It wasn't easy, she had long hair with fat curls that worked to escape her ministrations.

Offering, "Here," Déisi held the cap while she stuffed her hair up.

When they both sat back, Anya said, "It's taking a long time to get to wherever it is that we're going. We've been traveling a day and a half, where could we possibly be going?"

His hands clasped in his lap, Déisi stared out the side window not answering her. The area they were in was rural with dense green forests bordering both sides of the road. Signs along the way were in a language she wasn't familiar with.

From the start, they had taken long, evasive tactics to eliminate anyone from following them, that added a lot of extra hours to their travel time.

After more long hours, the car left the highway and parked in a huge crowded lot. Anya observed the tracks and trains and realized they had arrived at the train station.

Leaving the car, Déisi wound his big hand around Anya's arm and scanned the area.

The station was not as big as stations in larger cities, but it was busy, people hustled and bustled in all directions. Déisi spotted Kalo immediately.

His brother was waiting near the entrance casually leaning against a wall with earphones and wearing a ball cap. He looked bored and as if he was tuned out of the world.

Déisi knew better. Kalo was carefully observing everything and everyone. Not only was there a chance of someone seeing Anya and maybe catching an international missing person's report and turning them in, or, someone else could have had the same idea as de Vos and would be looking to steal her to use her too.

Déisi was on high alert. He was scanning the area just as carefully as Kalo was.

Keeping a tight grip on Anya's arm, Déisi guided her to his brother.

When he reached him, they bumped fists.

Kalo greeted his brother, "Bro, you made it," then nodded at Anya. When Kalo had approached, Anya had moved slightly behind Déisi, peering anxiously up at Kalo from under the bill of her cap. "Hi," he said to her with a grin.

Surprised she was actually hiding behind him for protection from this new possible threat, Déisi released her arm and slipped his hand around Anya's waist drawing her out. His mouth firmed in a frown, her body trembled under his hand.

Pulling her close to his side, in his own language, he said to Kalo, "This is Anyalia Marvaux. Anyalia," nodding at Kalo, he said, "this is *mi bréthaïdne*, Kalo."

Anya inched closer to Déisi's side, surprising him again. Then he realized she didn't understand what he said and likely feared meeting yet another strange man. He said in English, "Kalo is my brother, Anyalia."

Her green eyes floated from brother to brother.

They looked a lot alike, ruggedly tall, same muscular physiques, broad shoulders, strong hands and the same strong features.

Anya's gaze rose to Kalo's head.

He pulled off his cap and self-consciously patted his dark blond hair under her scrutiny.

Déisi's hair was black as midnight with eyes just as dark. They were cold and compassionless, whereas Kalo's dark blue eyes were cheerful, yet with the same icy steel as Déisi's tucked back in their depths.

She was being held prisoner, against her will. Anya said nothing.

Kalo glanced at Déisi with a quick wink that said, *Yah, she is a looker.* "Here," he said, handing a case to his brother. "The clothes and shit." He glanced at Anya, said with a smirk, "Pardon my language."

"*Bună,*" Déisi said taking the case. He looked around until he spotted restrooms. He took Anya's hand, said, "Come," and drew her across the crowded space to the bathrooms.

He pushed the door open to the ladies room and checked inside, it was empty. Holding the door open, he told Anya, "Go in." Then he said to Kalo, "Guard the door."

Nudging Anya to go inside, he followed her in, closing the door in his brother's grinning face.

The room was clean with several stalls, pink counters and peeling flowered walls. A wooden bench took up a wall, and a chair was off to the side.

Déisi set the case on the bench, opened it, took out a bag and set it beside the case. "You take off everything." Eyes narrowed in warning at her. "Everything," he repeated. "Including underwear, ah," a hint of color tinted his cheeks, "both top and bottom." His gaze directed from her chest to the apex where her legs met.

He cleared his throat. "Shoes and socks too. Put them in the sack."

Anya stared at him.

"Now, Anyalia, we have a train to catch, change now."

Taking the clothes that were on top, she started for a stall, he said, "*Na*, you will change right here, in front of me. I won't take the chance of you transferring something that I can't see."

She stalled, bottom lip pushed out. "I am not changing in front of you. You know very well there is nothing hidden on my body, or in my clothes." Her cheeks reddened at the remembrance of his hands feeling indecently all over her. "And, what on earth could you be thinking I have hidden on me anyway?"

"Ahh," his exhale irritated, he said, "Anyalia, we don't have time to argue. You fucking change yourself right now, or I will rip those clothes off you. Then I suppose after you're standing there stark naked you'll dress yourself quickly enough."

His hands on his lean hips, fingers digging into them in his aggravation. Broad shoulders hunched, he leaned menacingly towards her.

Clutching the clothes, she took a step back from him, her eyes darting to the door. "No."

Warning, "Anyalia," he moved between her and the door.

Clutching the clothes tighter, her lips clamped, she shook her head.

Glaring at her, Déisi dragged his frustrated fingers through his thick hair. Yes, his fingers could feel frustrated, he was feeling exasperation all the way to the tips of his fingers.

The big green eyes gleamed with welling tears, her plush lips quivered. Fuck. Why couldn't she just be one of the regular bawdy women he was familiar with and strip them off and move on?

His sigh grated in a short huff. "All right. I will turn around," he held up a hand as she started to object. "That's it. Now, you have 60 seconds." He turned his back to her and said, "Get started, I am counting."

Déisi figured that if she knew she had anything sewn into her clothes or shoes she wouldn't have sufficient time to get them out and transfer them to the new clothes.

He grunted pissed, this was the second compromise she'd maneuvered him into. First promising she wouldn't run temporarily if he left her un-cuffed, and now, keeping his back to her. He fumed. Not even a whole day passed and the woman was making him back down when he never did, not in his entire life.

She was small and helpless, but she had a helluva backbone.

He'd paid for the Town car to keep the dogs from the plane off her, and to reduce the nasty stares and comments from the other bitches, and hopefully ease her fears somewhat. It wasn't like him to have a heart, and he didn't much care for it. He sighed; it was going to be a long journey.

He heard a small sound of grief, then she sniffed as she kicked off her shoes, and he heard clothes rustling. In his mind he counted the seconds trying to keep the pictures of her nude out of his head.

When he got near 60, he grumbled, "You about ready? I'm turning around."

"No, wait-"

But he turned around, and gulped. "That son of a bitch," he ground out.

She was just finishing buttoning the top buttons of a relatively low-cut blouse. A thin sapphire blue that showed the top swells of her breasts, and was sheer enough he could see that the bra Kalo bought was too small, her breasts mounded out of it. And it was also fairly sheer as he could see her nipples poking straight through the bra and the blouse.

"What?" she asked innocently. "Is something wrong?" There was only a small mirror over the sink, she couldn't see how exposed she was. *Thank Dios.*

After snapping the top of her white jeans closed, she shoved her hair back, then sat on the bench and pulled on black velvet ankle boots with heels that were so sexy Déisi's brain went right to her wearing just them and silk panties.

He put a hand to his head with a groan, *da, and likely they were sheer and tiny too.* With a moan, he shoved aside the image, he was never going to make it to de Vos without popping a vein.

Her cap had gone askew, tresses were slipping out to curl around her shoulders. Rougher than he meant to, Déisi jerked the hat straight and stuffed the loose hair back up.

Answering her question of 'what's wrong,' with a, "Nothing," he stomped over and looked inside the case for a jacket. Rummaging through the rest of the clothes and not seeing a jacket, he slammed the case shut, and picked it up off the bench along with the sack containing her old clothes.

Handing her his jacket, he said, "Put it on and let's go."

Sliding into the jacket, her bottom lip stuck out again, she asked, "What's wrong? What did I do?"

"Nothing, come on." After helping her on with the jacket, he set his hand on her waist under the jacket and pushed her out of the room. Holding the door open for her, he groaned again as she passed through under his arm.

The jacket was bunched up over her hip showing that the white distressed jeans were soft and tight. So snug, her perfect little ass was cupped as if the light denim was made of a man's hands.

Snapping the jacket down to cover her, Déisi slammed the case into Kalo's stomach, grabbed Anya's hand and stalked towards the train with his brother's snickers in his ear.

When they reached their coach, Déisi bent his head and said quietly to Anya, "Just remember, you promised you would behave." Holding her elbow, he moved her to the side of the steps.

"Yes," she mumbled under her breath, "until we get on the train." The sharp squeeze he gave her elbow told her he heard her.

He spoke to Kalo in their language, "Stay with her, watch her, she's wily."

Déisi went back to the Town car. He knew the driver personally, which was why he hired him to drive them. He moved to the trunk that the driver popped, took out a shovel then strode a few feet into the woods to a small clearing.

He dug a hole and tossed the bag of clothes into it then lit a match and threw it on top of the clothes.

He observed the fire until there was nothing left of even her shoes. Then he threw the dirt back over the hole, trod back out to the car, tossed the shovel back in the trunk, shut the door and returned to where Kalo and Anya waited.

Anya watched him with wide eyes until he reached them then she turned away from him.

The trio stood off to the side as a few other people boarded. Déisi had deliberately brought them to one of the last doors at the end to come in contact with as few people as possible.

Regardless, every male that passed ogled Anya even wearing a hat and in his jacket like she was on a strip show stage.

With an irritated grunt, he grabbed the front of the jacket and with Kalo smirking at him, buttoned it up.

Expressing a huff, Anya tried to move from his hands, but he held the lapels until he was done, then let her go.

"Let's board," Déisi grumbled. He cupped Anya's elbow and assisted her up the steps.

Once they were inside the doorway, the attendant made his way to them. Kalo pulled the tickets from his back pocket and handed them to his brother.

Déisi's head bent, black hair hung over his eyes as he examined the tickets for accuracy before handing them to the attendant. More people boarded, Anya slipped in amongst them, and as the brothers spoke with the attendant, she moved down the corridor with the people.

When the people split off to cabins or other cars, Anya ran as fast as she could to a designated exit. It was a ways up through many cars.

The loudspeaker announced that the doors would be closing in four minutes. She hurried to the door and started down the three steps when suddenly the way was blocked by a man.

"Oh!" Startled, Anya stepped aside so he could board. But he didn't move and he took up the entire step area. "Excuse me, please, sir, I am in a hurry."

He didn't move, just stood there staring at her with a half-grin.

Getting seriously agitated and angry, she started to just push past him, but he was very tall and thick with muscles, and he didn't budge.

"Sir!" Anya's voice was on the edge of strident in her nerves, any second her kidnapping watchdog would be on her and abort her escape. "Please move, I need to go!" Frantically, she tried to shove past him but he refused to budge.

Using all her strength, she tried to push him out of the way, but he just smiled down at her like an unmovable truck.

"*Na, mi cochet svini Engleză,*" a hint of humor laced his heavily accented voice. "I am sorry my pretty little English girl, but I am afraid I cannot let you pass."

Bells rang, and behind him the door automatically closed.

The hair on the back of her neck rose, the pit of her stomach plunged at his familiar words and accent. Anya looked up at him and realized the worst.

He was obviously another brother. Same strapping build, muscles on top of muscles, same strong features. The only difference between him and Déisi and Kalo were his coloring and neatly trimmed, chinstrap scruff. He had dark brown eyes and hair.

He smiled. "*Mi bréthaïdne* would have my hide if I let you go." He held a cell phone in his hand. Evidently Déisi had alerted him to stop Anya's escape.

"I will have *her* hide instead, Luc."

Anya thought she was going to be ill. Déisi's deep, hard voice rolled through her, spiking pin needles of fright to every part of her body.

The train started moving. Anya's heart pounded with the pounding of the wheels on the track, beating faster as the wheels moved faster.

Chapter Seven

*L*uc Zukov grinned up at his brothers. Calling out his greeting, "Hey Dez, long time no see," he started up the steps and finally moved past Anya.

"*Na!* Wait Luc- don't move!" Déisi's warning was too late.

As soon as Luc was out of the way, assuming the doors would open automatically, Anya leaped down the steps and lunged for the door- but it remained closed and she slammed into it so hard she was knocked backwards.

Déisi jumped down the steps in one leap, grabbed her and clutched her against his chest.

Luc grinned at both Kalo and Déisi's ghost white faces. They had thought as had Anya that when she approached the doors they would open and Anya would have hurled out of the speeding train.

"Hell, boys," Luc informed the now obvious, "the doors are locked when the train is moving. She can't get out." He winked at his brothers. "Not your first time on a train, bros, you should have known."

Déisi was beyond livid. He held Anya for a moment crushed against his chest, his heart slamming against his ribs like a jackhammer. Then, he strung his fingers of one hand around her neck and held her in front of him.

Deep voice grinding, he cursed foully in his own language before switching to English. "You stupid bitch, what the fuck is the matter with you?" and shook her in his fright and rage.

"Hey, Dez-" both brothers stepped forward with concern of his rough treatment of Anya.

Déisi snarled, "Back off." His eyes hard bolts of flint warned them to not get involved.

"Bréthaïdne," Kalo said quietly, calmly, "she is a woman, and only half your size."

"Shut up, Kalo. You don't know about the fucking bus."

Then all three brothers spoke in their native language so Anya had no idea that Déisi was telling them how she'd tried to get out of the bus while it was going 70+ miles per hour.

His hand still gripping her neck, Déisi loosened his hold. Looking into the terrified green eyes, his voice cold, empty, he asked her, "You are more afraid of me than dying jumping from a moving train?"

She just blinked at him, panting, biting back the discouraged tears that were collecting. Her small hands gripped his wrist trying to pull his hand off her neck.

"Answer me," the aggravation grating his voice, his hard face scrunched dark in fury.

Anya jerked at his thick wrist holding her around the neck. Licking fearful dry lips, she said softly, tremors embracing every frightened word, "I- I don't know where you are taking me, for what, what you're going to do with me, to me..." she trailed off gulping her tears.

Wrath still radiating in his voice along with slight disappointment, he reminded her, "You promised me, Anyalia, you would not try to run."

Her eyes flit back and forth to each of his fearsome black eyes. "I- uh, said until we were on the train." She didn't need to state the obvious that they were now on the train.

"Ah, she's got you there big brother," Luc said with a chuckle in his voice ignoring the fierce look Déisi directed at him.

"So," Kalo, intervened seeing Déisi's wrath and inexplicable fear still wreathing his face. "Let's head on to our cabins, we don't want to attract attention." He moved back so they could all fit in the hallway.

His hand still around Anya's neck, Déisi shifted it to her nape. Cradling her carefully, his dark glare travelled her frightened face.

She was afraid of him, and he had been scared of what would have happened if she'd gotten the door open. Without another word, he dropped his hand to her arm and gently, albeit still rigid with emotion, drew her up the steps.

Kalo walked in front with Luc striding behind Déisi and Anya to block her from view as best they could, which with the three giant warriors surrounding the petite woman, it was fairly easy to do.

Kalo stopped at a cabin and slid a card into the lock, then swung the door open. He handed the key card and Anya's case to Déisi. "You guys are in here, Luc and I are next door. Luc brought your bag in earlier, Dez. So, listen, you need me to help you with her-"

Déisi hustled Anya inside the cabin and followed her in, then closed the door in his brothers' faces, both grinning like teenaged jackals.

The room was tiny of course, it contained a fold-down twin bed stretched under a window and another one was kitty-corner along the wall. A miniature bathroom was opposite to the bed with a table and two chairs. Another small table was off to the side.

A duffle bag was on the bed under the window, Déisi set Anya's case on the small table.

Her arms wrapped around her body, Anya moved as far away from Déisi as she could get in the tiny room.

He trod to the bathroom and peered inside to make sure there wasn't anything Anya could use as a weapon. He asked her, "You need to use the facilities?"

Her throat too tight to speak, she nodded. He jerked his head towards the bathroom indicating for her to go ahead.

Anya awkwardly slid past him trying to stay an arm's length away which was difficult in the small cabin.

When she came out, her face and hands were damp, she stopped just outside the door not knowing what to expect.

Déisi looked so angry, like he wanted to just beat her until there was nothing left of her except bones, and he'd probably break them and grind them to dust then burn them like he had her clothes.

She'd been flabbergasted when she saw him leave with her clothes and the shovel, and moments later smoke poured up from where he'd disappeared into the trees.

Her stomach doing flip-flops, Anya waited. Suddenly her head was dizzy, she put a hand to her forehead and stumbled back against the wall.

Déisi lurched right to her, grabbing her arm. "What is it? What's wrong?"

Her eyes scrunched closed in pain, her hand against her forehead. The fear clear in her shaking voice, she stuttered weakly, "I...don't know, I'm dizzy and my head...it hurts."

"Okay, come over here." Déisi rolled his burly arm around her and brought her to the bed against the wall and helped her to sit, and then sat down beside her.

His hand gentle this time, he cupped under her jaw and leaned in to look at her. "Are you still dizzy?" he asked, smoothing her hair off her face with his other hand.

She could only nod slightly. Déisi pulled out his cell and pushed a button.

Kalo answered, "*Yah*?"

Déisi spoke in their language, "Get a physician, bring him to my cabin. Tell him she is my wife and she has mental health issues, tells people she is being kidnapped, make sure he believes you."

"Okay." Kalo hung up.

Déisi grabbed some pillows and stacked them behind Anya's back and head against the wall and helped her get comfortable. He didn't know what else to do, so he held her hand and gently stroked her head, her face, her shoulder, once he started touching her he couldn't seem to stop.

It was only a few minutes before there was a knock at the door.

His palm on the side of her face, Déisi said quietly, "Anyalia, a doctor is coming, do not say anything to him about your…abduction. Do not tell him your name. Do you hear me? You tell him anything and you risk his life." He had learned that she would take risks with her own life but probably wouldn't with another's.

Her answer a pained whisper, "Yes."

"Bună." He left his hand against her face for a moment, then got up and opened the door.

Kalo was there looking concerned. Beside him stood an older, dark-skinned man in a black suitcoat and starched shirt that matched his white hair. He wore dark slacks and a blue tie, glasses perched on his sturdy nose.

"Vă medicului, mulţumesc, ah, that is, thank you, Doctor, for coming so quickly." Déisi motioned for him to come into the room.

Kalo followed on his heels. With the three men and Anya, the small room was quite crowded.

The doctor introduced himself to Déisi, "Good afternoon, sir, I am Dr. Fredrick Singh, and," he turned to Anya who was sitting back with her eyes closed and pale as a sheet, "this must be our patient?"

"Da." Déisi gestured for the doctor to go to Anya, then he sat on the edge of the bed and put his hand under her hair, back on her nape.

"Dr. Singh, this is…ah, Emily." He said to Anya, "Honey, this is Dr. Singh, he's going to fix you right up." Remembering her fainting on the plane, he had thought that was just her nerves. To the doctor, he said, "She was suddenly very dizzy, it has happened twice now, and she says her head hurts."

The doctor moved forward peering at Anya through his glasses, then he half-turned his head to Déisi. "I do not need you two big bruisers crowding the room, you may step outside while I examine the young lady."

Déisi's brows drew down with a shake of his head, said gruffly, "I do not leave my wife alone with any man, even a doctor."

He wasn't worried she'd tell him anything, Kalo would have ensured the doctor would think she was nuts. He just didn't trust any male alone with her except his brothers.

Standing nearby, Déisi knew Kalo was grinning like an idiot because Déisi normally could have cared less if a woman he was screwing was with another man. Déisi lowered his arm and held Anya's hand.

Singh's white brows arched slightly. He wasn't offended. He'd met many a husband who would not leave his wife alone with him. With Déisi's unfamiliar thick accent, the doctor mused, undoubtedly in the foreign guy's country, women were still treated more as helpless property to be protected.

He pulled down his glasses and peered over them at the brothers. "Very well, are both of you her husband?"

"*Da*," Kalo grinned nodding his head. At Déisi's frown, he said, "I guess I can wait next door. Let me know how she is, bro." He left and it was slightly easier to breathe in the small room.

"All right then." The doctor set a bag down on the bed and sat beside Anya. He said to Déisi, "You may stand over there." He inclined his head for Déisi to get up and move.

After a hesitation, Déisi scrutinized the doctor's face, then patted Anya's hand and reluctantly stood up. He moved to lean a shoulder against the wall while he waited.

"Now then, Mrs…"

"Emily," Déisi said firmly.

"Oh, all right then, Emily, honey," he smiled kindly at Anya while he unwound the stethoscope from his neck. "Tell me what's going on?" Putting the ear-tips in his ears, he helped her out of the jacket then moved the drum down just inside Anya's blouse.

A growl came from Déisi as he pushed off from the wall to start towards them.

Singh turned, peered at him over his glasses and said firmly, "The less you interfere, young man, the faster we will be done. I cannot examine her without touching her, eh?" He turned back to Anya with a smile and moved the drum of the stethoscope deeper into the top of her blouse.

Déisi snapped his back against the wall and crossed his arms tightly over his chest. Dark red crept up his face and the vein at his temple pounded as he watched the doctor do his examination. He was feeling proprietary and he sure as hell didn't like it.

But his eyes didn't budge watching the doctor's hands feeling under Anya's chin and a few other places. Muttering to himself, "The guy takes one liberty and he'll be picking glass from the window out of his head for a week."

The examination took only ten minutes, most of it was questions. Putting his equipment back in his case, Singh smiled kindly again at Anya as he told her, "You're just fine, sweetheart. From what you've told me about being under stress and considering your very low weight," his gaze streamed professionally over her body. "I think all that's needed is a hearty meal."

"What?" Déisi barked coming closer.

"Yes." The doctor stood up. "Your wife is on the edge of malnutrition." His eyes narrowed in rebuke at Déisi through the glasses. "You can't tell when your own wife is starving to death? Just look at her."

At his order, Déisi turned his attention to Anya. True, he'd thought her too thin, almost frail. He figured she wasn't eating today because she was terrified of him and their situation. But, he looked closer, there were dark circles under her tired eyes, her skin was wan, and yes, definitely, she was way too thin.

It just wasn't as noticeable because although thin, her curves were plump and stole all the attention. "*Bine*," a hand stuffed in a pocket, Déisi forked the other through his hair rumpling the dark mane. "She has ah, been ill."

His eyes on Anya, he said to the doctor, "I will see to it that she has adequate nutrition."

"Well then," Singh rose to his feet with a pat to Anya's thigh, he didn't see Déisi's eyes narrow at the touch. "You just need to eat, little one. If you feel worse, have them call me. But I think a few square meals and you will be right as rain."

Déisi walked him to the door. Pulling his wallet out of his back pocket, he said, "What do I owe you doctor?"

Singh shook his head with a smile. "Nothing, young man, it is a service of the train." He stepped outside the door, and motioned for Déisi to follow him.

Déisi stepped out and closed the door almost all the way.

In a low voice, Singh said, "I think she only needs to eat, Mr...uh," when Déisi said nothing, he continued, "but, there is something wrong. Your friend who retrieved me indicated some psychological issues. She appears...afraid. Quite anxious, her heart rate is unnaturally fast. Perhaps she is anorexic. She is quite frail. Is she under a doctor's care? If not, I would strongly recommend it."

"Da, bună, mulțumesc, thank you doctor, I will see that she is taken care of. I've been, ah, out of town, she gets nervous when I'm away, it must have affected her appetite."

Singh paused, then held his hand out. "Very well. She is your wife, I'm sure now that you see there is a problem you will ensure she gets help. Good day, then."

Déisi looked down at his extended hand, then shook it, and the doctor left. Déisi went back into the cabin, closed the door, and leaned against it.

Anya hadn't moved, she was still leaning against the pillows stacked at the wall, her legs dangling over the edge of the bed. Her gaze at him under heavy lids was steady but filled with trepidation and fear.

Déisi fished out his cell and called Kalo. When he answered, Déisi said, "Get Luc, we're going to the dining car in ten." His eyes never moved from Anya as he slipped his phone back into his pocket, but she lowered her gaze.

He sat down next to her. "Anyalia, tell me why you are so thin. I know this day has been harrowing for you, but that certainly doesn't explain it." He waited.

She said nothing, just stared at the floor.

His voice very gentle, he urged, "Tell me."

Her eyes rolled up to his, then away, then to her hands folded in her lap. Her sigh lowered her shoulders. "My granddad has gone missing. My stepmother does not want me to work or go to school, she wants me to marry this," she took a breath, "person.

"I ignored her demands that I stay home where this person...can reach me. I have been terrified for my granddad, I've been searching for him and going to school and work. I was so worried; I admit I didn't eat much. One afternoon I came home to shower and change clothes and my stepmother shoved me down to the basement and locked the door."

A shudder ran through Anya, she clasped her hands more tightly. "She said she would not let me out until I agreed to marry this man. He'd given her money to induce me to marry him. There was water from the small bathroom, but no food. It was many...weeks...she kept me there.

"One day my papa came downstairs to get a bottle of wine and I escaped. I slept in my car then hid in the bushes and changed into an extra set of clothes I kept in the trunk. Then I went right to work hoping I still had a job. I had hoped to earn enough money for a hotel room. Well, I didn't actually make it to work. You took me before I could."

Déisi remained silent, his expression gave away none of his thoughts, but the vein under the scar started beating a rapid tempo and his jaw clenched.

"Hey, Dez, wattup?" Kalo called from the hall.

Standing up, Déisi said to Anya, "Fix your hat, I don't want your hair visible." He opened the door but watched her.

She complied, tucking loose tendrils back up. Kalo and Luc stood outside the door.

Her terrible story about Anya's malevolent stepmother in his head, "Fucking bitch," Déisi murmured walking back over to Anya. He held his hand to her.

She eyed it warily, then cautiously took it. He helped her to her feet.

She tugged her hand from his grasp and whispered, "Where are we going? Are you going to…kill me?"

His brows slashed down incredulous. "What? You think I'd take you on a bus, a plane, and now a train across the entire damned world, get you clothes, and bring a doctor to see you, to just kill you?"

Her head lowered. "I don't know. You might be tired of me…you know, trying to run, and now being weak, and think I'm more trouble than I'm worth."

He cupped her chin, lifted it gently. Their eyes joined. He said quietly, "Anyalia, I am not going to kill you. And I'm not going to let anyone hurt you. Can you try to trust me?"

The Caribbean green eyes darkened to emerald, she moved her chin from his grasp. Her lips pressed tight, brows daggered down as she took a deep breath. "Trust you? Are you serious? You've kidnapped me and molested me, Mr. Zukov. No. I cannot trust you."

He contemplated her words, his gaze scanning her face from the deep emerald to the tiny obstinate chin to the small, but plushest lips he'd ever seen. Then said quietly, "My name is Déisi, or Dez as my *bréthaïdnee* call me."

"Speaking of brothers," Kalo said, "we're waiting…"

Chapter Eight

Ignoring Kalo, Déisi's gaze traveled over Anya's body. Her breasts pressed against the sheer sapphire material.

Déisi picked up his suit jacket and held it out. "Put this on."

She looked at him quizzically, then allowed him to help her slip into the jacket.

He stepped back to peruse her. "Button it," he instructed. When she did, he smiled. The jacket went almost to her knees. He nodded satisfied, her tits and ass were both covered. "Okay, let's go."

He took Anya's hand, locked the door and pulled it closed behind them. Kalo and Luc were in front of them.

The couple followed them a few steps then Déisi stopped walking. He said to Anya, "If you scream or seek help, or try to run again, you will endanger others and I will punish you."

Her lips twisted wryly. Her voice tight with sarcasm, she replied, "Is this the part where I'm supposed to trust you, where you aren't going to let anyone hurt me? Except you, I guess."

He cocked his head regarding her with a slight smile. "There are ways of punishing people that don't hurt them…terribly. But I must admit I was thinking of paddling your behind and then keeping you cuffed and gagged for the rest of the journey."

"You can't-"

He started walking tugging her along with him. "Just do as I say, Anyalia, and things will be fine. Trust me." Ignoring her snort of disbelief, Déisi followed his brothers down car after car until they reached the dining coaches.

Tables lined both sides of the wide cars. Kalo and Luc waited at a table. Déisi pulled out a chair that was against a window and helped Anya to sit, then he took the seat beside her, and his brothers sat opposite them.

"Anyalia," Déisi said, "I have been remiss in proper introductions. You know *mi bréthaïdne,* Kalo, and of course you have met our brother, Luc," he nodded towards the man with dark brown hair and neatly trimmed chinstrap beard.

Luc inclined his head with a smile. Like Kalo, he wasn't as cold and severe as Déisi, yet the same suppressed violence and aggression was present in all three.

Next to Luc, Kalo winked at Anya with mischief in his dark blue eyes.

Thinking any of them could, and would, break her neck in one move if they desired, Anya just looked at them without responding.

The three brothers spoke at length in their own language until a server came to take their order. He asked Anya first what she wanted.

Her smile stiff yet polite, she answered, "Oh, nothing thank you, just water if I may."

Kalo and Luc ordered blood red steaks with beer and shots of bourbon.

Déisi ordered just beer, he never got intoxicated when he was on the job. He requested the blackened swordfish. Then he said to the server, "The lady will have the spaghetti and meatballs with a salad, put a lot of ranch dressing on it and bring extra rolls and butter. And," he opened the wine list, "I think she could use a glass of rosé."

He closed the menu and handed it to the server saying, "Make it a sweet Enjoué. *Mulţumesc,* thank you."

A brow arched, the server's eyes flit to Anya then narrowed. He said, "I will require ID for the young lady-"

Speaking over him, "I will vouch for my wife. Just get the drinks," his powerful shoulders hunched, Déisi set his forearms on the table. Twining his thick fingers, his biceps bulged, and his hooded eyes didn't quite cover the threat directed at the server.

"Of course, sir," the server replied after clearing his throat.

Anya blurted, "No, Mister-"

Déisi cut her off, dismissing the server, "That will be all."

"Yes, sir." The server spun on his heels and quickly left the table.

Anya set a hand on Déisi's arm to get his attention. "Mr. Zukov, I- don't want anything to eat. I have no money, I can't pay for the food. Please call the waiter back and cancel my order."

Déisi had rolled his sleeves up. He stared at her hand, small and feminine on his muscled forearm. Her slender fingers creamy and soft, so delicate over the dark hair of his sinewy tanned skin.

He raised his eyes to hers and said, "You heard the doctor. You had the chance to order what you wanted, and you didn't. So you will eat what I ordered for you, every single fucking fattening bite of it."

Kalo said with a frown, "Geez, Dez, give her a break, you don't need to talk to her like that."

When Anya removed her hand from his arm, Déisi's hard eyes skewed over to his brother. In their language he said tersely, "Mind your own fucking business, and speak in our language. The less she knows, the better, you know that."

He then told his brothers what the doctor had said and then what Anya had relayed to him about her stepmother's mistreatment of her.

Both brothers were horrified and furious at the information, but they didn't look at her, they didn't want her to know they were talking about her and have her be embarrassed.

The server brought their drinks and a basket of warm rolls and tubs of butter.

Déisi pushed the glass of wine close to Anya, then reached for the basket. He took out a roll and set it on her bread and butter plate then knifed a hunk of butter and put it on the plate. Then he served himself two rolls, a hunk of butter and passed the basket to Luc.

Pushing the wineglass back, Anya said, "Mr. Zukov, please don't waste this stuff on me. I'm really not hungry, and I...uh, actually have never had alcohol before."

Déisi laid an arm across the back of Anya's chair, set the other on the table in front of her, and curved his body to her, slightly fencing her in.

Bending his head so their faces were closer, he said, "You almost passed out, twice now. The doctor said you would get ill if you didn't start eating healthy and regular. The wine will help you relax. Can you just for the evening do as I say without arguing with me?"

"But the money-"

Forcefully not gritting his teeth, keeping his voice quiet, Déisi said, "I will pay for everything, stop kicking about money for fucks sake." *Gah, he actually sounded like a damned husband.*

Her lips firmed, brows drew down, Anya insisted, "I refuse to be beholden to you. I will not owe you for anything so you can make me pay back with my bod-" she clamped her lips shut.

Kalo and Luc murmured quietly to each other trying not to listen.

Déisi curved in closer to her, his wide shoulders blocking her from view even from his brothers. Hell, she was kicking about a meal, good thing she hadn't realized he'd paid for the clothes and the Lincoln out of his own pocket.

"Anyalia, I will not expect payment from you, and," his voice darkened, "I would fucking not expect reimbursement with sex." His body rigid with anger, he watched the color flood her face.

"I've already told you, I'm not into skinny little girls. Besides, I could have taken you already, a dozen times if I had desired, without you owing me a thing. You are only a job to me, a body, a target, not a woman."

He took a deep breath, then exhaled the annoyance. "Now, drink the fucking wine, and eat the goddamned dinner."

Her eyes widened at his coarse words, then she turned towards the window and stared out, pulling her lips in to still their trembling. She was used to the foul cruelty of her stepmother, but the vitriol from the strange beast of a man was horribly disconcerting.

Déisi glanced over at his brothers. Both had disapproval scrawled all over their faces.

When Kalo opened his mouth, Déisi shook his head sharply. Sighing, Déisi turned back to Anya, put his hand to the back of her head turning her to face him.

He gently brushed his thumb over her cheek. His voice soft, he murmured, "Anyalia, I...am sorry." Hell, he couldn't remember the last time he'd said those words, actually he didn't think he ever had.

First compromising, and now apologizing, shit, what was happening to him? He was growing too soft. Grimly he thought of Kalo's words that she had his balls clinched in her small hand. He felt an involuntary twitch in his nuts.

Damn, mercenaries, enforcers like him don't get all fucked up over an entrant in their missions. He was becoming a pussy. Yet, seeing her so upset, well, shit.

Sighing again, he said, "I didn't mean to sound so harsh. But, the doctor said you need to eat. I don't want to see you get sick."

Earlier, seeing her in such physical distress had wrung his insides, he had hardly been able to think while he'd called Kalo to get the doctor. *Da, not only clinching them, she was now twisting his balls.*

"Hmm," her lips pushed out, she crossed her arms. "Fatten me up and keep me steady on my feet so you can sell me to a sex trader, or sell my kidneys, or whatever it is you have in store for me?"

His head fell back with a groan. "For the fucking love of *Dios.*" He glared at her. "Anyalia, I swear, tis nothing like that. I said I would see that no one hurt you, and I do not lie." He never lied, except every time he said he didn't desire her.

Déisi picked up her roll, split it in two and thickly buttered both sides. He grabbed one of her wrists, shoved half the roll into her hand, then picked up the rosé and pushed it into her other hand.

"Just, oblige me, please. So the rest of us can eat in peace." Fuck, he'd said the word please. Just shoot him now.

Luc nudged Kalo with his elbow, Kalo shot him a grin. Both watched the interplay between their big bad brother who scared the willies out of the most vicious of men, and the soft, delicate female. They had never seen Déisi be so gentle. The heartless soldier apologizing to and feeding a woman? Never.

Anya looked at the bun in one hand, wine in the other and couldn't help the smile at the silly picture she posed. She took a sip of wine and a bite of the roll.

Still penned around her, Déisi's shoulders relaxed, he sat back in his chair. His gaze fell on her mouth. First time he'd seen her smile.

She was already a stunning woman, her smile just made her heartbreakingly dazzling. Feeling his lower body stirring, he turned his attention to his own rolls and beer.

After the server brought their meals, Anya twirled a strand of spaghetti around her fork and said casually, "So, are you guys it or can I expect another brother to come jumping out at me?" She stuffed the noodle into her mouth.

Kalo and Luc grinned at her then at Déisi. In their language Kalo said, "Feisty little thing."

"*Da*, she is that," Déisi agreed, sprinkling salt and pepper on his asparagus and potatoes then added butter. "Don't let the petite shy aspects fool you, she's not just an empty-headed gorgeous female, she's got balls."

It was warm in the car. Watching Anya peel the jacket off and push it over the back of her chair, Kalo said with a bit of awe and a gulp, "Ah, I'm pretty sure she doesn't have balls."

Déisi looked up at his tone and saw both his brothers gawping at Anya. He hadn't noticed her removing the coat.

She was oblivious that her full breasts spilled over the too small bra and were slightly visible in the sheer blouse. They bobbled against the blouse with her movements.

Muttering curses, Déisi growled at his brothers in their language, "Fucking stop gawking at her tits you assholes. You son of a bitch," he said to Kalo, "you did that on purpose. Is everything you bought her like that?"

Never moving his eyes, Kalo nodded with a grin. "*Da, worse.*" He smirked at his brother. "Not my fault bro, the way you described her," his gaze swept her body. "Hell, that got me fired up. And," he licked his lips, "I have to say, your description did not do her justice. There's this dress I can't wait to see her in. So low cut it will expose half her-"

"*Bréthaïdne* or not, I'm going to fucking kill you-"

Unaware of the disturbance she was causing, Anya said, "You know," cutting off a piece of meatball she chewed it delicately, "it is not polite to speak in a different language that everybody present doesn't understand."

Déisi frowned, and his brothers grinned at her.

"To answer your question," Luc struggled to raise his eyes to her face, "we have two other brothers. Marshall is the oldest at 29, Dez is next at 27, Kalo is 26, I am 24, and our youngest brother, Kollier, is just shy of 18. He's the only one not involved in our kind of work. Dez insists Kolly stay out of the line of fire and in college."

At Anya's glance of skepticism at Déisi, Luc laughed. "Yeah, people think he's older than 27 because of that dour, brooding, steely eyed-"

"Luc," Déisi sighed, "shut up."

Nodding, Anya sipped her wine. "What about sisters? Where do your parents live?"

"We have no sisters and our parents are dead," Luc answered cutting a chunk of red meat.

Sympathy wreathed her face. "Oh, I'm sorry to hear that."

"Doesn't matter, Marshall and Dez barely remember them, and the rest of us were too young to remember them when they were killed. Dez was not even 10 yet at the time and he made a deal with his life to be able to keep baby Kolly with us. He and Marshall basically raised us."

"Luc," Déisi glowered a warning at him.

Luc smirked at him and stuffed the chunk of blood-rare meat in his mouth.

"So," Anya asked, "we've been traveling for so long, where are we going that's so far away?" Déisi had refused to tell her but the chattier brothers might blab.

Kalo gulped some of his beer then tipped his shot of bourbon into it and drank some. He told her, "The bus was hired because there were many of you to retrieve, and more added when you got on the jet. Privacy and security were important ergo the private plane."

He shrugged. "Tis on de Vos' dime so whatever. Anyway, none of those people have anything to do with you. Dez was instructed to get you and he wanted us as back-up muscle. As far as where we're go-"

"Dammit, Kalo," Déisi bellowed, "shut the fuck up. What are you, fucking social-media?"

Kalo shot him the finger with a grin, and said, "Pardon me, Anyalia, for the obscene gesture," and he chugged his beer.

Anya giggled at him and said, "Call me Anya, my friends do." She didn't tell him she only had a few friends from church that she didn't see often.

First he frowned at her words, but then at the unusual sound of her pretty laughter, Déisi's brows rose as he regarded her.

Anya's cheeks and the tip of her nose were shiny pink; her eyes sparkled and wobbled slightly. He took the glass of wine, only half gone, from her hand and set it out of her reach.

"Hey," her lip thrust out.

"You've had enough, you are not experienced with the effects of it." Déisi ordered curtly, "You have a lot more to eat, get going," he nodded at her plate. The men were finished.

She had eaten a quarter of her salad, one roll, half a meatball and some of the spaghetti, she set her fork down. "I'm stuffed."

"You can eat more," he growled.

"I can't," she said firmly.

"Come on, Dez, lighten up," Kalo chided him. "Look at her and look at the plate."

The three brothers took in her thin, petite frame then the plate that was huge and teeming with noodles and two huge meatballs. "Really, bro, the only things bigger on her than the plate are-"

"Motherfucker, Kalo, shut-"

"Those big green eyes." Kalo smiled at Anya then smirked at his brother.

"Ahh," Déisi groaned. Giving in, he stabbed one of her meatballs with his fork and dropped it on his plate.

Grinning, Kalo took the other meatball and Luc grabbed the plate and finished off the pasta and the half meatball. They'd also eaten several baskets of rolls.

Anya watched the men chowing down. They were big men and they ate big.

When they all finally tossed down their napkins, Déisi said, "Tis late, time to go back to our cabins."

"We're going to the club car and have some drinks," Luc informed him, his gaze swung to Anya's chest as they all stood up.

Déisi snatched up his jacket and helped her put it on. When he went to button it, Anya mumbled, "I am not a child," and turned from him and did it herself.

Frowning at her, Déisi said to his brothers, "We can't attract attention, you guys return to your cabin with us."

Kalo opened his mouth, then seeing his brother's set face, he sighed and smiled. "Okay, an early night for us."

Déisi put his arm around Anya, tucking her against his chest so it would be hard for anyone to get a good look at her. Kalo and Luc bookended them and they all went back to their rooms.

Kalo and Luc said goodnight then disappeared into their cabin.

Déisi opened the door and gestured for Anya to go inside.

Her hands tucked in the pockets of his coat, she stepped back from him. "I am not going to sleep in there with you."

The lids slid down over his eyes giving him the dangerous gangster thug look. "Get inside, Anyalia, I am not going to argue with you."

She took another step away and shook her head. "No."

"You are getting in this room, Anyalia. If I have to come and get you, you will be sorry."

Her mouth pursed, she glared at him.

His face darkened. Eyes barely visible under the dropped lids, his mouth creased into a hard line. He was so big he took up the doorway.

She suddenly turned and bolted- and got about five feet before he grabbed her, jerking her up in the air.

"No!" she screamed kicking her feet.

Grinding out a string of foreign curses, ending with a bitten off, "Goddammit," Déisi slammed his hand over her mouth and carried her kicking into the room, shoving the door closed behind them with his boot.

He dumped her on the bed.

She scrambled to the side to run back to the door. Déisi threw his arm around her, dragging her back and slammed her on her back on the bed and rolled part of his body on top of her.

Anya's chest panted at his, her frantic breaths wisped his face. Her natural fragrance that he had struggled to avoid inhaling whenever he was close to her, now wound itself around his senses.

She beat at him with her fists, he hardly felt them. He grasped her wrists and staked them to the bed, his chest pushing down on her. He felt her breasts, soft full pillows pressing against the hardness of him.

The large green eyes stared up at him in alarm and anger. "Get off of me!" she cried.

"You want me to teach you a lesson, *Engleză ilgáně*? You want me to throw you belly down over my lap, yank those jeans down and teach your bare ass what happens when you don't obey me?"

Holding her wrists next to her head, his fingers tangled in her hair. The silken tresses curled around his fingers, her pouty lips were drawing his mouth to them like a bear to honey.

One of his legs was between hers on the bed, his manhood was hardening as quickly as helium could fill a balloon, and in a moment she would be feeling it pressed against her thigh.

Then he would shift and move his hips to between her legs where he could rub his throbbing shaft against her tender sex. He was well aware of her inexperience, she had no idea how precarious her position, and how rapidly he was losing his control.

She bucked at him shouting, "Get off of me you big hoodlum, stop calling me a brat!" She grunted, trying to push him off her. But even tipsy as she was, Anya knew she would not be winning this fight. He was too big and too strong. And now she had goaded him into threatening to spank her.

Pressing her wrists into the mattress, Déisi held her with his leg, but shifted so his cock, now hard enough to pry open manholes wasn't shoved up against her sex as it wanted to be.

His voice low, he hissed, "You stop fighting me right now, Anyalia, or I'm taking off your pants and smacking your ass until you can't sit for a month of Sundays."

Anya paused, blinked up at those fathomless liquid black discs.

Déisi had surprisingly long lashes for such a tough masculine man. They curled around his dark eyes, his lips were full, yet carved as hard as the rest of him. His weight pressed her down into the mattress, she could barely move a muscle.

She could feel his heart beating against hers, his breath with a faint trace of the beer he'd finished after dinner was mildly warm misting her face. His strong jaw was dark and bristly with his 5 o'clock shadow, the scar white against the beating vein at his temple.

Anya should have felt repulsed, but instead, she felt, odd. His manly body pressing on her feminine curves brought tiny strange prickles through her body, starting at the apex between her legs.

That apex was growing strangely warm and tingly. Her confusion stalled her efforts to get him off her.

"You done fighting me *svini ilgánĕ*? If you are, I will let you up." *She'd better say yes or they would both have a problem.*

Alarmed at the new sensations spiraling through her virgin's body, Anya didn't move.

"*Bună.*" He rolled to sit up pulling her up with him. Leaning his back against the wall, he nodded to the bathroom. "You have one opportunity, that means right now, if you want to take a shower before bed."

Stiffly, she looked at him then to the other bed and back to him.

Getting her drift, he said drily, "I've told you, I am not attracted to you, you are only a job to me. I am not going to sleep with you, force myself on you. This is your bed, that one over there is mine."

His bed was under the window. He wanted to be between her and any escape she could try to manage. "Now, I won't repeat myself, go shower or you won't have another chance."

Damn, he'd never had so much trouble getting someone to do as he instructed, most people were so afraid of him they jumped to do as he said. But no, not this stubborn slip of a girl.

She stared at him for a few beats, then slid off the bed, stopped at the suitcase on the table, pulled out some clothes and went into the bathroom without looking once at him.

As soon as the door closed, Déisi let out his held breath. He got to his feet and adjusted his pants, loosening the material over the hard-on that strained against it.

Hearing the shower turn on, he sighed, it was going to be tough being with her until he turned her over to de Vos. The thought of that made his dinner threaten to crawl up his throat. Tossing a little innocent lamb to a ravenous lion was not what he wanted to be thinking about as he slept tonight.

When Anya came out of the shower, a flowery fragrance swirled around her making his dick hard all over again. What the hell kind of shampoo and crap did Kalo buy her anyway? At least he bought her pajamas and not some slinky nightgown.

Déisi didn't think he could have made it if she came out in transparent silk. The pajamas were pink and white and satiny.

Clutching her clothes to her chest, she was obviously uncomfortable being in front of him dressed in nightwear no matter how much it covered her up.

When she put up her clothes and combed out her damp hair, Déisi snapped, "Get into bed." The sharpness of his tone gave her pause. He stood motionless, hands in his pockets, gaze direct at her and unreadable.

Something about his tone made Anya move straight to the bed and climb in. As she pulled the sheet and blanket over her, Déisi trod over to her bed.

Long fiery lashes swept nervously up and down her cheeks, her body turned rigid in apprehension of his intent.

Bending over, Déisi reached down, grasped her hand, lifted it out, snapped a handcuff on it and then he cuffed the other end to the wrought iron bed leg.

"Hey!" She moved to sit up.

"Lay down," his voice barked commanding and tough.

"But why? I can't get past you out the door." Sitting up, she hated that her voice had a trebly whine to it.

"I warned you if you tried to escape you would be punished. You tried to get off the train, and now you screamed and tried to run when I told you to get inside the cabin. You will learn I mean what I say, and you will learn to obey me. Lie down."

"But, I can't sleep bound like this!"

He bent over further, set one hand on his thigh, the other on her shoulder and pushed her on her back. "I said lie down." When she lay still, green orbs glaring up at him, he was satisfied and left to take his own shower.

When he came out wearing boxers, and a T, he trod over to her.

She was curled partially on her side with her hand over the mattress, the wrist cuffed. The curly lashes rested unmoving on her cheeks, tiny lips closed as she breathed quietly in sleep.

He shouldn't, but Déisi sat down on the edge of the mattress and studied her.

The beautiful face strained in fear while she was awake, was now soft in repose. His hand of its own volition reached out and stroked the long, flaming flaxen hair.

His eyes went from the plush lips lower, to the equally plush breasts that rounded under the pajamas. He'd been growing hard even before he had sat down. This was a bad idea.

Déisi stood up quickly, turned out the lights and climbed into his own bed. At least with her cuffed he didn't have to worry about her sneaking out and hurling herself to her death from the moving train.

Gah, he sighed, even the toughest of felons didn't give him as hard a time as that one little woman. She refused to comprehend what kind of man he was and what he was capable of.

But then, she didn't know how much blood he had on his hands.

Chapter Nine

When Déisi's eyes opened with a yawn very late the next day, it was well past morning, he saw Anya was already awake and looking at him.

"Finally," she said shaking the chain around her wrist, "you're awake. Can you please take this off me now?" It was obvious she was frustrated and pissed but was trying to sound friendly and polite.

Déisi swallowed his smile. He had spent his life learning to read people to gage their degree of danger and whether or not they were lying. Her face was like a window to her soul, she couldn't hide her emotions.

He unlocked her and she hurried to the bathroom. Picking up the phone in the room he dialed and ordered food to be brought to the room.

When Anya came back out dressed, he was calmly waiting beside the bathroom. She gasped as he grabbed her arm and brought her straight to the bed, pushed her gently down on it, then clamped the cuff back on.

Lower lip shoved out in an angry moue, she whined, "Mr. Zukov, why are you doing this?"

Not answering her, he strode away to get shaved and dressed. As he emerged from the bathroom there was a knock at the door.

A curtain was positioned for privacy, which he hadn't closed between them last night, but now he closed it and opened the door.

The attendant came in with a tray that he set on the table. He couldn't see Anya behind the curtain.

"*Mulțumesc*," Déisi thanked him and handed him a tip. He shut door then opened the curtain to a fuming Anya.

"Listen Mr. Zukov, you unlock this- this thing right now!" she demanded, shaking the wrist with the cuff around it.

He moved the table to in front of her, took off the tops to the dishes and set them aside. He grabbed a chair and set it on the other side of the table and plopped down.

"Mmm," he mumbled hungrily, and dove right into his fried eggs. He ate two of the four he'd ordered then sat back to take a sip of coffee.

"This is delicious, smell it." He sniffed the air. "Doesn't that smell great?"

Her mouth a straight line, eyes narrowed furiously at him, Anya didn't move, but her gaze dipped to the food. It not only smelled great, it looked great. But she was not eating with the heathen shackled.

Déisi lifted a piece of buttered toast. Taking a few huge bites, eating half of it, he washed it down with a glass of orange juice. She still didn't move.

"Okay," he said to her. "This is the way it is. Every time you don't do as I say, or try to run from me, you will be cuffed, and if you scream or try to ask anyone for help, you will be gagged as well."

He watched her lips turn harder upside down, the emerald glower shooting bullets at him.

"And," he said, dragging the other half of the toast through gooey eggs, sopping them up, "until you eat every fucking, pardon me," he said sarcastically, "every piece of food that's on that plate," he nodded to her plate, "I will not take off the cuff." He popped the toast in his mouth and wiped his mouth with the back of his hand.

Her eyes sprang in incredulity to his.

His brows arched. "I wasn't clear enough? Okay, I'll be clearer. Unless you eat every bite I will not remove the cuff." He cut a sausage in three parts and ate one, chewing vigorously.

She watched him for a moment, then hesitantly picked up a glass of orange juice, took a few sips and set it down.

The black brows drew down. "I'm not playing here, Anyalia, I mean it. Don't eat and you'll stay cuffed all day, all night."

Lips pulled in, with a mean glare at him, Anya cut out a piece of crispy home fries and slipped it in her mouth. Stifling a moan, it was all she could do not to gush how delicious it was. She was not giving him that satisfaction.

Shaking his head while putting blueberry jam on another piece of toast, Déisi thought to himself, under that delicate exterior she's a tough one all right. Stubborn and brave wrapped up in the most beautiful feminine package he'd ever seen.

But, he gobbled down the toast in three bites, she learned now that he was the boss. He was confident he'd have no more trouble with her.

Anya put cream and sugar in her coffee and stirred it before tasting it to see if it was sweet enough.

"Why do you bother putting the coffee in? Just drink sugared milk," he teased watching her add more sugar. Déisi relaxed a little, she was eating and stopped scowling at him over being handcuffed.

She wrinkled her nose at him in response and sipped the coffee. Curious, she asked, "Mr. Zukov, are you married? Do you have children?"

He buttered his third piece of toast shaking his head. "Na. As you heard my loud mouthed brother, I spent years raising our three younger brothers, that was enough."

"But Luc said you were less than ten years old when you lost your parents. Surely someone else was raising all of you?"

Setting the toast down he shook his head. Looking at his plate and not her he said, "Na. When our parents were kill- uh, died, Marshall and I were already in…let's call it a boarding school."

A boarding school with the curriculum of murder techniques, hand-to-hand combat, martial arts and weapons training. "We were only…educated, there was no one to see to our care. We were on our own." She had 2 eggs on her plate. Knowing she wouldn't eat both, he forked one and dropped it on his plate.

"Luc said you had to make some kind of a deal, with your life, to keep everyone together?"

Chewing, bent over his plate, he looked up at her through a lock of black hair.

She was sitting primly, neatly cutting her food into small pieces and eating so daintily he thought he was at the queen's fucking tea party.

He never talked about their formative years. They had been hard, miserable, painful, the only good part was they allowed the brothers to stay together, but with strings.

Anya waited expectantly with interest on her face. A woman had never shown any interest in his past before, Déisi wasn't sure what to tell her, if anything. Then she smiled.

Her smile made him want to suck on her lips. Better to keep talking. "Ah, we, that is our parents were in the militia in our country, except it was with rebels not with the government. So we had to live in hiding, and in constant danger. When Marshall was not yet five and I was three, we were entered into…um, militia training."

Her eyes lifted wide, the brows pinched in distress. "What? You were babies! How could they-"

"Ah, Anyalia, it was the way of things, there's no use bleating about it now. Tis in the past."

Aghast, she asked, "How did your parents die?"

He shrugged, set his napkin on his plate and sat back holding his coffee cup. "A civil war within our country, our parents were on the losing side. They were," his eyes drifted to the window, he squinted at the remembrance. Even as small children they had been forced to watch. A lesson for them.

He thought he was well over it, but his exhale actually brought him physical pain. "They were executed."

"Oh, Mr. Zukov, I am so sorry. To lose them at so young an age, you must have been devastated."

He shrugged again. "Not really. They were away most of the time fighting, leaving us to our own military training, we seldom saw them. Even when our mother was pregnant, she fought as long as she could, delivered each baby then went right back out. We took care of each other including the baby, he was only a few weeks old when..." he took a breath, "they were killed."

They were both quiet for a while. Then Anya said, "Luc said you made a deal for your youngest brother, the baby, Kollier was it?"

Sipping his coffee, he nodded, his face an iron blank. "*Da.*" Shoving the hair back off his forehead, he looked at her then away.

"Because he was an infant, after the execution, the...leaders, wanted to...dispose of him. Babies were too much trouble and no one had time to care for them. So," he took a deep breath, "I made the deal that I would give my life in service to the military if they would let us keep Kollier and let us all stay together. Anton de Vos bought my papers years ago."

"Oh, Mr. Zukov you poor thing, never having any choices, any chances."

The last thing he wanted was pity. Déisi dragged his blunt fingertips down his face and rubbed his chin. "Like I said, tis done and over, water under the bridge."

"And now," she said softly, "you have been ordered to bring me, somewhere. Your job." She set her coffee down. "Can't you tell me where, why are you bringing me? Anything?"

His hard eyes stated he was not telling her anything.

She asked, "What country are you from?"

A shoulder bumped as he answered, "Tis of no consequence. We were moved around so much, hidden, fortunately there were teachers here and there to teach us, we lived amongst all different kinds of people with different accents, languages, we often mix words of different languages together."

His lip ticked up. "Which is fine, so few people can understand us when we are speaking. But," he set the empty coffee cup down, "as to your question about what country we are from, my brothers and I were brutalized, forced into military servitude, never shown an ounce of kindness, our parents murdered, bah," he rolled his shoulders. "We claim no country as ours."

He looked so disturbed, enraged, resigned. Anything Anya could say would only worsen his feelings so she didn't say anything.

They sat in silence for a few minutes, then she said, "So, you didn't say if you have wife, or a significant other. Judging by that woman on the bus, women are attracted to you. Considering the types of people you associate with, I guess you play the field. Or, unlikely as it is, Mr. Zukov, is there an open minded wife or girlfriend sitting at home waiting for you?"

His eyes narrowed at her, but her fresh face was void of guile, or sarcasm hinting that he fucked anything that walked in front of him because no good woman would have him. And if one was unfortunate to be his wife, he would screw around on her without a trace of guilt, shame, or secret.

As he was thinking earlier, her face was an open book; she couldn't hide anything, that's why he could tell when she was planning on trying to escape from him.

Instead of answering the question, he said, "I've told you my name is Déisi. You call me Mr. Zukov. Coming from a young woman less than ten years younger than me makes me sound like an old man or a school teacher."

She had the nerve to giggle at him. "You are of course neither of those. But," the smile left her pretty face, "you are holding me prisoner. I've seen how people fear you, like the waiter, and how violent you are, the way you struck Darryl on the plane," she shuddered with the memory.

Déisi had only backhanded the man the first time, but with so much power and strength Darryl was thrown across the bus like he was an empty soda can. Then when Déisi punched Darryl for slapping her, the man hurtled even harder, further, and was knocked out. And Darryl Dassey was by no means a small man.

Déisi's gaze scrolled over her face, his own features hardened. She was saying since he acted like a thug, a barbarian, that she wanted to stay as impersonal with him as possible. That they were so polar opposites, he was not good enough for her. That they could never be more than brutal abductor and helpless captive.

Huh. Where the hell had that thought come from? What in the hell made him even consider that they could be more? He studied her through tapered eyes.

She was wearing the snug, white jeans, and a short-sleeved, pink blouse that did nothing to hide the plumpness of her breasts. She was barefoot and her hair was rumpled like she'd just awakened or been made love to.

His body started burning, Déisi abruptly stood up. "I need to speak with my brothers," he stalked to the door.

"Wait! The handcuff- Mr. Zukov you said if I-" the door slammed behind him.

Chapter Ten

Déisi had to get away from Anya.

He knew his brothers would only taunt him about her, so he strode through the coaches until he came to one which was designated the smoking car.

He opened the door to a cloud of smoke, a crowd, and a small bar.

Wearing black jeans, boots, and a burgundy sweater, he moved to the bar, pulled out his pack of European thin cigars from a pocket in the t-shirt he wore under the sweater, and lit one. He ordered a beer then moved over near the window that was partially opened at the top.

"Zukov," a lusty voice drawled his name.

Groaning inside, Déisi's skin quivered at the sound.

Busty Paulina pushed through the crowd to get to him.

Ignoring her call out, he leaned a shoulder against the window. Holding the bottle and cigar in the same hand, he tipped his beer to his mouth.

Paulina immediately wrapped her sturdy arms around his empty arm and squashed her big breasts against his huge bicep.

"Ah, Zukov, those muscles, I'd love to see you put them to good use, on me." Her lashes batted without a hint of reticence.

"Hey Paulina," he said flatly. Chugging half his beer, he extricated his arm from between her tits hoping her overpowering perfume was not clinging to him.

"Zukov, Déisi darling," holding a cocktail in one hand, she cooed, "you are so hot. You know how to dress, you are half GQ and half," she moaned running a hand up his thick chest, "crude savage. Such a raw man, uh," guttural sensual groans crept up her throat.

"Listen," her hand stroked back down and over his taut abdomen. "God, you are so hard. And as I remember," with a leer, she drew her hand down further to grip his manhood.

Just what he wanted to hear, confirmation that he was a barbarian. Scowling, he grabbed her hand and pushed her back.

"*Basta*, enough, Paulina, stop mauling me." He had a better understanding now of how Anya had felt being pawed against her will. By him.

"Oh, come on, hunky," she pouted with a smile. "You finally drop off that scrawny bitch? You have time now for me." She snuggled up against him trying to slide her hand over his fly.

Again he pushed her away. While Anya's pout was adorable, sexy and unaware, Paulina's was annoying, deliberate and unattractive.

Muttering, "I need another beer," Déisi elbowed her out of the way and went to the bar. Stubbing out his cigar, he ordered another beer and a shot of whiskey. Paulina followed him, set her glass on the bar and hugged herself against his back.

"Come on big boy, I can tell you are lusty and robust, an alpha dominator." She rubbed her melon tits all over his back, cooing, "And damned big. I can't wait to ride you; we can have so much fun together."

Thinking of Anya's pout with Paulina rubbing all over him made Déisi feel trashy and weird. He chugged the beer right down, gulped the whiskey in one shot, and ordered another beer with a double whiskey.

Turning, he pushed the big blonde away again demanding, "You stop touching me, Paulina, or so help me *Dios* I'll knock you on your wide ass."

"Oo, I'd love for you to try, handsome." She rubbed against him again wriggling her breasts over his chest.

Wishing it was Anya who was all over him, that wanted him, Déisi tossed back the liquor, slammed the shot glass down. Draining his beer, he slammed that down on the counter, and ordered a fourth beer and another double as he gripped Paulina's shoulders and set her away from him.

But like a yo-yo, she came right back at him. He slugged down the beer and whiskey without stopping and ordered yet another.

"Hey bro," Kalo said in their language as he came up to him. "I can't believe you'd tear yourself away from that hot little piece you have in your cabin. You know, *Anya*." He stressed her name smugly pointing out that she had told him to call her Anya as her friends did, and never said the same to Déisi.

"I know if it were me, we'd be sharing one of those tiny beds right now with me impaling that sweet little body writhing under me." He grinned at Paulina, greeting her in English, "Hi honey."

Downing the alcohol, Déisi scowled at his brother. "You know man, sometimes you never know when to shut up." Like he needed a picture of his brother slamming Anya in his head.

"Zukov," Paulina drawled in her most sultry voice, "who is your friend?"

A rare mischievous grin tugged up the side of Déisi's tough face. "Ah, you haven't met my brother." He set a hand on Kalo's shoulder and introduced them. "This is my brother, Kalo. Kalo, this is Paulina. She is also on her way to de Vos under Darryl Dassey's supervision."

Panting eagerly, "*Ohh*," Paulina turned her attention to Kalo. "You are one nice big hunk too. How many Zukovs are there? And are you all this huge and good looking?"

Letting Paulina rub up against him like an un-spayed cat, Kalo grinned and told her, "There are five of us hot specimens.

Yep, we all pretty much look the same, 'cept a bit of different coloring."

Paulina stroked her hands up his chest and over his shoulders then propped her breasts on his chest. "Ah, that sounds like something to put on my bucket list, fuck all five Zukov brothers. Not at once of course," her giggle spurt libidinous and crass. Grinning slyly, she murmured, "Well, actually on second thought, that sounds like fun. When can I meet all of the-"

Déisi took the opportunity to slip away from the pair. His personal rule was never to get intoxicated on a job, he always needed to be sharp, have full use of his faculties, and another rule was to never, ever, get involved with a woman on any mission.

And here, he'd run from Anya's mesmerizing draw, rattled by her words referring to him as a brute and basically a male whore, and gone and gotten stinking drunk.

Huh, like he couldn't handle himself, couldn't control himself around a babe as young and inexperienced as her. Which was half the problem, she had no idea how gorgeous and sexy she was. He got steel hard just thinking of her.

The day de Vos showed him her picture he had been instantly captivated. Not only exquisitely beautiful, she was laughing with her grandfather, her smile so sweet and loving. He had to see her. Had to.

And he had to keep the other men de Vos would hire from going after her, they would have seriously hurt her, and enjoyed doing it. De Vos didn't care what condition she was delivered to him in, as long as she could provide the goods.

Déisi strode through coach after coach, his brain running in circles. He'd never felt this strong an attraction to a female before. His entire existence had always been nothing but use and dump.

It was the life he lived, the sort of people that orbited de Vos and his abominable ilk, as well as Déisi himself. He couldn't point the judgmental finger at de Vos, when Déisi was as ruthless, hollow, violent and despicable as him.

Now that Déisi has seen Anyalia in the flesh, he was ten times more besotted than he had been with the picture of her. He'd made a dangerous bed for himself to lie in. Bed. Great. That made him picture a naked Anya on her back, arms raised to him beckoning him to come to her, those green eyes sultry and radiating desire...for him.

Cursing under his breath, he muttered, "Ah bloody hell," he should not have drunk so much. He would be shit protection for her if he needed to be.

He stumbled back to their room. It took him two tries before he got the door unlocked and opened.

Anya was sitting on the bed, of course, she was chained to it.

Late afternoon and the breakfast tray was still there. His eyes dipped to it, she'd eaten about half her food, then he raised his eyes back to her, and smiled.

She was pissed. Her little face was all red, cheeks shiny, green eyes spitting fire. The great *Dios* himself could not have made a prettier, sexier, angel.

Déisi started towards her and stumbled again.

Her lashes flew up, then lowered, she lost the angry look, her face now filled with trepidation. A sober Déisi was a dangerous man; she didn't know what to make of an obviously drunk one.

He picked up the tray and took it and set it outside the door on the floor. He'd given strict instructions that he wanted no one in his cabin, no maids, no attendants. If he wanted them for anything he would call them.

He came back into the room and trod over to her. His lips bunched at her shrinking away from him against the wall.

"Anyaaalia," damn he was slurring, he cleared his throat. "Listen-"

"Take this off of me!" she demanded shaking her wrist.

Aw, how cute, she was mad again. Moving closer, he drawled, "What will you give me if I do?"

Her forehead wrinkled puzzled, brows rose. "I- you know that I have nothing to give you."

"*Da*, you do," he purred. His lids covered most of his dark irises so she couldn't see his pupils dilating, or his cock swelling in his jeans.

"I don't understand." She held up her free hand warding him off as he moved closer. But he kept coming until he stood with his legs against the bed, then he bent over setting his hands on the mattress.

"Uh, can you step back, you smell of smoke and liquor." Nose wrinkling, her voice filled with disapproval.

Smiling, Déisi purred, "Ah, tis the scent of men, don't you like it?"

"Mr. Zukov, please-"

"Déisi," he growled, and leaned towards her.

Suddenly, the train changed tracks and the coach jerked and jolted sideways throwing Déisi forward.

Anya squealed, and he had to throw his hands against the wall on either side of her head to stop himself from falling on her.

Holding steady, his eyes bored into hers then dropped to her lips, they were parted from being startled. He took advantage of it, slanted his head and covered her mouth with his.

Anya immediately protested, pushing at his chest, but he moved one hand from the wall and cradled the back of her head holding her immobile while his mouth ravaged hers. Damned if she didn't taste as sweet as she looks and acts.

Déisi's brain burned and swirled, he forced her lips to stay open. Slicking his tongue along her top lip, he nipped the bottom one then thrust his tongue into her mouth. He felt her pushing at his chest but he couldn't stop.

Relentlessly, he kissed her, chasing and sucking at her tongue, shoving his tongue down her throat before tasting her all over again. Then, Anya responded.

She moved her free hand from his chest and clutched his sweater at his bicep as she accepted his plundering and tried to follow his moves.

Déisi about came in his jeans and died on the spot. Her innocence was crystal in her kiss, it was beyond enticing. He thought he would explode from the thrill of it, the taste of her, fresh, tender, sweet. Her natural scent stole up his nose tantalizing him further like he was a rutting animal.

His brain a red haze of pure sensation, keeping his lips hard on hers, Déisi reached for the buttons on her blouse. He had most of them undone before she even realized he was pulling her blouse apart.

Her lips froze on his; her hand went back to his chest and pushed at him again. She tried to turn her head from his rampaging mouth but he kept her still with the force of his kiss. He pushed the sides of the blouse off her shoulders and reached for her pants.

Tugging at the top button, he netted the back of her neck with his long fingers holding her still and groaned into her mouth, "*Anyalia*," then lowered his head to first suck at her neck, before dropping to the swell of her breast.

Stunned from his heady kisses, Anya gasped and panted to catch her breath.

Still working on opening her pants, Déisi sucked her flesh with rumbled growls, filling his face with her curves. Licking the mounds, biting and sucking them until red spots rose.

"No-" she gasped. "Please, stop, Mr. Zukov-" she pushed futilely with her free hand. But he was a rutting bull and she was helpless to stop him.

"Déisi," he mumbled against her breast and brought his hand up to cup it. "*Gah*, Anyalia," he groaned. "You are lush and beautiful all over."

He caressed her breast over the silk bra and pushed his face down her cleavage seeking a nipple while forcing her to lie on her back. "You will be just as tender and soft inside wrapped around my cock, *babia*."

"No, please, Mr. Zukov, Déisi, stop!"

He reached behind her back to unclasp her bra, the other hand unzipping her pants.

Anya yelled, "Stop! Please stop!" and punched at his chest. Her cries of alarm finally knifed through the whirlpool of blind desire that enveloped him.

Déisi pulled back, eyes bleary with lust and liquor gazed through a mist of confusion at her.

Her distress was clear on her expressive face. Panic radiated from the green irises, rapid breaths fast and shallow and frightened panted through her parted lips and hitched her chest.

His gaze fell to her heaving breasts wet and red from his mouth, tongue, teeth. Like a moth to a flame, he lowered his head to her bosom-

Anya put her hand on his head and pushed it back exclaiming, "Please, stop."

Shaking his head to clear the haze, Déisi licked his lips and moved back from her. Only then did he realize what he was doing.

Her shirt almost off her, pants undone, marks from his mouth all over her neck and breasts, and her eyes glowing with terror, of him.

"Fuck," he cursed. Swiping the back of his hand over his mouth, he raked his palms over his hair. His chest rising and falling like a rough current, his eyes shifted to her chained wrist and he cursed again.

His stomach sinking like a rock, a hot flush shot up his neck. Hell, he was raping a woman who hadn't said yes, a virgin, and for fuck's sake, she was fucking restrained. And they weren't playing a consensual bondage game.

Mi Dios, he dragged his hand over his hair again and sucked in a heavy breath. He was a disgusting animal, what the hell had come over him?

She struggled to sit up, her chest huffing from her efforts to stop him. Staring at him with those big frightened, beautiful eyes, it felt like a dagger stabbed into his heart, and his balls. Déisi knew what had come over him.

He'd been lusting after since he'd first seen her picture, and his mind was gone by the time he held her in his arms when he was abducting her.

What a piece of work, what a man. Snatching a powerless woman off the street, restraining her, then sexually assaulting her when she couldn't defend herself. Not that having two free hands would have made a difference.

If her voice hadn't cut through to his enflamed mind, he might have completed the act, against her will. And without protection. His erection was clawing to get out of his pants and get to her, inside her. His eyes fell to her open blouse.

Licking his lips, his heated gaze lowered to her open pants, the haze of overwhelming lust was ascending again, making him deaf and blind to anything but getting inside her. He was again the mindless rutting dog.

But words slammed into his head. Anya was a virgin. He would hurt her with his savagery, he- he needed to get the hell out of there.

He pushed off the bed to his feet, took out his keys and unlocked the cuff then about raced out the door. Next door, he pounded on the cabin door.

The door opened and he was surprised to see Kalo was back from the bar and not banging Paulina somewhere.

Kalo opened his mouth to make a crack but then he saw how disturbed his brother was. "What's going on, bro?"

"I need you to stay with her. I…need to go," Déisi mumbled almost incoherently.

Kalo looked at his mussed hair, his gaze went to Déisi's jeans where the hard bulge was clearly outlined. Kalo's brows slashed down. "Tell me, *bréthaïdne*, you didn't hurt her."

His expression sheepish for the first time in his life, Déisi muttered, "Ah, not exactly, sort of, oh shit," they could hear her muted sobs through the wall.

"You son of a bitch, Dez! You fucking forced yourself on that girl? I can't believe you-"

Déisi choked, wiped at his face. "Ah, just stay with her, I gotta go, I need a drink," and he staggered away down the hall.

Stunned, Kalo watched his brother, who was always calm and in control in every situation, always, become unglued over of all things, a woman.

Sucking in a few deep breaths, he called to Luc, told him to go after Dez, then went next door and opened the door and went inside.

Chapter Eleven

Anya had pulled a blanket over herself and was huddled under it, she had nowhere to go, nowhere to hide.

Kalo walked slowly to her. She pulled the blanket up higher, holding it tight to her chin like a shield.

Kalo said softly, "I swear, Anya," he held his hands up, "I won't harm you, I won't come any closer."

Crying, "Where is *he*?" she frantically looked at the door expecting Déisi to come charging in and pounce on her.

Sitting down to ease some of her alarm at his presence, he saw she was fully dressed and sighed with relief. His brother might have been all over her without her acquiescence but it didn't look like he had raped her as he'd feared.

Kalo said quietly, "He is not here. He's ah, staying away for a bit." He looped his fingers together setting them in his lap. "Listen, Anya, I swear, Dez would never harm a female, especially you." His lips pulled in at her look of cynicism.

He said, "We are not just brothers but best friends. We have had women all over the world, uh," his face colored slightly at her frown.

"I mean, what I'm saying is, women throw themselves at him all day long, but I've never seen him act the way he does with you. Anya, truly, he obviously has feelings for you, *na*," he said shaking his head at her look of raised brows in disbelief and lips crooked in derision.

"*Da*, of course he is sexually attracted to you, who wouldn't be? But," he ran on quickly at her lips tightening, "the gentle way he treats you, getting a doctor for you, covering your body up so other men can't ogle you, making sure you eat so you don't get sick. He's never been that way before, Anya, ever."

"Gentle?" She snorted with disgust. "If that's his gentle side I'd hate to see him tough."

Nodding with a lop-sided grin, Kalo agreed, "*Yah*, I know. He is a coarse, rough, aggressive man. We all are." The grin left, in its place was a sadness. "We had to be, Anya, we had no choice. We were trained to be, and wouldn't have survived if we hadn't hardened into tough, ruthless men. And he had it harder than the rest of us.

"He withstood more beatings to keep the heat off the rest of us, and sold his body and soul to keep us together, to keep our baby brother with us. But, honey, he just left me in the bar, that whore Paulina was rubbing and touching him all over, shit she-"

Anya's soft face stiffened. "Uh huh. He feels special towards me. That's why he was making out with that- that woman, then came here and assaulted me. I guess he left to go back to her to have sex, or be with some other woman. Please, Kalo, stop talking."

Rolling his eyes at his blabbing mouth, he said, "*Na*, no, you get me wrong. Paulina was all over him, but he was yanking her hands off him with anger when I came in. He sicced her on me, and as soon as her head was turned, he split faster than you could say snowflake, and came straight here to you."

Kalo smiled at the fight he'd had to put up to get the bitch's claws off of him and get away with his hide intact. Lifting his arm he sniffed his sleeve and made a face. Her stinking perfume was all over him.

He watched Anya trying to absorb all that he was telling her and secretly prayed that his brother would get Paulina's perfume off him before he came back to the cabin or Anya would never believe anything he or Dez ever said again.

Women were notoriously unforgiving when they smelled another woman's perfume on a man, or saw lipstick on their collar.

He forked a few fingers through his dark blond hair then said gently, "Anyway, honey, Dez doesn't normally take on the female, ah, abductions. He is sent after the worst of the hard-core felons. But shit, you have to understand." He paused before continuing.

"The men de Vos originally picked for the job, of uh, snatching you, well," his shoulders bunched with his exhale. "They were more than willing to send one of your fingers, or other body part to prove de Vos was serious about harming you if he didn't get what he wanted. That would be after they joyfully raped you over and over, brutally, without a care to your wellbeing."

He smiled kindly. "Your sad tears would have brought them much laughter and sadistic urges to cause more of them to fall. They wouldn't have stopped assaulting you, run from you and tell me to come in and sit with you, protect you."

Face stricken white, her voice low, terribly quiet, Anya asked, "And what does this de Vos person want?"

Kalo hesitated, Déisi hadn't wanted her to know why she was taken. But, she would find out soon, and she might be more compliant if she knew where she was going and why.

He sucked in a heavy breath, let it out slow. "De Vos has your grandfather. He wants something from him and Dauphine refused to give it to him. De Vos threatened him with torture, mutilation, death, if he didn't spill, but your grandfather wouldn't give it up.

"So de Vos came up with the idea of kidnapping you, and bringing you to your grandfather and..." ah shit, her face was turning green. Déisi was going to kill him.

"My granddad?" Her voice tight and shrill, she cried, "He's hurting my granddad? What does this man want from him?" Tears welled immediately and spilled over her cheeks.

Ah shit, big mistake, no wonder Dez had kept the mission from her. Well, he'd already let the cat out of the bag. The girl would undoubtedly badger him mercilessly until he spilled it all.

"De Vos thought if he had you in front of him, he could force Dauphine to talk. If he didn't spill the information he wanted, de Vos would threaten to…harm you." He paused again, he never should have started.

Anya's beautiful face was stricken stark white.

Knowing she'd never let up on him now, Kalo went on, "He had, as I said, wanted a body part at first to prove to your grandfather he could access you, then he decided to just get you and bring you there. Déisi was present for another job when he heard the discussion of the other mercenaries offering to do the mission, to…hurt you, take you."

Kalo leaned forward, his expression earnest that she believe him. "None of us brothers would kidnap or harm a woman. But those bastards were willing to…harm you. So, Dez volunteered for the job. He felt he could keep you safe until he figured out what to do.

"He couldn't just put you in hiding, because eventually, after cutting off pieces of him one at a time to get him to talk, de Vos would have killed your grandfather. Dez was trying to help-"

Anya jumped up with her hand over her mouth and ran to the bathroom slamming and locking the door.

Kalo could hear her retching inside. "Aw fuck," he muttered. He got up and went and knocked on the bathroom door. "Anya, uh, honey, come out, it will all be okay, I swear, please don't be upset." He waited, pretty sure she was not about to come out.

Grabbing handfuls of hair on both sides of his head he tugged them in desperation, he'd made a colossal mistake. He considered taking the door down, it wouldn't take but one shoulder hit or kick, but it would likely only frighten her more.

Not having any idea what to do with a sobbing woman, one that was now so terrified she was physically sick, he stepped outside of the cabin to think.

Déisi and Luc were coming down the hall.

His eyes were bloodshot, but Déisi was walking straighter.

"Why are you out here?" he demanded as he approached Kalo.

"Ah, I sort of upset her." Kalo rambled what he had told Anya and how she reacted.

His head hanging, shaking it, Déisi said, "Great. I assault her, and you terrorize her with thoughts of mutilation of both her and her grandfather. We're a hell of a pair, huh?"

Luc offered, "We aren't used to women like her, Dez, dainty, ladylike little things. We're used to rough and tough, fuck 'em and leave 'em, the kind that don't care for pretty manners and nice talk. She's…different. We don't know how to deal with her kind."

Kalo snorted with a choke of shame. "Tis a good thing we aren't the marrying kind, because the chicks we dig aren't either. That little miss is the kind you want to take home to mother, if you had one, and raise children with. Good thing that's not for us, huh? We can stick with our whores and be happy."

"*Da*, sure, good thing," Déisi mumbled miserably.

The brothers stood for a bit, thoughtfully quiet.

His chest swelled with a deep breath, exhaling roughly, Déisi said, "She hasn't had anything to eat since this morning. Give her some time to compose herself, then bring her to the dining room. She'll feel better if she's not locked in a room with a bunch of horny assholes."

"Speak for yourself, dick," Kalo grumbled.

"Huh," Déisi groused. "At least I didn't scare the living shit out of her. Now she has to worry about getting cut into little pieces and her grandfather being tortured and murdered."

"Shit," Luc chuckled. "Between the two of you, you sure know how to freak out a female. Maybe I should be the one to be with her for the time being."

He nodded at Déisi. "She thinks you're a rapacious dog, and you," he winked at Kalo, "you've given her nightmares to last a lifetime. I think she could do with a fresh, calm, innocuous face."

117

His mouth opened to deny his brother, then Déisi thought about it. What he said was true. But, hell, he wanted to be the one to comfort her, not be the one she needed comforting from.

"Okay. But make sure she puts that eye-catching hair up in a hat. All right," his sigh laborious, he said, "Kalo and I will head for the dining car and wait for you there."

Grinning at him, Kalo said with a smirk, "More coffee?"

Shooting him the finger, Déisi said a bit queasy, "*Na*, I just poured about a gallon of it down my throat. Listen," he held a hand out to Luc, "don't say anything that could possibly upset her further. If she asks questions about her granddad, tell her we will discuss it at the table. I think she might feel better if she sees other people than just us mercenary bruisers right now. Okay?"

After they left, Luc hung outside for a while then knocked and went into the cabin.

He heard the shower so he sat in the chair closest to the front door to not startle her when she came out and saw him there. Although, between his two lug-headed brothers, she had to assume one of them would be inside the room, especially since she wasn't cuffed. He saw the handcuff on the edge of the bed.

It was fifteen minutes before she came out, damp curls dripping down her back. She was fully dressed, of course she hadn't come out expecting to be alone. She eyed Luc warily.

He held both hands up as if in surrender. "I come in peace. The other two jackasses are in the dining car. Dez said to bring you there when you've had some time to, uh, regroup. You okay?"

Her small hands curled on her hips, sarcasm saturating her tone, "Oh, sure, I'm great. Your brother just about rapes me, and your other brother tells me my beloved granddad is in terrible danger, as am I. Yeah, sure, I'm great." Tears welled, she choked them back.

"Ah, um," he wanted to go to her but decided she'd feel safer if he stayed where he was. She was a slender petite thing and he was a muscle-bound hulk.

"I know it all sounds…hopeless right now, Anya, but you don't know my brother, Déisi. He always makes the impossible, possible. Trust him. Yeah, I know," holding up a hand, he nodded with a grin, "so far tis tough to trust any of us, but," his face turned serious. "But I know us Zukov brothers; we could stop the world from spinning if we had to."

As he spoke, he could see her shoulders lose some of their stiffness, lips a little less tight, the fingers gripping her hips loosened.

Luc said, "So, you ready to go to the dining car? You have to be dying to get out of this cave, huh?"

She smiled wryly at that. "I guess."

He handed her the hat, she took it with a droll roll of her eyes. She twisted the long locks on top of her head then plunked the cap down on top of it.

The dining car was half a dozen cars or so up the line but it only took a few moments to get there.

As they passed people, several men moved to approach them, their eyes on Anya, but one look from the tall, broad shouldered young man with a boxer's physique deterred them.

There were actually several dining coaches strung together.

Déisi and Kalo were waiting in the furthest car.

Facing out, Déisi saw Luc and Anya enter the first car, his groan alerted Kalo who turned around.

Normally, after Anya put her cap on, Déisi would pull the bill down low to conceal as much of her face as possible, and he made sure she wore his jacket, but Luc hadn't been as careful.

Déisi could see the interest in the males the second Anya stepped into the first car. As before, Luc glared at them and most looked away.

But, she walked gracefully through the coach, breasts moving against the thin pink blouse, the sensual sway of her hips, even with the hat on and her head down, she was still sexy as hell. And totally unaware of the way her beautiful body moved with that sensuous grace. Déisi s teeth grit.

They made it to the second car before a man ignored Luc's threatening glower and stood up. Luc nudged Anya behind him.

Tugging his pants up, the man swaggered towards them, his eyes rudely scrolling up and down Anya's body.

As they neared, he said to Luc, "She your girlfriend, bro, or what? Maybe she'd like new company?"

It was obvious Luc was a tough guy, he and his brothers with their brawny bodies and hard faces, had mercenary written all over them. The man assumed she was a piece of property to maybe be shared, or loaned out at a price.

Luc kept moving, keeping Anya tucked close to his side, he growled, "Get out of my way, bro."

The man grinned crudely. "No, wait boy. How about a little share time? How much you want?" He reached in his pocket for cash. "I'll bring her right back, soon as I'm done."

Not wanting to cause a scene, his eyes cold and tapered, Luc hissed, "You don't fucking back away right now, asshole, you won't have an ass to sit on. You get me?"

In the third car, Déisi and Kalo were on their feet.

But, seeing the lethal menace in Luc's brown eyes, the man backed off, snorted at him, swept Anya with a vulgar look, then went and sat down.

Kalo muttered to Déisi, "Okay, now I get why you wanted her covered up."

Luc walked Anya to the table.

Déisi pulled out a chair on the inside. She sat down, lashes fluttering, revealing how unnerved she'd been at the scene that just occurred.

Déisi sat down across from her, Kalo beside her.

Feeling uncomfortable over his behavior, Déisi figured he'd ruined any chances of being with Anya. Then, his eyes narrowed at her, he remembered, she had responded.

He might have been drunk and forceful, but he knew when a woman was responding to him. But, he sighed, he'd moved too fast, had been too rough, too forceful, dominantly aggressive. She wasn't one of the regular floozies he fucked with. She wasn't a whore, and he had treated her like one as well as scared her.

Anya spoke directly to him breaking through his musings.

"Mr. Zukov." Ignoring his frown at her use of his surname, she said, "Since your brother was kind enough to tell me what you would not, now that I know my…destiny, how soon will we be to where my grandfather is being held?"

Anya gave Kalo a small grateful smile, he didn't return it. At Déisi's fierce gaze at his shooting off his mouth, Kalo just nodded briefly. No one answered her.

Anya spoke coolly, bravely, but the trembling of her hands gave away her fear. "What were you going to do," she directed to Déisi, "wait until I was in front of this- monster of a man with my granddad beaten and broken, and then I would be told what was going on, without any warning-" her voice caught. Kalo patted her hand.

The brothers shared a look before Déisi answered her.

His arm crooked across the back of his chair, he somewhat slouched while toying with a butter knife on the table. "Anyalia," his voice cold, hard, dark eyes hooded, "this is my mission. I don't have to tell you, or anyone, anything I choose not to."

Her lashes flew up with a gasp. Color burst over her cheeks, hurt spread through the green eyes.

Kalo and Luc stared down at the table with their mouths shut.

Déisi's black discs chilling, ruthless lasers cut straight across the table into her eyes.

A visible shiver rolled over her shoulders at the violence she could see suppressed inside the casual slant of his body.

Silence permeated the table as the server came over and took their orders.

Anya was about to refuse to order anything, her stomach was in knots, but seeing Déisi's lids lower further over his ominous eyes, she asked for soup.

Déisi looked like he was going to push her to order something more substantial, when he saw her twisting and pulling at her fingers with nerves. He was feeling a prick of guilt, she was right.

It would have been a terrible shock to just be brought in front of de Vos without any warning, and, as she said, seeing her grandfather in dire straits and being informed of what de Vos would do to her if Märtin Dauphine refused to cooperate.

His original thought had been, why have her fret all the way there about something she could do nothing about? Fear her grandfather would be dead before she got there, fear of the torture and death that could be done to her. He hadn't wanted to put her through that helpless torment.

He had to admit, it was better that Kalo had blabbed. He glanced up at his brother and saw the look on his face that he knew what Déisi was thinking. Surprisingly, there was no mocking grin, no taunt of 'I told you so.'

It was a serious, dangerous, grim situation, one none of them found any amusement in.

The brothers spoke quietly, in English, about trivial things, people they knew, sports. Anya pushed her spoon around the soup bowl not really eating much of it.

At the end of the meal, Déisi wiped his mouth with his napkin and set it beside his plate. Finishing his glass of water, he looked at Anya and said, "Tomorrow, at the first stop for the train, we will disembark. Then take a car. We will be at our destination by noon."

Her hand went to her throat to stifle the sound that threatened to escape. "To- to," her eyes closed, she took a breath, "to where my granddad is?"

Déisi hated to see the terror in her beautiful face. Other than when he had attacked her, she'd been relaxing a bit more and more, now the rigid spine and shoulders, tightened mouth showed she was back on edge.

He wished she would allow him to hold her, comfort her, but he knew she would deny him. Huh, he'd never had the desire to just hold a woman before. Comforting someone? Him? Had he lost his mind?

Nonetheless, his features and voice softened, he said quietly, "*Da, dulci ta,* sweet one, tomorrow we will be where your grandfather is being held."

She had questions, but didn't know what to ask. Dismayed, scared, Anya just sat and blinked at him.

Déisi stood up, his brothers followed suit. Kalo stepped aside and Déisi pulled her chair back and held his hand to her.

Frozen in despair and confusion, she couldn't think, couldn't move. Déisi reached down and took her hand and helped her to stand then rolled his bracing arm around her shoulder.

The pink blouse slid soft under his palm, her hair flowed in waves and curls over his arm. He felt her stiff and shaking at the same time, her frame so slender under his husky arm.

He wanted to hold her against his chest and crush her in his arms until she felt secure and protected. But instead, he bent and kissed the top of her head. Whispered, "I promise, *mi dulci* Anyalia, I won't let anything harm you."

He nodded to Kalo, his brother started down the aisle. Holding her tight against his side, Déisi trod with her behind Kalo, and Luc followed close behind them.

People stared, but this time no one approached them. The three burly brothers with severe faces and hard bodies were too intimidating to even consider engaging.

At their cabins, Kalo and Luc said goodnight.

Not giving her the opportunity to protest, scream, or run, Déisi quickly ushered Anya into their room.

Inside, she stood not moving, unsure of what to do. Her eyes glued on him like she was a tiny mouse and he was a snake twined around a branch hanging down ready to seize her.

Keeping his distance from her and his hands harmlessly tucked in his pockets, he said, "Go on, honey," motioning with his head to the bathroom, "get ready for bed."

She still didn't move. He gathered up her pajamas she'd left on the side of the bed, went to her and put them in her hands. "I won't attack you, Anyalia. I swear."

He lightly set his hand on her back and moved her to the bathroom, giving her a little push inside and closed the door.

Pulling her sheets and blankets down ready for her to climb into when she came out of the bathroom, a wry grin touched his mouth, he was experiencing a lot of firsts this week.

Seeing to the care and comfort of another person was so out of his stratosphere. It was easier to just go with the flow and not question, analyze, or berate himself over his odd behavior.

When Anya emerged from the bathroom, Déisi gestured for her to get into bed. She eyed the cuff still attached to the iron railing. He unlocked it and tossed it on his bed.

Standing over her, he said, "I am the only one that can take you to de Vos, to your grandfather. I would assume you would not run from me now?"

Of course, she might be so frightened out of her mind that she would run and hide so she couldn't be brought to de Vos. But even in the short time Déisi knew Anya, sure, she tried to run from him because she didn't know what he was up to with her. But, she wasn't a runner from trouble where she could possibly be of help.

She loved her grandfather and there was no way this brave little woman was not going to do everything she could to help him, even if it put her own life in jeopardy.

Silent again, Anya nodded then curled up as he laid the blanket over her.

Her mind clearly a tizzy of racing thoughts. Déisi crouched beside the bed and smoothed a few tangles of hair off her face. "Try to not think about tomorrow. I told you, I won't let anyone hurt you."

A tint of green in her skin indicated the idea that her grandfather was hurt made her nauseous. Her forehead furrowed as she asked, "What about my granddad?"

"I will do all I can do to get him out," *if he still lives.* "Now, go to sleep, you get scared or whatever, want to talk, I won't mind at all if you wake me. Okay?"

A small yawn slipped out, she mumbled, "Okay."

He kissed the top of her head and left her to get ready for his own bed. The tender kiss mystified him along with all his other peculiar behavior in regards to Anyalia.

Sighing, he closed his mind and slid into sleep.

Chapter Twelve

Early the next day, after the train came to its first destination stop, the brothers and Anya exited the train and sought the autos they had rented ahead of time.

Kalo and Luc said a quick, "See you later," and they hopped into a separate vehicle and took off.

After closing her door, Déisi went around the car he chose for them. He tossed their baggage into the backseat then climbed in behind the wheel.

Buckling her seatbelt, Anya looked around the silver and blue luxury car he'd rented. "Gosh, Mr. Zukov, this car is sleek and beautiful, it must have cost a fortune."

Turning the ignition, the powerful Jaguar Sx3 growled awake. "*Da*," he shrugged, "tis all right. Listen, Anyalia," he turned to her watching her smooth the skirt of the sundress Kalo had bought.

Smothering his groan at the flowery dress with thin stringy straps that tied in neat bows over her feminine shoulders, with its billowing short skirt, fit her to a T, showcasing her rich curves, her tiny waist.

She crossed her graceful legs drawing his gaze to the high-heeled sandals his idiot brother thought were so sexy. Great. He was taking her into a warren of immoral men, and Kalo thought it was cute to accentuate her sexy kitten allure. Of course, she could be dressed in a cardboard box and her innocent sensuality would be apparent.

Tearing his eyes from her breasts that bounced slightly with the movement of the car, he swung off down the main highway.

When he didn't finish his sentence, staring out the window at the passing scenery, she asked, "What were you going to say?"

He glanced at her then back out the front window. A shade of irritability in his voice, Déisi said, "Can you please stop with the Mr. Zukov shit? We've shared a kiss." He observed pink brightening her cheeks. "I think we've moved past that formality. What do you say?"

Anya turned her head to look at him.

Déisi was a big man, the luxury SUV was a good fit for him. His long legs weren't cramped up; he rested a confident hand casually on the wheel of the powerful car, and laid his arm across the back of the seat.

He had taken a shower just before the train had stopped, his hair was still damp making it even blacker and shinier. Although he'd shaved, his jaw was still shadowed. When he looked at her, the normal hardness in his dark eyes softened, the strong jaw not clenched as usual. His features lost some of their menacing sharpness.

"Anyalia?" he prompted.

She turned to face back out the window. "I…don't know," and twined her fingers in a strangling hold.

Then swiveling back to look at him, reproach in her tone, but embarrassment in her eyes, she said, "We did not *share* a kiss. You forced yourself on me, and," her cheeks turned redder, "it was a bit more than just a kiss." Clearly she recalled his mouth all over her breasts as he struggled with the opening on her jeans.

Her blush made them both think of his assault on her. Both aware he'd just barely managed to come to his senses and get control of himself before he carried through and raped her.

His own cheeks darkened with shame. The guilt of his actions tightened the corners of his eyes in a wince. He skewed a glance at her that roved from her fiery hair over her blushing face, down the full breasts to her legs and back up.

Looking back out the window, his voice husky, he said, "I should not have done that, Anyalia, I'm sorry. But," his gaze swept her again, "we did share a kiss. You responded. *Na*," he said quickly when she shook her head, "don't try to deny it. I know when a woman is reacting to me. Hell girl, you want me to show you my scrunched up sleeve where your little fingers were clutching it, holding onto me with all your might?"

"Oh!" She pressed both palms to her burning cheeks. "How dare you!"

He glanced at her and back to the road. "I dare because you did. You kissed me back, Anyalia. So, tis ridiculous to call a man by his formal name when his tongue has been down your throat."

Gasping her indignity, she snapped her head towards the side window, away from him. Mumbling, "You said you had no desire for me, I recall your exact words, you've repeated them. You said skinny little girls don't make you..." her mouth shut mortified at the picture it drew, of him with an erection.

"Hard," he said it for her. "*Da*, well, I guess I was wrong." He had told her that for her benefit, so she wouldn't feel slimy when he had his hands all over her during the pat down on the plane.

And later at dinner on the train when she thought he expected payment for the food with her body and he had tried to convince her, and himself, he didn't see her as a woman, only as a job. They sat quietly, pondering their thoughts.

A few miles went by and he glanced at her. Seeing she was wound tighter than a clock, Déisi reached over and pried her wringing hands apart. Engulfing her hand with his larger one, he rested his hand on the compartment folded down between them and held hers gently.

Her brow furrowed as if she was deciding whether to tug her hand away. She asked, "Where are Kalo and Luc? Why aren't they with us? Aren't they coming too?" The tenseness tightening her voice evidenced she was petrified of where they were headed. Her fear heightened thinking Déisi's brothers weren't going with them. There was strength in numbers.

"Ah," he squeezed her hand, "they'll be there, *dulci ta,* but you won't see them. That's how we work." He smiled at the slight softening of her rigid shoulders at his reassuring words.

After a couple of hours of Déisi asking her about her childhood, her studies at the university, chatting about his brothers, he pulled in front of a diner. They stopped for a quick bite.

While Déisi paid the bill, Anya stepped outside.

Wherever they were, it was warmer than her home. Anya strolled a few feet down the stone walk peering in shop windows.

They were in a small village with cobblestone streets and antique street lamps. All of the signs again were in a language she didn't know. Déisi had spoken to the server and gave their orders of meat pies and chips as Anya couldn't read the menu or speak the server's language.

Her stroll was pleasant, above the sky was bright blue, the balmy breeze tickled her hair. A bookstore gave her pause to stop and peruse.

Out of nowhere a car came screeching up to the curb and two men jumped out.

Anya had barely enough time to let out a scream before they grabbed her and hustled her into the car.

As the car doors closed, Déisi came out of the diner. Hearing her scream, he raced to the car, a gold Renault, as it took off.

"Motherfucker-" he swore under his breath looking up and down the street. His car was parked behind the diner; they'd be long gone before he could even get to it.

Seeing the Renault flash around a corner, Déisi turned and sprinted down a short alley emerging just as the car was going by. When the Renault had to go slow on the sharp narrow turn, Déisi raced to it and flung himself on the hood.

The four men inside cursed as Déisi gripped the metal under the windshield.

Anya was entrenched between two men in the front seat, one Déisi recognized. Darryl fucking Dassey. Bastard must have thought he could ransom Anya to de Vos and get a ton of money for her.

Moron, Déisi thought as he clung to the car. De Vos would snag Anya and never let Dassey get away with it. He'd pay for his greedy stunt with his life, and in very excruciating ways. De Vos was not a forgiving man, especially when someone tried to cheat him.

The driver slammed on the brakes then jerked the wheel, swerving, trying to dislodge Déisi. But he had fingers of steel, and this wasn't his first pony show.

Déisi managed to tug brass knuckles out of his pocket and jam them on one hand. Then he pulled his shirt off and balled it around his fist. Clinging to the swerving car, he bashed his fist through the driver's side window. Glass shattered all over the screeching driver.

Reaching in, Déisi lifted the handle opening the door, grabbed the man behind the wheel and jerked him out of the car.

As the man went slamming, scraping, bouncing on the stone road, Déisi muttered, "That's why you should always wear a seatbelt," then he climbed in the car. His brass knuckles had flown out the window along with the man.

Ripping his shirt off his arm, he reached in front of Anya and punched Darryl Dassey in the nose hard and fast like a sledgehammer hitting a nail. Blood gushing, Darryl screamed slapping both hands over his nose.

Leaning over Anya, Déisi pummeled Darryl with one fist again and again then pushed the passenger door open and shoved him out.

Out of control, the car rolled downhill picking up speed, the passengers bounced and jerked as it careened side-to-side while it continued its hurtling plummet.

With a squeal, Anya grabbed the wheel causing the Renault to fishtail even more jerkily back and forth across the road forcing other vehicles coming at them to swerve, dodge out of the way, a few veered off into the grass with horns blaring.

One of the men in the backseat produced a gun. Waving it at Déisi he shouted, "You are fucking dead you fucker!"

Like lightning, Déisi threw his upper torso over the seat, grabbed the gun, smashed it into the man's face then grasped the man's head and bashed it into the head of the hollering man next to him knocking them both out.

Déisi clamored with some difficulty over the seat to land in the back. Pushing one of the doors open, he quickly shoved both men out of the careening vehicle. Their screams were silenced almost immediately.

The Renault swerved and bucked, throwing Anya back and forth. She tried to hold onto the wheel to steady the car but she was tossed against the passenger door.

Leaning over the seat, Déisi grabbed ahold of the wheel. He yelled to Anya, "Can you reach the brake?"

She slithered down the seat to smash both feet on the brake.

Tires squealing with the stink of burning rubber roiling, the jouncing vehicle slowed.

Déisi crawled back over into the front seat, nudged Anya aside and took control of the car.

After a moment of corralling the out-of-control vehicle, Déisi drove it back to the diner to where he'd left the Jag. With a heavy breath, he put the car in park and shut it off. Wiping both hands down his face, he shoved his hair back and turned to Anya.

She was huddled against the passenger door, eyes as huge as satellite dishes, her chest heaving with stunned rapid shallow breaths.

Finding his shirt, Déisi shook the glass out of it and shrugged it on. "C'mere, baby." He reached for her, but she was frozen, blinking, panting, shaking, eyes wide in shock and disbelief.

He gripped both her arms and pulled her across the seat. Cleaving her his chest, he wrapped both arms around her.

His palm cradling her head against his shoulder, he stroked her hair murmuring soft, calming words in his language. Then in

English, he said soothingly, "Tis okay now, *dulci ta,* I've got you. You're safe, *babia,* baby."

It took Anya a few minutes to calm. Eventually, her breaths deepened, slowed, she leaned back from him.

His palm warm, Déisi held it against Anya's face. Brushing her bouncy curls back, he tucked a few strands behind her ear. Their eyes joining, cupping her chin, he bent his head to press his lips on hers-

Leaning back from him, Anya let out a long exhale. Her words shook out, "Why, Mr. Zukov, why did Darryl do that?"

Stiffening, his fingers tightened around her jaw. "Déisi, Anyalia, for *Dios'* sake, call me Déisi."

When her eyes dropped from his, he gentled his touch. Sighing, he replied, "I think Dassey thought he could, ah, sell you to de Vos."

Lashes flying straight up, she gasped, "Sell me? Mr.-" seeing his mouth firm, she said quietly, "Déisi, why all this? What is this all about?"

He curled her into his embrace. One big arm around her, the fingertips of his other hand embracing the side of her face, he kissed the top of her head.

"De Vos didn't say what he wanted out of your grandfather. I think it has something to do with his work, his science. Märtin Dauphine, your grandfather, must have found something, or created something that de Vos thinks will be worth a lot of money, or power. Anton de Vos does not deal in small anything."

Anya moved back and then away from Déisi. "This whole thing is a- a nightmare. First you grab me off the street, force me into a bus, then a plane then a train, molest me. Kalo tells me some homicidal freak has my granddad and he wants to chop pieces off Granddad and me."

She took a breath, pressed a hand over her heart. "I don't understand," her eyes tilted up at him. "I just don't understand. You...how on earth did you..."

The image of Déisi throwing himself onto the hood of the car, literally breaking in, beating the men inside and tossing them out like they were paper dolls. The mere strength it took, not counting the speed and agility and everything else the man had engaged to rescue her.

"Who does that? Why did you risk your life-" her lips pushed out, she turned towards the window. "I know, you don't have to say it. You were only doing your job, protecting your investment."

"Anyalia, don't be ridicu-"

She moved to open the door. "Can we just go? The sooner we get this over the better. You can deliver me, get paid, and move on to your next mission."

Back in the Jag, his hand on the wheel, Déisi faced her. He reached out to touch her arm. "Come on, Anyalia, you aren't just a paycheck to me, I don't need the money."

"Sure," Anya snorted, jerking her arm away. "A wealthy mercenary. An indebted, rich mercenary, sounds a bit oxymoronic doesn't it?" Sighing miserably, she said quietly, "Can we please go."

"Anya-" seeing the set of her jaw, Déisi dropped his hand. Squaring himself behind the wheel, he turned on the ignition and easily whipped the Jag out of the lot and back to the highway.

Chapter Thirteen

As they entered a big city, Anya goggled all around at the Eastern European architecture.

Buildings of white and beige and mustard-yellow brick, many with brownish-red and orange roofs, some with medieval towers, crowded on top of each other.

Steeples and Orthodox bell domes filled the ancient skyline. Outdoor cafes clustered with tables and colorful umbrellas popped up along narrow, cobblestone and pebbled streets.

Elaborately carved bridges arched over rivers, statues stand proudly in parks and along tree-lined boulevards.

Her face plastered against the window, Anya asked in awe, "Is this where you're from, mist- uh, Déisi?"

He responded with a noncommittal grunt.

Anya looked at him, he had reverted to the cold, tough gangster that had kidnapped her.

His jaw worked, eyes hooded, skin darkened. He didn't take his eyes off the road except to continuously glance in all the mirrors watching for another tail. Déisi was silently chastising himself. He was losing his edge. First, Anya had taken him unaware trying to jump out of the bus, and now that fucker Dassey following them and snatching her.

Not moving his head, his jaw clenched harder. It was her. Right from the very start he had let her get under his skin. But that was over now. He would not let a little girl with amazing eyes keep a grip on his balls, as Kalo had said.

He'd shut women out before that chased him, threw themselves at him, he would do it now. Except, the air slid out of his lungs, it took work to not look at her, or those legs flowing out of the short skirt. Beside, Anya wasn't chasing him. She didn't want him. It wouldn't take any effort to shut her down. *Da*, it was him that needed to shut down.

He drove outside the city for a few miles then along a road that ran through a bit of forest before coming to a compound.

The compound consisted of a stone, main two-story building with groupings of smaller buildings built of wood off to the sides.

Entering an underground garage, Déisi parked the Jag. Getting out, he moved around the front of the car to open the passenger door.

Anya didn't move. Her fingers were coiled together so hard in her lap the skin was white. He didn't blame her for being terrified. She had a right to be.

Bending over, he wound his fingers around her upper arm and gently pulled her out. "Come, Anyalia, we need to go inside." And he meant it.

The garage of the main building was endemic with thugs, mercenaries, assassins, continuously going in and out. He didn't want to expose her longer than necessary.

Her body was a stiff as a board. Déisi rolled his arm around her and pulled her tight against his side to shield her as much as possible.

The men that frequented the compound would take one look at the beauty and try to fight him for her. It was the world he lived in. The world innocent Anya had been plunged into.

Normally he would have just casually strode past as two or more males fought sometimes to the death over a woman one man had and the others desired. For the moment. Once they had their taste, the broad would be tossed to the side like stank dog turd.

Before Anya, he could only shake his head at the males going at each other for some unnamed bitch. Fighting over a broad was never anything he'd ever even consider. There was enough fish in the sea without getting his knuckles bruised over a broad.

Anya had watched damned orgies and was harassed by men on the bus, the plane, even from strangers on the train thinking she might be a moll, a girlfriend of a gangster. A female to be passed around or sold.

Déisi knew the picture he and his brothers presented when they were together. They were big, muscled, hard-eyed, the aura of ruthless violence resonated from them. The life they lived, women were cheap, and interchangeable.

A heavy sigh strained his big chest when he glanced at the precious woman under his arm. Déisi finally admitted to himself he wants Anya, body and soul. But, shaking head, he told himself, he has no business trying to drag her into his brutal world, she didn't belong there.

Yah, try and tell his used to be cold and dead heart that. His heart had started beating again, and it and his cock both wanted her.

They rode the elevator silently to the 1st floor and stepped out into a marble lobby.

Nodding at men that looked as tough as him, Déisi drew Anya across the white and gold glossy floor to another room.

Several people passed back and forth as Déisi brought her up to a gold, glass-topped desk.

When the woman sitting behind it saw him approach, her eyes widened and she lit up. She immediately rose to her feet with a very welcoming broad smile for Déisi.

She hurried out from behind the desk and tricked across the shiny floor in high stilettoes while tugging down the slinky short dress that clung to her body.

Another smutty Paulina type that was thrilled to see Déisi.

Anya tried not to feel like a bucolic ingénue in her simple girlie dress as she scanned the lavish exotic area.

The building, the biggest part of the compound, was a mix of ancient and modern. The architecture was old European but the posh furniture and fixings were pure modern; glass, gold, steel, uber grandiose.

As was the woman who leaped at Déisi. Throwing her arms around him, she hurled her buxom, statuesque body against his stalwart body.

"*Oof-*" she knocked the air out of him hitting him so hard. Déisi had to release Anya to keep himself from being knocked backwards.

Anya stepped from the woman with thick brunette hair painted with salon-fresh highlights. It fluffed in curls in a pouf around her head, and down over the shoulders of the chartreuse saran-wrap of a dress. The scoop neckline exposed an ample bosom, which she was polishing all over Déisi.

Huh, Anya thought, it's a wonder he seems so enthralled with my breasts when he has the most curvaceous women dropping at his feet begging him to take them. By the looks of this one, Anya thought ruefully, any second she'd be tripping Déisi and throwing herself under him.

Anya's lips pinched as she looked down at her own summer dress with its flouncy skirt and flowers. She looked like a plain schoolgirl next to the sophisticated woman in her flamboyant attire.

Déisi gripped the woman's arms and had to tug hard to pull them from around his neck. When he got them loose he gave her slight push, caught Anya's wrist and pulled her partially in front of him. "Fabiana, this is Anyalia Marvaux. Inform Anton that we are here."

"My handsome Déisi, why do you always push me away?" She nudged Anya aside trying to cuddle against him, her hand stroking his chest. "Take me with you, sugar, you excite me so. *God*," she gushed. "You are damned pure raw power."

She worked her way into his arms. "I've waited for you, Déisi, you know I've always wanted only you."

Lifting her hand off his chest, he said drily, "*Yah*, you waited for me while lying beneath other men. Now, tell-"

"My handsome jαύdraς, that accent has always slayed me, those shoulders," a finger trailed down his ribs. "You make me wet, Zukov. I've only been with other men to learn...techniques that I can pleasure you with, things I can do to, for, you."

Impatience edged Déisi's rough voice, "Fabiana, cut it out, we have no time for this shit."

Speaking as if Anya wasn't standing there, Fabiana said, "Jαύdraς, you know I'll take care of you. I'll let you do anything," she coyly clinched his collar, tugging it, tilting her head up to him with a wanton smile. "Anything you want. You mercenary types always like it rough, maybe a little violent, eh? You can do it all with me." The smile was a purr of invitation as she listed, "Cuffs, whips, nipple clamps, buttplu-"

"*Basta*," Déisi broke in irately, pushing her away again. His voice stiff, he ordered, "Get de Vos. Now." Anya didn't need to hear this shit. She already thought he was a rapacious whoring ape.

"Yes," Anya said snidely, "he's had so much action with handcuffs the past few days," she sighed with an eye roll and smile. "I'm sure he'd like a bit of a break from them. Wouldn't you, *mi dulci ta*?"

A choke burst from Déisi at her words. He gaped at her, studying her to see if she knew what she was saying. She was such an innocent- his eyes narrowed, her cheeks were bright pink. She was working hard to look casually from him to Fabiana.

Appalled at Fabiana's brazen behavior, Anya was deliberately taunting the older woman, with technically, the truth. He had been using cuffs, keeping Anya restrained.

A short grin ticked up at her attempt at his language. Little minx, if they were alone- "*Yah*, baby, I'm bored with the restraints." His voice lowered seductively along with his lids. "I have other ideas for later, *mi dulci ta*."

Her brows like despising brown pencils slashed down between her brown eyes, Fabiana scowled at Anya then Déisi who gazed with blatant lustful hunger at Anya. "Humph! You will tire of this," her sneer raked down Anya, "juvenile, soon, and I will be here, waiting for you." Hips snapping like a spurned pendulum, she stalked off down the hall.

They watched her go to a door, open it, and say something to someone inside the room.

Déisi said, "Anyalia," his hand on her arm, "you-"

Fabiana was already stomping back into the room in her ultra-high heels. A hand on her wide round hip, her petulant nose in the air, she announced, "Mr. de Vos is in the denătria, he said to go in."

Déisi quickly ushered Anya towards the entryway Fabiana had gone through.

"Déisi darling," Fabiana shouted after them with a deep-throated sexy voice, "I'll wait for you, right here!"

Feeling the weight of his hand on her lower back, Anya said sweetly, "Your girlfriend? She seems nice."

"Anyalia, don't-"

"Déisi Zukov, my man," a booming voice called out as the couple entered a room.

The room was round decorated in white panel, burgundy colored leather furniture, and filled with half a dozen men.

Anya had thought Déisi was a scary looking man, but these men, she struggled not to bolt and run, or wrap her arms around herself.

The man who greeted Déisi came forward.

He was big, but not as big as Déisi, his hair was thinning around a hard faced, sharply hacked head. He had a square jaw, and was dressed in a white suit with a pale blue tie. Slits of mean sunken eyes hopped from Déisi to Anya where his pupils enlarged and sparked.

Déisi's hand tightened on her waist.

Anton De Vos crossed the room, stopping a few feet from them. "Ah, this is our lovely Anyalia, yes?" Lewd greed expulsed from the narrow brown eyes like a foul lantern bathing her in a deviant light. He held his arms out as he moved to her.

Déisi shifted her to stand slightly behind him.

De Vos frowned at him. Seeing the unmistakable lethal warning in Déisi's onyx depths, and his frown darkened to a grimace. Dropping his arms to his side, with a nod of understanding, a sneer of a grin lifted the corners of his cruel mouth.

Under arched brows the mean eyes gleamed with vile spite. "So that's how it is, eh?" He swept Déisi with a condescending gaze. "You would step between me and my property?" The nasty gaze swung to Anya and down her body, lingering on her breasts, drifted lower, then back to Déisi's stone cold face.

De Vos said to him, "Ah, of course, a lusty young man such as yourself would be unable to keep his wick out of such an exquisite honey pot." His eyes narrowed at Déisi.

"Well, son, her cunt belongs to me. You can move on to another bitch. There's a million of them out there, maybe not as fine as this one," his base gaze returned to impudently scroll over Anya's body. To Déisi, he scarped, "Maybe you can make up for her in volume."

Her face vivid red, with a mortified gasp, rage flew up Anya's body. She took a step towards the abhorrent man, but Déisi held her back.

"Where is Dauphine?" Déisi demanded.

De Vos tore his attention from Anya and back to his jαύdraç, his enforcer. The two men stared each other down.

The other men in the room shuffled their feet, grumbling, unsure of what they were expected to do. De Vos was the boss, but no one ever fucked with Déisi Zukov, AKA *na čelu vlad,* Death Comes. His fearsome reputation was infamous around the world, the underworld.

With a false smile and false sorrow, de Vos said to Anya, "Unfortunately, my dear, your grandfather, is not well. In fact he is quite ill. He is in a bit of a coma, he is unable to speak at the moment."

De Vos' breath expelled with coarse, frustrated anger, and desire, his eyes once again trailing over her figure. "Even to save your luscious skin."

Anya put a hand over her mouth. Déisi squeezed her waist, murmured in her ear to hold it together.

De Vos continued, lids sinking over sly eyes, "However, my little beauty, under delirium, he thought you were here and he spoke to you, telling you that you know where the information that I want is. That," he yawned as if bored, "well I guess he thought he was also speaking to your deceased grandmother."

He sighed with the inability to comprehend romantic love. "Because he told her don't forget her Romeo." Thick lids like a croc levered slightly assessing her reaction. But Anya was only hearing that her grandfather was seriously ill.

"I need to see him." She pushed from Déisi but he kept ahold of her. Urgently, she beseeched, "I must see him. Please, Mr. de Vos, please take me to him."

De Vos regarded her thoughtfully, his gaze flit to Déisi whose face was a block of ice. Veritably unreadable. Back to Anya, he said with a shrug, "Of course. This way, he's in a room upstairs."

Struggling against Déisi's iron hold, Anya cried urgently, "Please, please Déisi, I have to see him. Let me go!"

"You wait here, Jαύdraç, I will take her. Don't worry, I will take good care of her." With a leering grin, de Vos held his hand out to Anya.

Still Déisi held her back. "*Na*, she goes nowhere without me."

"Déisi, please-"

He rolled his arm like a band across the front of her. "*Na*, Anyalia, you go nowhere without me." His voice low, against her ear, he said, "I swear I will carry you out of here right now and take you somewhere that this fucker can't get to you. You do it my way, or that tis it."

"Zukov," astounded, de Vos started angrily, "my best soldier defies me? You would fight, perhaps even kill, your mentor?"

"*Bah*," Déisi spat. "You were never my mentor. You bought my debt papers from Khaliar. I finish this job and tis my last."

Brows rounded, de Vos gaped. "What? You can't do that. Your debt is for life, you can't-"

"*Da*, I can. I've paid back with my life, a lifetime, 17 years, for the life of my baby brother. Something I never should have had to do."

Eyes fired with fury, de Vos snarled, "You can't just walk away! You are my jαύdraç, I own you." His eyes flicked to Anya. "I own her. You took her for me."

"*Na*. No more. You can't stop me, Anton, and you know it. Even with all of your men here with their weapons, you know you cannot stop me. Take us to Märtin Dauphine. I will not ask again." His hand moved to Anya's waist where it tightened so hard his fingers dug into her flesh.

She took one look at Déisi's chilling, black fissures of slate, her stomach clenched. An enraged Satan could not have looked more powerfully hellish. Her blood froze, she bit her lip to quell the tremors.

Though Déisi held no gun in his hand, the cringing of every man in the room was palpable, indicating they all knew if they tried to stop him, none of them would leave the room alive.

He had a death-grip on her, Anya was not going anywhere without him.

Chapter Fourteen

De Vos' lips blew out, then he sucked them back in, he stared hard at Déisi.

Déisi dared him to call his bluff. He had bluffed with Anya one time, the time when they were leaving the plane and he told her he'd hit her, knock her out, if she tried to run or scream. This time he wasn't bluffing, and de Vos knew it.

Déisi's only concern was keeping Anya out of the crossfire of combat. There was a divan by the nearest wall. At the slightest movement he interpreted as a violent act against him, he would hurl her under it as he launched into action.

"Unpredictable as always." De Vos shook his head with a small smile. "You can't walk out on the papers, Zukov, you know that. You renege on them and the authorities will incarcerate you in the filthiest, deadliest pit of all prisons in Algiers.

"Yes, you have wealth beyond all measure, but," de Vos cocked his head with a haughty sniff, "what good is all that wealth if you are imprisoned or have to hide for the rest of your life?"

His lip curled at Déisi's implacable face. "Sure, you can take care of yourself, but your brothers? You want to give lifetime prison sentences to your brothers? All of them? Even the youngest, Kollier? To exist forever either in hiding or prison, abort his studies, his youthful dreams of a grand future?"

The vein under the scar hammered, it was the only thing on Déisi that moved. An inscrutable mass of chiseled granite, the midnight eyes didn't waver, lids narrowed over them until only a shimmer of deadly threat shone.

De Vos' breath discharged with fury. He exploded, "Fine, you ruthless bastard." He strode towards the door, a handful of the men dashed right behind him.

"Come, Anyalia." Déisi cupped her elbow and they followed the men out the door with the rest of the soldiers behind them.

De Vos traipsed down a hall and up a wide staircase, down another hall then stopped at a room. He nodded to the soldier next to him.

The soldier opened the door. De Vos held his arm out indicating for Déisi and Anya to go in.

Holding Anya back, Déisi said to de Vos with a tight smile, "After you."

Hesitating, then de Vos' angular face rose in a true smile. "Always the cautious one, eh, Zukov?" His chest puffed big, de Vos strode into the room, a few men followed, then Déisi and Anya.

The room was dim, containing a table, two chairs, and a bed. More like a gurney. A body lay on the gurney partially covered by a sheet.

"Granddad!" Anya strained at Déisi's grip.

He let her go but stayed at her heels.

Anya rushed to the bed, then stopped with a pained sob. She bent over the still figure lying on the bed. Reaching out with a shaking hand, she tenderly touched the side of her grandfather's face.

Tears slipped out and dropped on the sheet that covered to his chest, his shirt above it was torn and bloody. Märtin Dauphine's wrists were manacled to iron posts attached to the bed.

Anya turned with tear-filled furious eyes to de Vos. "You-you restrained him? He's badly hurt," her voice crumbled. She turned back to her grandfather.

His face was covered with cuts and bruises, his eyes swollen and blackened. She swung back to de Vos. Taking a step towards him with her fists raised, she shouted in outrage, "You animal! You've beaten him! You-"

Déisi curled around her, blocking her from de Vos and his men. She could do nothing but turn back to her grandfather. Bending over his beaten body, she stroked his battered face as the tears fell.

Smiling grimly at Déisi, de Vos said, "I saw the way you looked at her picture. How you quickly volunteered for the job to abduct her. Hell, a blind man can see how you look at her now, how you want her."

At Déisi's stoic expression, de Vos sighed. "I must say, born and bred to be a killer, I thought any atom of compassion, mercy...love," a resigned sigh, his eyes twitched to Anya seeing her shoulders stiffen.

Then his gaze shifted back to Déisi. "Every good and decent thing inside of you should have been beaten, whipped, tortured out of you. I never thought you would ever fall, and fall hard, for a skirt.

"As I said, always the unpredictable one, my son. But, I should have known, the way you cared so much for those fucking siblings of yours. Or is it just plain scorching lust you feel for this girl?"

He tucked his hands in his pockets and shrugged. "Anyway, I took precautions and had Dauphine bolted down. I thought if you were so into her, you would try to take Dauphine for her. And, as the ghost that you are, you would have had them both gone before I could do a bloody thing to stop you."

Through streaming tears, Anya said loud enough for de Vos to hear, despising contempt ringing in her voice, "What is it? What does he have that you want, you miserable excuse for a man?"

The room was quiet for a moment, except for Anya's weeping. Then de Vos moved near her. Déisi stopped him with a look from getting any closer to her.

With the bearing of a general, tone temperate, de Vos explained, "Your grandfather has been working on chemical warfare with the military. He has created a…gas of types. This gas can be sprayed with long-range high-powered rifles, from planes, helicopters, from anything, and from a great distance.

"It paralyzes people. For up to eight hours, maybe more. That means soldiers can charge in, kill whomever they want, such as al-Qaeda, Isis, Mexican cartels, and leave the innocents untouched."

Arrogance in his tone and stance, he went on, "The gas can be sprayed to as few as desired, or masses, entire cities. The soldiers can slip into countries they war with, freeze everyone and infiltrate their top secret buildings, steal restricted information.

"Or, for someone like me," he smiled, miming as if he was twisting the end of a dastardly moustache. "They can get into places like banks, Fort Knox, jewelry stores, munitions, on and on, pharmacies, whatever, and take for me anything I want, all I want."

Holding her grandfather's hand, de Vos' words traveled around Anya but weren't settling into her brain.

On the other hand, Déisi's body was rigid with the ramifications of what de Vos was saying. "De Vos," his voice dark, "it can be a weapon of mass destruction in the wrong hands."

Anya wiped at her tears and looked over at de Vos. Her voice heavy with concern she told him, "It will do only harm. Someone waiting for emergency health care could die, a woman having a baby, houses on fire won't stop burning, people driving- the accidents, and - and helpless women, children, can be taken…and used."

She shook her head adamantly. "No, Granddad wouldn't have had a part in this- this evil. It needs to be destroyed. I won't get it for you."

De Vos took a step towards her, Déisi moved between them.

"You both will do as I say. You, little missy, want your granddad's life to be spared, so you will get the formula for me.

He can't create the gas without the formula, it's obviously too complex to recall all of the components."

His smile curled with the shaking of his head. "But, when Dauphine realized the danger of this chemical, he lied to the military he was creating it for, said it wasn't working, and he hid the formula. He wanted to see if he could create an antidote for it before destroying it, just in case someone else managed to invent it."

De Vos stepped back, his hands on his hips, the sides of the white suit coat held back by his wrists. "Now, Ms. Marvaux," tone of commanding brass, he said, "you will go and get my formula."

He nodded to Déisi. "You bring them both back, her and the formula. One without the other and Dauphine dies. And of course you will not be paid. You'd better fuck her fast and hard, get it out of your system, Zukov."

His voice dropped to a coarse whisper, eyes stripping Anya, he sneered, "Because she will be mine. And," his mean gaze lifted to Déisi, "you will give her up. You know it, and I know it. Your brothers mean more to you than some random cunt you've only known a short time. You would never place your little brother's welfare above this lovely slut.

"There're women on every corner, son. Put your energy into one of them. Now, get the fuck out of here and bring me my formula."

Anya jumped at him with a scream, her hands outstretched like claws. "You inhuman monster-" Déisi's arm latched around her waist, holding her back.

"Ah, I love a little fire in my bitches," de Vos smiled taunting her. Then he said harshly, "The sooner you go and get my formula and return, the sooner you can get medical care for your grandfather. I would suggest you stop dicking around, Jαύδραζ *my enforcer*, and get a move on. I know you won't let anything, or anyone get in your way."

Mouth turned up in a nasty grin to Anya, he said, "He has told you, sweetheart, that he is not *one* of the best assassins in the world, he is *the* best."

150

Her lips parted, green eyes raised up to Déisi. She took an unconscious step back from him.

"Ah," de Vos chuckled seeing her blanch. "Apparently not. Well, then, child, at least you know he will keep you safe from others. From him? Maybe not so much. Just don't do anything to piss him off and that lily white, slender and fragile neck of yours, should be just fine."

He grinned at her bewildered fear. Turning his serious, angry eyes to Déisi, de Vos barked, "Go on. The old man may not be able to hold on for long."

"We have to go, Anyalia," Déisi said flatly.

She nodded, bent to her grandfather and kissed his clammy forehead. She whispered, "I'll be back, Granddad, I promise. I will be back for you."

Wiping her eyes, she stood straight and trod past Déisi and de Vos, heading for the door so quickly she was already stepping through the doorway before Déisi caught up with her.

"Dammit, Anyalia, don't fucking leave my side-"

But she was grabbed suddenly, pulled into iron arms.

Before she could scream, the man said with amusement, "*Bréthaïdne* you need to keep your eyes on your girlfriend, she's quick."

Faster than a wink of light, Déisi was behind Kalo with a forearm across his neck. He slapped him lightly in the head then released him, and Kalo released Anya.

Déisi growled at his brother, "What part of 'guard the door' did you relate to 'grab Anyalia?'"

Kalo laughed at him. "Just wanted to show her how quickly shit can fall." He looked at her, his face of mirth hardened. He said seriously, "You need to stop running from us, honey, away from us is straight to danger."

Shoving her hair back, Anya wiped at her eyes. "I don't want to be with you, any of you. A- a wild wolf pack, a family of killers. I don't need you, I will do this on my own." She strode down the hall to the staircase.

Déisi looked at Kalo who shrugged, and Déisi traipsed after her. Kalo stayed to make sure de Vos and his men didn't come after them.

Her high-heeled sandals clicking across the marble floor, short skirt slapping back and forth with her angry strut, breasts bouncing, Anya fumed her way to the elevators.

"Anyalia, wait!" Déisi jogged after her.

Fabiana rushed in front of him. "No, my deadly warrior, let her go, I am all the woman you need-"

Déisi shoved her aside. "Fuck, *Anyalia*!" he roared as Anya stepped into the elevator and the door closed in his face.

"Motherfucker," he cursed at the door while jabbing at the button. His head whipped around as he searched for the stairwell.

Spotting it, he raced to it while shouting to Kalo who was grinning at him, "Fucking see that Luc is on point, you know what to do-" and he shoved the door to the stairs open and hurried down the flights.

The door opened with a ping and instead of going to the garage, Anya flew out the front of the building.

There was nothing but other buildings and vast lawns. She stood still, frantically looking for a way to get transportation when tough hands snatched her hard against his chest.

"Dammit Anyalia, don't you ever fucking do that again. You stay with me, do you understand me?"

Twisting around to face him, Anya pushed at him. "Let go of me. I don't need you, a- an- assassin. I'll get the formula and bring it here and he will set Granddad free."

Déisi held her like a steel fence. "*Na, babia*, you bring him the formula and he will kill your grandfather and keep you."

She struggled in his arms, he gripped her jaw holding her to look at him.

"Anyalia, he would never let you go, never. I've known the man most of my life. He desires you, once he has you and the formula he won't need your grandfather, and he sure as hell won't let him go and run to the military and tell them what de Vos has.

152

"The military would stop de Vos before he could make the gas. *Na, babia,*" he shook his head sadly. "He will murder your grandfather and will never let you go. If he tires of you, he will kill you too. He has no conscience, he would snap you out like a light."

His fingers tightened on her jaw, forcing their eyes to fuse. "If you want to save your grandfather you must stay with me. I promise," he sifted tangles of hair off her wet cheek. "I will get him out. I swear to you. But, you must listen to me, do as I say, without argument. And," he brushed his lips across hers, "fucking do not run from me again."

She tried to lower her eyes, but he squeezed her jaw and lifted her head, forcing her to look at him, see his grave integrity. "Trust me, Anyalia."

He'd said that to her before, and she'd thrown his words in his face. This time, the air seeped out of her in capitulation. Déisi held her, waiting, but she said nothing. At least she stopped fighting him.

Déisi stared hard at her eyes because what he really wanted to do was untie those strings at her shoulders, let the top of her dress tumble down so he could cover her succulent breasts with his hands. He was dying to feel their soft suppleness, knead them, put his face in them, kiss, suckle, like on the train- *damn*, he leaned into her.

The mist of his sigh warming her face, before he could stop himself his mouth fell to hers. He sucked her lips, then pushed them apart to slide his tongue inside sweeping everywhere, tasting her depths, savoring the tender delight of Anya.

His big hands stroked her back, pulling her tighter against him, wedging her full breasts against his chest. He wanted her bodice pulled down and his shirt off. He wanted her skin on his, slanting his head he kissed her with more and more heat.

She yielded, briefly allowed him passage. Reciprocating his foraging with her own soft strokes from her inexperienced tongue, a tiny moaned mew wisped into his mouth and she broke from him, pressing her hands to his chest.

Catching her breath, she murmured, "I…we need to go." But the frail thread of control Déisi had was breaking, his hands grew rougher, more sensual, stroking over her nape, down the sides of her waist and around to the inner curve at the beginning of her bottom.

His mouth hard on hers, his kiss voracious, breath heavy, he pulled her so she could feel the long, hard, raging length of him pressed like a throbbing iron rod against her.

Anya turned her head, gasped, "Déisi, stop, please."

His grip loosened, her voice brought him around. Still holding her, he leaned back and looked around. They were standing out in front of a compound teeming with killers for *Dios'* sake. He'd allowed them to be vulnerable.

Forcing himself to release her, Déisi dug his fingers into his scalp and scraped them through his hair, wiped his mouth. "Anyalia, forgive me."

She shifted her head from him, the fiery blonde curls covering the side of her face. "We need to go."

"*Yah*," he nodded. "This way." He reached for her hand. When she moved away, he grabbed it anyway. Holding onto her, he led her to the side of the building to get back to the garage.

Déisi helped her into the Jag, then hopped in and left the garage with a squeal of tires.

It wasn't until they hit the main street that Déisi slowed. He said, "We need to pause, *babia*, uh, Anyalia. We need to plan where to start to search for the formula. Perhaps your granddad's home?"

"No, I mean, yes, we need to go back to my country. I think I know where he hid it, or at least a clue to where it could be hidden."

His black brows arched as he glanced at Anya.

He didn't question her, just fished out his cell, spoke in his own language to his brothers, and headed for the airport.

Chapter Fifteen

*T*hanks to his connections, Déisi was able to get Anya plane tickets without her having ID.

They landed in Washington State after a day and a half of napping in three different airports while waiting for their connecting flights.

When they finally landed for the last time, Déisi rented another Jaguar SUV and drove to a hotel. They wearily checked in and went right to their room.

He hadn't wanted to purchase a suite with two beds, but he made himself. At least they would be in the same room. The pair hadn't been apart since the entire escapade started, and Déisi didn't plan on starting now.

Besides protecting her, he didn't want to be apart from Anya. *Da*, maybe obsessive, he didn't know how he was going to let her go when the mission was done. He might not be able to.

Even if she didn't want to stay with him, he was as they said, a ruthless man who played by his own rules, taking what he wanted. He was as bad as de Vos, but then, he had never denied that he wasn't.

Anya was in a hurry to get help for her grandfather, but between the stress and running around, jet lag on top of it, she walked towards one of the beds and dropped on it, curled up and was asleep by the time Déisi ordered room service.

At the knock at the door, Déisi let in the attendant with the tray of food.

After the attendant set the tray on the table and left with his tip, Déisi locked the door and paused by Anya's bed. The pull to lie down with her was excruciating. He moved away and crashed on the other bed.

The next morning, rested, showered and fed, they headed out to a deluxe street of fancy shops. When Anya had told Déisi where they needed to go, he told her they required an upgrade in their attire.

Anya maintained that the sundress she wore was adequate. Not arguing with her, Déisi motioned for a clerk to come and assist her.

After giving the clerk instructions on what he wanted, Déisi whispered to Anya, "I will be right next door, do not leave this building. Promise me?"

Rolling her eyes, Anya complained, "Have you always been this bossy?"

He nodded seriously. "*Da*, when I know what tis best. Give me your word, *babia*." Coiling one of her long fair curls with fire highlights around a finger, he brought her face inches from his. "Please." The unfamiliar word tasted odd on his tongue.

A soft smile lifted her lips. "Since you ask so nicely, yes, I promise. Okay?"

His gaze on her lips, he nodded. "*Da, yah*, okay," and kissed her lightly before leaving her in the clerk's capable hands then he went next door.

Déisi had a duffle of clothes but no suit. Since he owned plenty but they weren't in the country where they were currently, he bought a new one, off the rack. Something he seldom did. His height, breadth of shoulders, and the leanness of his hips usually dictated a tailored suit to his specifications.

He did however, have luck finding a black suit with the faintest pinstripes that fit reasonably well. Added to that, he bought black dress boots, a starched white shirt, and a wine colored tie. Retrieving clean underwear and a white t-shirt from the car, he changed into the suit.

He combed his thick black hair, paid the salesman, and went next door to collect his date.

Waiting by the window, hands clasped behind his back, Déisi stared out, his thoughts deep in planning.

"Déisi?" she said, her sweet voice soft.

He turned, and his stomach plummeted.

A vision of perfect beauty, he grew hard just standing there looking at her. Interesting, Anya's dress was the exact shade of the tie he'd chosen.

The wine colored dress embraced her curves, demure and sexy at the same time. The capped sleeves made of fine lace, the same lace along the bodice, just low enough to draw the eye, making a red-blooded man crave to see more.

The skirt several inches above her slim knees, she wore black stilettoes he died to have digging into his back while her bare legs wrapped around his waist. In her hand, she held a clutch covered in black sequins.

"*Mi dragă,* when I think you can't be more beautiful, ah, you take my breath away." His mind a blur of desire, and something else, he mindlessly moved towards her.

"Sir?" A polite voice interrupted.

Déisi had eyes only for Anya. She stood shy, uncertain.

The clerk cleared her throat and said, "The bill…"

Without taking his eyes off Anya, Déisi pulled out his wallet, took out a credit card and handed it to the clerk then took Anya's hand and brought it to his lips.

Lids heavy with desire and, admit it, infatuation, he kissed the back of her hand. Then he turned it over, looking up at her through a flop of swarthy hair, their eyes binding, he pressed a kiss to her small palm.

Embarrassed, Anya murmured, "The clerk insisted I try on this dress. Really, Mr. uh, Zukov, I can't allow-"

Frowning, he pressed his lips harder to her palm and said, "Déisi, Anyalia, don't backtrack on me."

Color staining her cheeks, she said, "Déisi, I have no money. I can't pay for this dress. And even if I had money with me, I could never afford this. It's- it's crazy expensive. I can't allow you to buy it. The sundress I had on will be quite sufficient I'm sure." She turned and started for the dressing room.

Making a mental note for next time to have tags removed before she sees anything, he moved right with her but as she neared the fitting rooms, he nudged her to the side, stopped her with his hand stroking up the side of her face.

He brushed her cheek with his thumb, it grew redder under his gentle caress. "Anyalia, you heard de Vos, I'm loaded. Seriously. This dress is nothing, peanuts."

"But I can't afford it, you can't-"

A groan rumbled in his chest. "Please, Anyalia, can you please not debate everything with me? We are going to the highly elite Fondateur Hotel. You are aware it is one of the most expensive restaurants in the region. We must dress the part so we don't stand out and attract attention. We don't know who might be following us."

"But-"

"Shh," he lowered his lips to lightly brush hers. "I know you have no money," he sighed with a beleaguered smile. "You went on enough about it on the train. Seriously, sweet," he lifted her chin so she met his eyes, "this mission must be a success if you and your granddad can walk away alive.

"Now, get that pretty little ass of yours in there and retrieve your belongings, or I will do it and burn them and then you will be forced to wear the dress anyway." And the lingerie he knew she had on under the dress.

He was already learning the look of her body, her breasts weren't bouncing like they were in the sundress with no bra. Damn, that was the last time she goes out the door without a fucking bra. Even Kalo had been shamelessly ogling her.

Gah, there was that damned sting, the irrational territorial feeling. He pinched his brow, he needed to get his head on straight and get the mission done, and move on before he lost more than his sanity over her.

She demurred, "Déisi, I was brought up that one earned everything that was given to them, and a good woman doesn't accept expensive things from a man who isn't her husband, or at least a long-time boyfriend. We need to-"

He put his hands on her shoulders and turned her to the fitting rooms. "Go. Come back out in this dress or you will not like what I do." He hated to default to threats with her, but if he was to save her and Dauphine's lives she has to do what he tells her. Déisi watched the mutinous set of her tiny chin transform to resignation.

"Fine," she said with a twist of her head, chin in the air. "I will keep all the tags so I know how much to pay you back," and flit into the room.

Eyes rolling heavenward, Déisi started for the clerk's counter. *That woman*, he groused silently, *she was enough to make ten men crazy*. Check that, he was the only man she would be driving crazy.

He told the clerk to go to Anya and cut the tags off the dress and bring them to him. The tags were already off the shoes, purse, panties and bra and in his pocket. By the time he signed the credit card receipt and stuffed his wallet back in his pocket, Anya came back out.

Déisi suppressed the smile at seeing a bag in her hand containing the sundress and sandals. He actually really liked that sundress. Thinking about her wearing it when they were alone, his fingers still itched to tug at the strings that kept the top of the dress up.

The clerk discreetly slipped him the tags to the new purchases.

Thanking the clerk for her assistance, Déisi set his hand on the small of Anya's back, and guided her out the door and to the newly rented Jag.

When he opened the passenger door, Anya's gaze swept over him. Her rosy cheeks betrayed her embarrassment, but she said, "You, um, look really handsome, Déisi."

"Huh," his snort scornful. "I could never be handsome with this mug." He traced the scar at his temple with a finger.

Sliding into the car, Anya said softly, "It's true you have a strong face, hard and cold as iron." He nodded, staring at her legs as she pulled them in. "But besides the menacing aspect, you have that...uh, cliché thing, you know, rugged, handsome in a tough way."

His brows arched, Déisi made no comment as he closed her door and went around to the driver's side. He hated that his insides felt warm and mushy at her words.

Sure, women chased him relentlessly, but they'd told him it was his scary looks that intrigued them, made them hot. They liked the predatory danger of his barely leashed violence. With his tough looks they figured he was aggressive in bed. They were right.

It wasn't a long drive to the Fondateur Hotel and Restaurant.

Sitting at a light, Déisi swiveled slightly towards Anya. "So, we can't get into the back part of the hotel because the owners reside there and only people with invitation are allowed in that section. Have you thought about a way to get to the room we need to find?"

Looking out her side window, Anya replied, "We're having dinner, that's our...what you call, um," she tuned to face him, "yes, our cover. It is our cover to get into the building. I remember Granddad telling me how he and Grandmother pretended to go to the restrooms and snuck out a side door and found their way to the room."

Anya smiled wistfully at the memory of her granddad's story. "They were only looking to sight-see, have some fun, and," a teasing glint in her eye. "I think they were looking for a bit of privacy to, well, you know. Grandmother's family would never let Granddad alone with her, so they were always trying to find private time in public places."

She sighed with a dreamy smile. "They were so romantic, don't you think?"

"Mmm," Déisi murmured as he swung the car up the long entrance to the Fondateur. "I leave the romance to the writers, I don't know romance from Chinese checkers."

Before he put the car in park, a valet was at his door and opening it. Another valet opened Anya's door and held his hand to her.

By the time Déisi got his ticket and made his way around the car, the valet was still holding Anya's hand and whispering to her.

Déisi strode up and rolled his arm in a proprietary manner around her shoulders and glowered down at the smaller man.

The valet raised his eyes to the brawny male with destruction written all over his hard face, and quickly released Anya's hand.

As Déisi ushered Anya up to the grand doors, Anya whispered, "Really, Déisi, you must stop giving everyone the evil eye. I swear you're scaring the life out of people with that threatening glower you give them."

A doorman swung the door open for them to enter.

Déisi's hand dropped to her waist. "You are imaging things, *mi babia*, I don't give everyone the evil eye." *Only the males that put their hands on you.*

The couple strode through the busy lobby of the ritzy hotel.

The walls were powder blue with white trim and white cutouts. Cushy blue carpet stretched over the vast room, and that was surrounded by glossy white tile with miniature blue diamond designs.

Huge windows embraced by blue drapes were pulled back to let the sun shine on the white divans and chairs. The front desk was teeming with guests and attendants assisting them.

Déisi glanced around until he saw a sign designating the dining room, and led Anya in that direction.

Up a short set of wide, blue carpeted stairs, they made their way down a hall.

Conversation spilled out of the dining room into the hall. The aromas sifting out with the talking and laughing, cutlery clinking on fine china, were mouthwatering.

Paused at the entrance while waiting for the maître d, Déisi and Anya both scanned the room, first to make sure there was no one there they recognized, and second, to find that side door her granddad had described.

"Two sir?" The tall thin man in a tux tilted his head back so he could look down his supercilious long nose at the pair. "Do you have a reservation?" His haughty gaze flit from one to the other.

"*Da,*" Déisi said, discreetly handing the man some bills. "We do. A private table if you will, towards, ah," he saw the side door, "that wall over there. It appears out of the way." He slipped his arm around Anya's shoulders pulling her against him.

"Ah," the maître d looked at the bills in his hand then to Déisi with a conspirator's smirk. "Romance is on the menu tonight I see. Of course, this way," and he swept off through the crowded room.

The couple followed him.

Well across the length of the dining room, the maître d stopped at a table and cocked his head at Déisi. At Déisi's nod of approval, the maître d set two menus down on the table.

Déisi helped Anya into her seat then took the one across from her.

"Your waiter is Seth, he will be right with you," the maître d announced then flounced off.

"Oo," Anya giggled, "someone's going to have a heart attack when I order a Big Mac."

Reaching his hand out to set over hers, with a smile, Déisi agreed, "*Yah*, keel right over, he would in this place."

The server instantly appeared at their table.

Déisi ordered a bottle of wine.

When the server glanced at Anya about to ask for ID, Déisi stared at him, his expression a total blank.

A brief gulp and the man wrote the order down and left right away.

"Déisi," Anya admonished with a crooked smile, "you did it again."

His dark eyes swerved to hers. With all innocence, he said, "What? I was very careful to not express any intimidations."

Anya rolled her eyes. "Uh huh. Yeah, but you can't seem to hide the threat that glitters from those daunting black peepers of yours."

Squeezing her hand, he said quietly, "We may be here to do a job, *babia*, but that doesn't mean we can't enjoy the evening, and I want to see your cheeks and nose get pink like they did from the wine on the train."

The steward brought the wine, and Seth their server returned setting bread and butter on the table. He took their order without making eye contact with either of them.

Déisi asked him, "Where are the restrooms? We've been traveling all day and would like to freshen up."

Seth indicated a hallway next to a door that the couple had already determined was where they were going to sneak out.

Dismissing him, Déisi mumbled a curt thanks. "*Mulţumesc.* We will be gone a few minutes, just serve the food even if we have not yet returned."

As soon as the waiter left, Déisi stood up and pulled her chair out. "Ready?"

She hesitated, then pictured her granddad's appearance and she got right up.

Déisi took her hand to stroll through the dining room making their way to the side door. They slipped out the door and entered a carpeted hallway.

Signs were posted everywhere indicating proceeding further would be in violation and to return to the public areas. They were now in the forbidden, private section where the owners resided.

"I…" Anya swallowed, her eyes dashing all over waiting for someone to leap out and arrest them for trespassing.

Feeling her hand cold in his, Déisi said, "Relax, *babia*, if anyone stops us we just say we were lost coming back from the restroom." Craning his head in both directions, seeing numerous doors, he asked, "How will you know which room it is?"

"Um," her gaze slid over a few doors then down the hall. "That way," she pointed down the corridor. "Granddad said it was at the end of the hall. I remember he said the glass doors were double and very ornate with gold, and something about a beautiful purple bird."

Grinning at her, Déisi squeezed her hand and they started down the hall. "This is kind of fun, huh? Like an adventure, treasure hunting?"

"Hmm." Sure, if her and her grandfather's lives weren't on the line she would be feeling the excitement of doing something wrong, not real wrong, more like searching, like a scavenger hunt.

Anya admitted, "I do feel a little thrill. I've never done anything bad before, it is kind of exciting," she squeezed him back.

Déisi gave her a big grin. She blinked in surprise, then smiled.

"What?" he asked.

Shaking her head, she replied, "It's nothing, just that I've never seen you really smile before. You look really..." she trailed off, her face coloring slightly.

"Look like what?" They were almost to the end of the hall.

In a tiny breathy voice, Anya murmured, "Handsome. I'm repeating myself from earlier, you look really handsome, Déisi." She had always beheld him in such fear and confusion she hadn't noticed how really good looking he was.

Sure, women were constantly falling all over him, but Anya contributed that to him being so big and muscled. He had such a powerful, dominant presence, confidence and strength exuded from his strapping body and harsh face.

His neck warmed with the compliment, this was the second time she'd called him handsome when he'd never heard that from a woman before. Feeling a ping in his heart, he said, "Anya-"

"Here, this might be it." She stopped him outside a set of double glass doors that were trimmed in gold, and a design of an elegant colorful peacock was etched in the glass in both doors.

Déisi turned the knob, they both held their breath, it was locked. He knocked lightly and they waited.

After another knock and short wait, with a brief smile at Anya, Déisi pulled a small pouch from inside his suitcoat pocket. He'd come prepared.

It took mere seconds for the lock to make a snick sound. Tucking the tools back into the pouch, he stuffed it in his pocket. Gingerly turning the knob, he slowly pushed the door open then stuck his head inside.

The grin huge on his roughhewn face, Déisi said, "This is it, come on," he pulled her in and closed the door.

In awe, they perused the opulent room.

It was as her grandfather had described it; magnificent. Cathedral ceilings with stain glass windows the length of the wall, luxurious furniture all in cushiony white as was the thick rug.

A huge stone fireplace covered the far wall, the satin drapes were gold, and all the decorations, paintings, mirrors, everything was gilded in gold.

Their attention landed on a large painting on the wall.

Anya smiled in delight. "Oh, Déisi," she gushed, roaming up to the painting. "It's just as he described. Dark reds and greens in a rich velvet."

She stopped in front of it, gazing up with wonder. "Romeo and Juliet, isn't it glorious? So gorgeous."

He came to stand beside her and studied the painting. "*Da, mi dragă*," he smiled down at her glowing face. "But tis nothing compared to your beauty."

She kept her eyes on the painting. "You're being silly, but it's nice of you to say anyway."

"Anyalia," frowning, he put his hands on her shoulders to turn her to face him. "Why do you disparage yourself like that?"

Her head down at first, then she looked up at him. "It's okay, really, don't worry. I'm used to being called plain, homely. My stepmother always said, well," she shook her head, "never mind. We have a mission to complete, right?"

Aghast that anyone could describe this ethereally exquisite angel as homely, Déisi had to bite his tongue for now and force himself to turn his attention back to the painting.

They studied the painting for some time. Then, "What do you think it tis, Anyalia? Why did your granddad direct you to this painting?"

She crossed her arms, her view traveling the span of the stunning painting. "I don't know." She reached out to touch it, but he grabbed her hand. "*Na*, there could be an alarm."

Her brows drawing down, she looked all around then set her head against the wall to see if she could see behind it. There were no wires or anything that she could tell attached to the painting.

"I don't think there is. Granddad wouldn't have mentioned the painting if it didn't mean something. Didn't have something, didn't hide something that I could access." Very lightly, she ran her fingers under the frame.

Déisi sighed, as long as the thing stayed on the wall, if it was wired, they couldn't be accused of attempting to steal it. He copied her, sliding his fingertips up the sides and top that she couldn't reach. Feeling the entire frame, he shook his head. "There is nothing, *babia*."

Anya stood back, crossing her arms again and continued to scrutinize it. "We need to check the back of it."

"Ah, sweetheart, if tis wired-"

"I don't want you to get into trouble, Déisi, after all, he is my granddad. You can go back to the table and-"

"*Na*, no way, I will not leave you." His sigh a deep giving in, "Okay, I'll do it, you're too short. Step aside."

"No, Déisi, really, if I get arrested I can bond out, they can't say we stole something if it's still on the premises."

Ignoring her protests, he put his hands on both sides of the painting and lifted it off the wall. Gently setting it on the ground, he turned it around and leaned it against the wall.

They stared at it, scrutinizing every inch.

Then, "There," Anya pointed at a tiny raised piece of the frame.

Déisi followed where she indicated, his brows jumped. Crouching, he picked at the raised wood and a part of it slid to the side. Taped inside, was a key.

Whispering, "Oh my gosh, Déisi!" Anya couldn't keep the thrill out of her voice.

He peeled the key off, handed it to her, and quickly replaced the painting. Wiping his palms on his slacks, he bent to look at the key she was examining.

Tucking his hands in his pockets, he said, "Anyalia, there is no way to know what that key can belong to. A locker, a desk, a safe, a jewelry box, it could be anything."

She gave him a 1,000 watt smile. "I know what it belongs to. Granddad and I have a safe deposit box that can only be opened with both of our keys. I have mine, and this," she held it up between finger and thumb, "is his."

Déisi rattled off a string of foreign words while dragging his hands through his hair.

Shaking his head, he said kindly, "Don't get your hopes up, honey, tis a safety deposit box. De Vos, with his contacts, hackers, money, he would have already scoured all those avenues of your grandfather. Searched his house, his deposit boxes, mail, any other addresses he ever used, friends, family."

Her impish smile brightening the green eyes, she said, "Maybe, but, he wouldn't know that Grandmother's older sister who lived with them had a lover. He died, but, Granddad had kept his passport and papers and over the years managed to have his own picture affixed to the passport as he kept renewing it.

"Jonathan King was from a country so small most people have never heard of it. It went unnoticed so Granddad kept the deception going. I don't know exactly why he did it, I'm sure to keep some of his work separate, safe, hidden.

"When we opened the safety deposit box together, he had used Jonathan's ID, and had Jonathan as the primary owner of the box. So, even if Mr. de Vos had searched for anything under my or Granddad's name, no flags would have gone off." She tucked the key into her sequined clutch.

With a small smile, Déisi said, "I can't wait until we get you guys out of this and I can meet this clever Brainiac granddad of yours, he would make an amazing asset to my brothers' team. Okay, let's get out of here before we're discovered."

He put the painting back up on the wall and they quickly left the room.

Hurrying down the hall, fortunately they didn't run into another soul. They made it back to the side door undetected and slipped right back into the dining room.

By the time they reached their table, Seth was setting their dinners down.

The steward hurried right over and opened the wine. He poured a drop of wine into Déisi's glass. When Déisi sipped it and nodded that it was acceptable, the steward filled their glasses, set the bottle in a wine bucket off to the side and he left.

Seth the server asked if they needed anything else.

Déisi reached out and took Anya's hand, smiling at her, he said, "*Na*, we have everything we need right here."

With a nod, Seth said with a clip, "Yes, sir, enjoy, I will check back." He quickly scurried away, the big fierce looking man scared the shit out of him.

Squirming in her chair, Anya whispered, "Déisi, we have the key, we need to go to the box." She was anxious to retrieve the formula and get back to her grandfather.

"*Na, babia*, the bank won't be open until tomorrow, and you need to get your key. Let's toast to our miracle, eh?" He lifted his glass to hers. Seeing her frown, he asked, "What is bothering you, Anyalia?"

Her eyes dropped to the table, she was so humiliated at her situation. Lifting them back up to him, she said bleakly, "My key is at my house. My, uh, stepmother, she, I mean, I will have to sneak in and out. If she catches me-"

"Motherfucker," he spat. At her frown, he said quickly, "Sorry." Damn, he needed to make sure when he cursed it was in his own language. "Sweetheart, I will be with you. No one, trust me," his eyes darkened, "will lay a hand on you again. Ever."

He held his glass out to her for her to clink in a toast. "Now, salute with me, everything will be fine, I swear to you." The side of his mouth tilted up in encouragement to make her smile. She did, and relaxed a little.

They enjoyed dinner, wine, then desert, and coffee for Déisi.

He was sipping his coffee when he saw Anya blink, then the color drained from her face. "Anyalia, what is it?" He turned around but couldn't tell what had suddenly alarmed her.

She bit down hard on her lower lip. Uttering, "I- I'll be right back," she set her dessert fork down.

"Anyalia-"

"I- I," she took a breath, put her hands on the table to push her chair back. "I need to go to the ladies room."

He caught her wrist. Holding her still, puzzled brows pulled down, he said, "You just went not five minutes ago, what is going on?"

A man was rapidly approaching their table, the closer he got, the whiter Anya's skin turned. He stopped a foot from Anya.

It was too late for her to get away. Her body rigid as ashen rock, she gripped the edge of the table and looked up at him.

The man greeted her with a big smile, all bright white teeth gleaming. "Hey dollbaby, what the hell are you doing here?" He glanced at Déisi then partially turned his back to him as if he wasn't there.

"Uh," Anya's lashes flapped a mile a minute. "Raoul, what are you doing here?" Hearing an antagonistic growl from across the table, she peered over at Déisi and saw his narrowed eyes laser in question at her, then shift to the man, a hostile warning surfacing from the dark depths.

Raoul moved closer to Anya, the growl from Déisi rumbled, deeper, louder.

Ignoring him, Raoul said, "Anya, I must speak with you, it's about your grandfather. Come with me," he reached for her arm.

The growl low and guttural, Déisi snarled, "She is not going anywhere."

"Granddad? You have word of him? Is he home?" Anya rose to her feet. Anxiously, she said to Déisi, "I have to talk with him. I'll be right back."

Déisi went to rise, "*Na-*" but Raoul was already pulling her across the room. Fishing his wallet out, Déisi raised his hand to catch Seth's attention.

Raoul pulled Anya down the hall towards the restrooms.

After only a few steps, Anya dug her feet in, forcing him to stop or drag her. "Tell me, tell me right now, Raoul, is Granddad home? Is he all right?"

The suavely handsome man in his expensive suit palmed dark wavy hair off the side of his forehead. Dark brown eyes gleamed as he raked her from top to bottom, pausing at her breasts like most men did. "Damn, girl, nice dress, you look hot." He tugged on her arm, urging, "Come on, come with me."

But she resisted. "No, stop, tell me about my grandfather." Her fearful tone turned demanding, "Tell me right now!"

The patronizing smirk marring his olive skinned good looks, he tightened his grip on her arm to the point she gasped, and jerked from him.

Raoul sneered, "There's nothing to tell you, Anya. I heard he was missing. It was a ruse to get you away from that prick in there. What the hell are you doing with him anyway? He looks like some kind of a thug, a brawling beast."

"Let go of me right now, Raoul." Anya jerked her arm, but he held her tight.

Raoul's eyes narrowed in repulsive pique at her. "You wouldn't have sex with me but you'll fuck that brute?" Still holding her arm, he clasped his tie with a few fingers wriggling it like he was way above whatever Déisi was.

"It is none of your business what I do, Raoul, or with whom. Attempted rape, a split lip, bruises, and a black eye are not my idea of making love, now let go of me."

Shaking her, he said angrily, "You wouldn't give it up, Anya, and we were dating for fucks sake. I had rights."

Her brows hopped appalled. "Are you serious? I asked you for more time, you knew how sheltered, how inexperienced I was. But instead, you tore my clothes and tried to rape me, you hit...me," an involuntary wince twitched at the memory.

She accused, "You would have done worse if the mailman hadn't rung the bell and I was able to run out the back, in my bare feet into the woods."

"Oh boo hoo, you wouldn't have hurt your stupid feet if you hadn't left me. This time, you are not getting away. I paid that bitch of a stepmother of yours to keep you locked up until I returned from London for you, and I plan on getting what I bought."

Anya hit at him while trying to wrench and twist from his grasp. "No! I am done being anyone's prisoner- leave me alone!"

"Not this time, dollbaby." He stuck his hand in her hair, wrapping it around his fist. "You come quietly with me or I swear to God I'll knock you out and carry you out."

Déjà vu tingled up her spine, it was the same thing Déisi had threatened to do that day to get her off the plane compliantly. Except now, she realized Déisi would never hit her, or any woman. He had been faking, trying to scare her into behaving compliantly.

But Raoul, she looked up at him. Entitlement in the curl of his lip, cruelty in his eyes, he didn't care about her, he only wanted to possess her, and of course, have sex with her. And he had already proved he had no compunctions about beating her and forcing her to submit.

Jerking her arm, he snarled, "I will have you home, and with your parents' blessings, tied to my bed so fast, you won't have time to even think about running away-"

"She'd not going anywhere with you, you fucker. Let go of her." Déisi had come up a different hall hearing every word the bastard said to Anya, and his body was burning with rage. On his fierce face was the familiar look of Lucifer blackening his features, eyes lethal as obsidian sin.

Raoul's grip loosened as he checked Déisi from head to toe and back up with a sneer indicating he was beneath his station. "This is none of your business, dickhead, you may crawl back under whatever shit-assed, gangster rock you came out from. Take off, bro before I hurt you." He assumed Déisi would back off due to Raoul's superior status.

Anya took the advantage of his loosened grip and jerked out of his grasp. She looked from one man to the other, both were livid.

Raoul because he didn't like anyone thwarting his desires, and Déisi, damn, she cringed inside. He stood calmly poised, face now implacable, but his eyes were dark as death.

"Anyalia," his eyes on Raoul, Déisi handed her a ticket. "Give this to the valet. When he brings the car, get in, lock the doors and wait for me."

When she just stood frozen blinking at him, he lifted her hand and tucked the ticket in it and closed her fingers over it. "Go, do as I say," he commanded quietly. "I will be there in a minute." He shifted his body to directly face Raoul.

Raoul stepped closer to Anya declaring, "No fucking way, shithead, she's not going anywhere with you. She's with me now, you can take a hike. Anya," he turned to her, "ignore this big fucker, I will get rid of him. Now, you remember I'm partial to Porsches. The one I have is cherry red. Go downstairs and wait out front for me. I will be right there to pick you up."

His attention swung back to Déisi. The sneer back in his gaze sweeping Déisi's body, he said, "This fucker doesn't know I am quite experienced in martial arts."

Exasperated at being talked to and ordered about like she was a child, Anya looked from one to the other.

Raoul was smirking, Déisi's face a blank mask. At the moment she didn't know which one was scarier. Huh, Déisi of course. She knew his background, that de Vos man said he was a professional killer, a trained assassin, she'd seen his anger.

Raoul only attacks helpless women. Something she was getting damned tired of being. She opened her mouth to tell both jackasses to stop behaving like schoolboys in the schoolyard, but then saw their fixed expressions.

There would be nothing she could say, or do to stop whatever was going to happen. Sighing, maybe they would just talk it out.

Sure. They looked like they just wanted to chat. She turned her back and strode towards the staircase, and didn't look back.

Down the stairs, her heart was thumping like mad wondering what was happening up there. She kept going, her lungs tight with apprehension. Maybe she should just try to get a taxi, go home.

Maybe her father would be there, maybe he could help her. Or, maybe she should call the police. Thoughts just rambled through her head as she tried to decide the best course to take.

De Vos was in another country, it was doubtful either his country's authorities or hers, would, or could help her. And, sadly, her father barely knew what day it was without Maisa telling him.

The doorman bowed as he opened the door for her.

Anya stood on the walkway of the elaborate hotel debating what to do.

Chapter Sixteen

"Madam?" The valet came straight over to her. His approving gaze rolled over her face and body, she was easy to remember. He glanced around quickly, so was the big bruiser she'd come with.

Ambivalent, Anya faltered, then tentatively handed the claim ticket to the valet.

Accepting it, he nodded. "Yes Ma'am, the Jag. I will be quick." He strode to the board with the keys to the cars on hooks with numbers, plucked off the keys to the Jaguar and took off jogging through the lot.

People passed by Anya, some noticing her with interest. She saw nothing as she stood biting a nail, an old habit she thought she'd overcome.

She was still unsure of what to do when the silver and blue Jaguar SUV swept up the U shaped drive with pompous flair. The valet parked it, exiting with a flourish. He ran around to open the door for Anya.

Still, she hesitated. Then, a frustrated sigh emptying her lungs, she climbed in the passenger side and the valet closed her door. He immediately turned away to address the next guest who was standing waiting with his ticket held out in his hand.

Inside the comfy, luxurious vehicle, Anya's eyes were on the keys the valet had left dangling in the ignition. Remembering

Déisi's instructions to lock the doors, a flash of Darryl Dassey throwing her in his car made her move quickly to do as he said.

After ensuring the doors were locked, she sat back and again perused the keys. She didn't need Déisi. She could go get her deposit box key, retrieve the formula and go to de Vos and demand he release her granddad.

As much as he stated otherwise, Déisi was only going to leave her and the formula with de Vos, collect his earnings and take off. Surely de Vos wouldn't still kill her granddad after he got the formula.

As the developer, Granddad would more quickly and expertly create the compound than any other scientist. Then, Granddad could putter away pretending to create it while he and Anya plotted their escape.

Yes, nodding her head firmly, she could do it, she didn't need him. Her eyes shifted from the keys to stare back out at the busy hotel searching for the tough man with the thick black hair and confident stride.

Did she want to do this alone? Was she getting kind of used to having the big lug hanging around giving her orders? A tiny smile lifted the side of her mouth, not really. At least not his annoying dictatorship. Bossing her around, telling her what to do, physically forcing her to do as he instructed if she resisted.

His cold, ruthless manner, aggressive and violent behavior, the way he had of just looking at a person and that person wilted, shook, and usually hurried away from him. Shaking her head, no, she certainly did not miss the bullying man.

Yet, her fingers drifted to her lips. His kisses, darn the man, he could make her head spin with just his kisses. Thinking of the day he assaulted her on the train, her bottom squirmed on the leather seat in remembrance.

True, she had been shocked, appalled, scared...and yet, thinking about his hard hands on her, touching her roughly. His face, mouth, all over her breasts, oh, she could feel the heat not only filling her cheeks, but it burned between her legs.

She should be furious the way he continued to take liberties with her, forcing himself on her. The frisk on the plane had been devastatingly mortifying.

But, now, recalling on the train his thick manly fingers undoing her clothes, skimming those strong hands over her skin, gripping her breasts with fevered intensity, a shiver ran through her body.

Scolding herself, Anya shook her head with a snap, ordering, "Stop it, girl. He is a hired killer, certainly not boyfriend material. He is going to dump you the second he gets the formula to his boss and collects his pay." The thought churned her dinner in her stomach.

Never to see the muscle-bound bully with the hard lips that kissed so savagely, then amazingly softly, ever again? The passion heavy in his sooty eyes as they drank her in, the untamed hunger for her he unsuccessfully tried to hide?

Her eyes flicked back to the keys. Did she dare? Would he have her arrested for stealing the car? Somehow she doubted it. But, a certain smile twisted, he would undoubtedly punish her if he caught her. And, she sighed, he would catch her, she had no doubt about it.

Tap-tap

Startled, she eeked, "Oh!" jumping at the light knocking on the window. Deep in her revelry she hadn't seen him come out of the hotel or paying the valet. Anya peered out at Déisi.

It was amazing that such a harsh-faced brutal man could look so debonair in his suit. Broad shoulders and thick chest filling the jacket, the material swung looser around his lean hips.

He didn't appear at all damaged, no bruises, no black eyes. The suit was as pristine as it had been at dinner. His tie still knotted neatly at his throat, jacket buttoned, only his hair was slightly mussed.

"Anyalia, open the door." Black brows drew down at her hesitation. He watched her look from him to the keys in the ignition. His growl of, "Don't even think about it," came through the closed window.

She leaned over and pushed up the lock on the driver's side then moved back as he opened the door and slid in.

He smoothed his tousled hair with his hands drawing Anya's gaze to his knuckles. Her skin shriveled with her blanch.

Seeing her looking at his hands, he pulled out a handkerchief from his pocket, and calmly wiped the blood off his knuckles.

"Déisi, what happened?"

Stuffing the hanky in his pocket, he turned the car on and drove down the long curved drive out to the street. His eyes on the road he said without inflection, "There is nothing to talk about, Anyalia. The fuck- uh, jerk will not be bothering you again." He tugged at his tie, dragged it loose and off, and tossed it in the back seat.

"No, Déisi, please tell me you two didn't fight!" But obviously they had, he didn't get bloody knuckles from knocking on the car window.

Exhaling roughly, he grunted, "We are not going to discuss it."

Angry, turning in her seat towards him, she retorted, "Yes we are, you got into a physical…altercation with a man who- who- you don't even know-"

"Who fucking tried to rape you, and he beat you. Seriously, Anyalia," he glared at her before turning back to the road.

"You think I would let a man get away with hurting you? Even if the action was done before I met you? You think I would leave a danger like him out there to harm you again? Please," he snorted, "you don't know me very well."

Glancing at her glaring green eyes, her palms were on the seat between them bracing her in a half-kneel. The front of her dress scooped low exposing a good deal of her cleavage. His eyes fastened on it.

A horn blared drawing his attention back to the road. Expelling a deep breath, he commanded, "Put your seatbelt on."

Shaking her head, she lamented, "That is true, I do not know you, at all." She sat back and latched the seatbelt over herself.

He grunted again without responding.

179

Anya cocked her head slightly to look at him.

His face was just as harsh from the profile as head on. His mouth closed, strong jaw working, the vein under the scar at his temple hopped with his ire. Both powerful hands gripped the wheel. She saw the blood hadn't been his, there wasn't a scratch on him. Her stomach roiled.

"Déisi, you didn't..." she quailed at saying *kill*- "uh, hurt him?"

He stared out the window saying nothing.

"Déisi, answer me. Tell me what you did."

Never taking his eyes from the road, his lips remained pressed closed.

Anya's face paled at the implication that he had at the very least, seriously hurt Raoul, since she hadn't seen the other man exit the hotel.

Laying her head back against the seat, Anya closed her eyes. She was upset, but, Raoul had viciously attacked her. He had seriously injured her during his assault. Also, he had paid her stepmother to keep her prisoner for him. Truthfully, part of her was glad he'd gotten his comeuppance.

Déisi had done what her granddad would have done if she had told him what had happened. Except, she didn't know if Déisi had...killed him. Granddad would not have gone that far. Right?

It didn't appear as if the big block of solid man at the wheel had any intentions of telling her what happened. And, he was clearly still enraged, the vein pulsed at his temple, jaw grit, his fingers strangled the wheel.

Letting out a heavy breath, there was nothing she could do about it now. Shooting Déisi a brief glance, his mouth was clenched, huge hands gripping the wheel so hard he could probably break it if he wanted to. He was a grim, brutal man and he terrified her.

Blinking, Anya's gaze flit back to the front window. Nonetheless, somehow he made her feel safe. Her eyes flicked back to roll down his manly chest, and lower. Even as angry as he was, when his gaze had drifted over her cleavage, he had grown noticeably hard.

Cheeks flushing, she could see he plainly desired her, and, as heat prickled between her legs, she shifted in discomfort. Her lungs filled with disconcerted air, she was worried she was beginning to feel the same about him.

Sensing her eyes on him, hearing her fretful breaths, Déisi reached out and took her hand. Twining their fingers together, he moved them to set their linked hands on the seat between them.

Her head twitched to him, then she looked back towards the window, but did not try to pull her hand away. They drove like that until they reached her home.

Pulling up the driveway, Anya's skin paled, her body turned rigid as a board. Her fingers squeezed his so tightly he feared she'd hurt herself.

Déisi felt her agitation skyrocket, and it made his innards burn with anger. No one should dread going home. Sure, he and his brothers were different, they were brought up under bizarre circumstances.

Releasing her hand to put the car in park, it infuriated him that Anya's stepmother abused her, and her father stood by and let her. His base inclination was to go in and make retribution, however, he glanced at her sitting completely still, mangling her fingers in her lap, she would hate him if he did.

Turning the car off, he got out and went around to the passenger side.

When he opened her door, he was met with wide, disturbed and embarrassed green eyes. "Déisi, I…have to warn you, my dad gets…confused, and my stepmother, is, uh, not exactly a nice person. She-"

"*Da babia*, don't fret, I won't hurt them. And you are not them, there is no judgement here. Come," he grasped her arm helping her out. "Let's go in, get the key, and get the hell out of here."

Strengthening her tremulous smile up at him, Anya climbed out of the car, tucked her hand in the crook of his arm and led him up the walk to the house.

A quick glance to the backyard brought a sad frown. Her grandfather's cottage sat forlornly amidst the grove of leafy trees. The door hung open by one hinge. "They haven't even bothered to fix Granddad's door."

Déisi patted her hand. "No worries, sweet, I will take care of it." His face stiffened when the front door opened and a woman strode out. Anya's clutch on his arm tightened.

The woman had blonde hair, it frizzed around her sharp shoulders. She was dressed in tight jeans and a tighter blouse. She had the faded looks of a cold-hearted beauty.

The mean expression that tightened her lips and brought lines around her eyes and mouth destroyed whatever beauty she once possessed. Maisa Marvaux was not giving into age even with the changing of her middle-aged body. Swinging her hips, she strutted to them as if she walked the runway.

When they were a few feet from the woman, Anya said softly, "Maisa, this is-"

Whack-

Maisa slapped her, snarling, "You filthy whore, you finally deign to come home? Well you won't-" her shrill voice was choked off from Déisi's huge hand wrapped around her throat. Dark hazel, petrified eyes looked up at the fierce man, his face contorted in rage.

"No! Déisi! Let her go!" Anya grabbed at his arm trying to pull him loose.

He uttered a string of blistering words in his language, eyes and mouth spitting with fury. Cursing the older woman, he squeezed his fingers.

In English, he snarled at Anya, "*Na*, no one harms you, *mi dragă,* no one." Steam about poured out of his ears, his nostrils flared like a bull scraping the ground about to attack.

Wrapping her fingers around his brawny forearm, Anya said quietly, "Please, Déisi, I'm asking you to let her go."

The tendons on his arm swelled along with the vein beating furiously at his temple. Lids so low the dark eyes were almost invisible, his fingers maintained their fierce grip.

Anya repeated softly, "Please Déisi, let her go."

His fingers slowly unclenched from her neck. He dropped his arm, flexed his shoulders and stretched his neck as he regained his composure.

Gagging and coughing, Maisa's hands went to her throat. Exaggerating a choking squawk, she screeched, "Anya, you little slut, where did you find this- this- animal!"

Her words fired Déisi back up. His shoulders bunched, fists clenched. He warned her, "You will not speak that way to her if you desire to keep your tongue…attached to your mouth."

Maisa stepped back from him in horror. Then, she took in the hard, scarred face, huge shoulders broad in the expensive suit jacket, biceps bulging in his anger, and the horror receded to, a coy admiration.

Quickly forgetting his strangling her, Maisa's voice took on a flirtatious invitation, "Anya, dear, who is your…friend? You haven't introduced us properly."

Glancing at Anya, Maisa said with a snipped sneer, "Why are you dressed like that?" Her lascivious eyes back on Déisi, she rebuked Anya, "You let this man buy you expensive clothes? I always knew you were a cheap tramp. Now, introduce me!"

Anya's mouth dropped in bafflement. Her stepmother had just about been strangled, threatened with mutilation, and she was flirting with Déisi! Anya was in an alternate universe, she just knew it.

Déisi had only wanted to frighten Maisa, not harm her, but Maisa didn't know that. She was flirting with a dangerous, violent man.

Déisi rolled his arm around Anya's slender shoulders and protectively pulled her close. His body literally vibrated with his fury and the struggle to hold himself back from doing injury to her stepmother.

Considering he had never hurt a female in his life, it was shocking that it took everything he had to keep himself from pummeling her into the ground.

"M- Maisa," Anya took a breath to steady her voice. "This is," she raised a brow to him, did he want her disclosing his name?

"Déisi Zukov," he inserted with a sharp nod. The black in his eyes like a sword of warning.

So infuriated with Maisa slapping Anya, his accent deepened, he was barely intelligible. His English lapsed as he threatened, "You never touch her again. You do, female or *na*, I take care of you. I fucking bury you. You understand this, Mrs. Marvaux?"

Gasping, "Oh," Maisa backed away from the enraged, ire-spouting savage.

Features marred with his livid rage, Déisi leaned into Maisa, accent wringing, stunting his English further, "And *da*, I buy her clothes. I buy her diamonds and house soon, none of this your fucking business."

"Um," Anya moved around her stepmother pulling Déisi with her into the house. He allowed her to tug him along, but shot Maisa a menacing glare over his back at her.

Maisa blinked, swallowed hard, then followed them inside.

Over her shoulder, Anya told her, "We are going to my room to get something. We will be only a minute and then we will be out of your hair."

Maisa stormed after them shouting, "You will not Anya! Nice girls don't take men to their bedrooms. You will not pay him with your body for his gifts to you in *my* house-"

Ignoring her stepmother, Anya hurried to the stairs, drawing Déisi with her as she quickly ran up them. She didn't let out her held breath until she reached her room. Pulling him inside, she closed the door.

"Anyalia," he started then saw her look of horror.

She was gawking at the destruction in her room.

Every drawer was pulled out and dumped, the closet emptied, her clothes tossed on the floor. Her pictures on the wall were pulled down and torn apart, bed cut up, destroyed.

The room that once was pretty with peach and silver wallpaper, white trim, white furniture, and peach comforter and ruffled curtains, was now slashed from one end to the other. Even the wallpaper was in shreds in parts.

"Oh no..." her little pained cry wrung Déisi's black heart.

The door opened and Maisa peeked in. Seeing Anya distraught, she shrugged then explained, "Some men came, asked to see your room. They, uh, paid for the privilege, so," her angled shoulders shrugged again like it was no big deal.

"You- you- you let them-" Anya chugged like a train.

Déisi put his hand on Maisa's shoulder and pushed her out of the room and closed the door in her face. He moved to stand behind Anya, pulled her quaking spine against his chest and wrapped his arms around her.

"I'm sorry, Anyalia that all this evil has touched your life. This is Anton de Vos' work."

She trembled in his arms. He bent his head to kiss the top of her head, then moved his mouth lower to kiss her brow.

He murmured against her ear, "We will fix all of this. You, your granddad, I promise *mi babia*," he continued whispering soft words in his language until the trembling ceased.

Anya took a deep breath and moved from the comforting circle of his embrace and shoved her hair back with both hands.

Her voice steadier than she had expected, she said, "I know. It's just so...shocking." Shaking her head to chase away the chills, she started walking to the opposite side of the room.

He trailed her. "Did they get it?"

Now the smile she conjured up was genuine. "Nope. No way, jerks."

When she reached the wall, she dropped to her knees.

Standing behind her, Déisi leaned over to watch.

She pried at a corner of the border that trimmed around the room bisecting the wall and floor, and lifted a piece of printed peach wallpaper. The paper had covered a hole.

Anya stuck her hand in. Even if it had been seen by one of the people sent to search the room, it was unlikely any of their hands would have been small enough to fit inside the hole, they wouldn't have even noticed it.

"Ta da!" Anya exclaimed, gleefully holding up the key she'd pulled from the hidey hole. Standing up she showed it to Déisi.

"I thought it was all fun and mysterious adventure at the time when granddad made this hole, the printed wallpaper hid that it had been cut to lift over the hole. At the time I never dreamed what…horror it could relate to." Her shoulders rolled as a shiver bristled over them.

"*Da.*" Déisi's grin was big and natural, something that didn't happen very often. His accent softened, he said gently, "Tis all terrible sweetheart, but the good thing is that your granddad was shrewd enough to expect trouble and ensure the information was kept hidden from those that would use it for evil. Come, let's get the fu- uh hell out of here."

"Okay." Anya stood for a second gazing around her damaged room. Because of Maisa's ill treatment of her, and Raoul stalking her, with Granddad gone she really had no desire to live in the house anymore.

She would have to figure out how she could afford her own apartment. She would have to cut down on her classes and get a second job. It would take longer to get her degree, but it would be worth it not to have to come back to this place.

Sighing out her melancholy, she smiled up at him. "Let's go get my grandfather."

Anya found her passport in a drawer, gathered up some clothes and tossed them in a suitcase.

When she went to pick it up, Déisi grabbed it. "Listen, I'm not helpless," Anya protested.

"*Da*, I know. Why should you struggle with something that is ten times easier for me to do? Let's not bicker about women's lib shit now, we need to go."

Her mouth open in retort, he was already out the door.

They planned on just leaving without saying anything to Maisa, but she was lurking outside the bedroom door waiting for them.

Ignoring her, Déisi nudged Anya to walk in front of him so he was a buffer between her and her stepmother. Nevertheless, Maisa followed them asking a million questions.

"Anya, where have you been? Where are you going? Did you come for something specific in your room or were you just looking for a place to have sex with this man? I mean, this is not a hotel you know, nor a whorehouse. You want to fool around you need to go-"

Déisi swung around so fast Maisa had to stop up short to not run into him. With a few foreign curses, he shouted at her, "Will you shut the fuck up you prattling bitch?"

Red spots at being spoken to like that sprang on Maisa's lumpy cheekbones. "Listen you- you ruffian, you can't talk to me like that! This is my house! That little tramp will not-"

His brows drew down so hard and fierce his eyes were all but glittering black diamonds.

Maisa took a step back from him expecting him to strike her, her hand hovered at her throat.

Eyes narrowed in fury, his voice low and tight and quiet, thick with his guttural accent, Déisi leaned into her. "I won't say this again, vile woman. You will not speak with disrespect to Anyalia, and you ever lay a hand on her again I forget you are female. Tell me this you understand?"

He waited while Maisa's shocked hazel eyes roamed over the wide shoulders, heavy chest and down where they stalled at his fly. The red spots grew darker, her tongue moistened her lips.

"Uh," not moving her gaze from his groin where even flaccid his manhood bulged noticeably, her eyes widened as she licked her lips again.

"Madam Marvaux!" Déisi roared, getting her attention. "You harm *mi* Anyalia in any way, I hurt you. You should be whipped and arrested for locking her in that fucking basement and starving her."

His big fist in her face, his eyes screwed into slits, he snarled, "I fucking want to kill you for that. I will not, only because

Anyalia would not want it." A look of disgust smeared the fury curling his lip, he shook his head and stalked down the stairs.

Already at the door, Anya's head was craning in different directions.

When Déisi and Maisa reached her, Anya asked, "Where is my father? I would like to say hello to him."

"Humph," Maisa sniffed. "He is at the supermarket. If you want to wait for him you may sit in the kitchen, or go to your grandfather's cottage."

"Maisa," Anya said, "why has granddad's door not been fixed, or the damage from it being searched not put right?"

Shrugging one shoulder, Maisa replied aloofly, "When is it my job to see to his business? I am not his servant. He can repair it when he returns. Actually," she twirled a piece of frizzy hair around a finger while her heated gaze continued stroking up and down Déisi's muscled body.

"I think we may fix it and rent it out. We should be getting some money out of it. The funds your grandfather gives us barely pays for gas in our car."

"Really, Maisa, this is Granddad's house, he owns this property. He was gracious to live in the cottage and let you live in the big house because of me. He shouldn't have given you any money in the first place."

Her snort dismissing Anya's words as irrelevant, Maisa said snidely, "I swear, *Princess*," she sneered her old derisive nickname for Anya. "Your family is the cheapest, most-"

"That's it, we're leaving." Before he totally lost his temper and did something Anya wouldn't forgive him for, Déisi set his hand on Anya's lower back and pushed her gently out the door.

Maisa glared at them, her mouth yapping cross insults as they strode to the driveway and hopped into the Jag.

At the sight of the luxury SUV, Maisa's mouth dropped. She started across the lawn with words of apology on her lips. Hey, if the hot looking savage had money as well as sex appeal, well, why should Anya reap all the fun and benefits?

Her body shimmying in eager desire, she ran after them calling out for him to stop.

Déisi thrust the car in gear and gunned it down the drive and to the street leaving the horrid woman and the ransacked buildings behind.

Chapter Seventeen

*A*nya sat silently twisting her fingers together and staring blankly out the window.

Déisi's heart bled for her. He couldn't believe her stepmother treated her so despicably, and her father apparently did nothing to stop her cruelty. "Anyalia," he said softly, "when that bitch locked you in the basement, why didn't your father let you out?"

One shoulder bumped up in feigned indifference. Anya replied, "It wasn't his fault, he has terrible bouts of absentmindedness. He wouldn't have known I was down there. If he asked where I was, she would have told him I was away with friends. There was a bathroom and cot down there. He never even saw me the day he came for a bottle of wine. When he went to the cellar part, I dashed up the stairs and out the door."

Nodding, Déisi muttered, "I see." He fished his phone out of his pocket and pushed a few numbers.

When someone answered, he spoke a few words in his own language then hung up and slid the phone back in his pocket.

"I heard you say my address, what are you doing?"

Combing a hand through his hair, Déisi said, "I called someone to make repairs to your granddad's home, and sort the inside. It will be ready by the time he returns home."

Her lips parted in surprise then curved into a gentle smile. Anya set her fingers on his sleeve. "You…are so…kind, sweet, Déisi, thank you. I can pay you-"

"For the love of the saints, woman," his head dropped back with an eye roll. He clasped her chin tilting her face up to his. "Please, as long as we know each other I do not want to hear the words money, pay back, any of that shit again. One more time and I will have to punish you. Okay?"

Before she could answer, he said with a slight sour scowl, "And never describe me as sweet. I am a soldier, an enforcer, I am not *sweet*." His tongue stuck out as his mouth twisted more in embarrassment than in chastisement.

Anya laughed. "But you are sweet. But don't worry," she leaned over and kissed his cheek. "I promise, I won't tell anyone." Then her lips pushed out with a frown. "What do you mean punish? What do you mean by that?"

Now he laughed at her. "You mention money again, my sweet, and find out." He chucked her chin playfully then put his attention on the road.

Déisi drove into the main part of town. Pulling up a long drive to a posh hotel, he parked at the curved front of the main entrance. Opening his door, he said, "I'll be right back."

"Why are we here?" Anya asked, her eyes huge taking in the opulence of the ten-story establishment.

"The earliest flight out of here that I could book doesn't leave until later tomorrow. I don't want to be in anything de Vos owns in this country where he can possibly trap us."

"Oh. But this place is…I mean…it looks very expensive, I don't think-"

Bending in the door, he stroked her cheek. "Ah, *mi babia*, do not start. Just wait for me, keep the doors locked. *Da*?"

Ever since his verbal battle with Maisa, he had yet to calm himself. The entire drive his accent had thickened to the point Anya had to ask him to repeat himself several times.

He didn't wait for her response, just locked then shut the door and strode into the hotel.

He was gone long enough for her nerves to start jangling again. It was the longest Anya had been relatively alone since she was taken.

Watching guests coming and going, families with children bouncing up and down and laughing, she thought back to the day she was snatched off the street and carried into the bus. She'd been frantic, breathless with fear. Terrified of the other people on the bus, what was going to happen to her, and she'd been most frightened of Déisi.

He had been cold, rude, rough to her. As horrible as he was with his hands all over her while he patted her down, he had protected her from everyone, including Darryl Dassey, Anton de Vos, Raoul, and now, she smiled briefly, her stepmother.

She remembered Déisi had been truly concerned when he thought she was ill on the train. He'd had his wallet out, he was going to pay the doctor with his own money. It couldn't all be to protect what that hideous man had said she was, property of Anton de Vos, could it?

She stared without seeing out the window. She didn't really know Déisi, unsure if she could trust him. He might have his own agenda, maybe he wanted the formula for himself. She turned to look at the ignition, he had taken the keys.

Uncertainty and panic started their toxic grip on her again.

Anya grabbed the door handle, she needed to go back home. Go to her father, get money from him so she could return to De Vos. Images of her grandfather's battered face floated into her mind, her eyes blurred with tears. He needed her, she had to go, she couldn't trust anyone.

The panic surged, flooding Anya's racing heart. She fumbled with the door, opened it and slid out. Her head flung back and forth, which way to go? What to do? She would hide until Déisi came out of the hotel then she would run inside and use their phone to call home.

Maisa would have to let her speak to her father. If she refused, Anya would…her heart raced faster, she would promise Maisa that she would see Raoul. That is, her mouth quirked at the corner, if he was still alive. But, Maisa wouldn't know what happened with him anyway, so she could promise, and hope, that Raoul would not be around to get to her.

She dashed down the walk, hurrying around people and luggage, and around the side of the hotel where she could be hidden and still be able to see the front entrance for Déisi to come out.

Her stomach pitched in a sickening hollow at the thought of never seeing him again. Shaking her head, she combed her hair back with her fingers, she told herself she was only just used to him being around, that was all.

Still, she was already feeling empty inside thinking about never seeing the tough lug again.

Swiping at a tear that was about to fall, she peered around the corner. He hadn't appeared. "What on earth could be keeping him from-" Suddenly, an arm moved in front of her, fencing her against the wall.

"All this work and you were going to leave this behind, *babia*?" He reached into his inside coat pocket and drew something out.

Every part of her rigid, Anya blinked at her sequined purse held up in front of her face. Her head dropped forward, how could she have forgotten her purse that held the key? She was so stupid. She'd left it when she had gone off with Raoul in the restaurant.

Thank goodness Déisi always keeps his head and awareness of everything going on around him, including her silly purse.

His arm blocking her from fleeing, her back against the wall, Anya turned slowly to face him. She looked up at the big man, bracing herself for his fury.

Thinking he might finally be angry enough with her to hit her, she curved her head away and closed her eyes. Instead of a punch, his large hand softly cradled the side of her delicate face and turned her gently to meet his gaze.

Her lashes flipped rapidly, he didn't look angry. There was actually a small smile on his hard face.

"Anyalia, you will learn to trust me and stop running from me. When will you realize that I would never hurt you, I've told you this. Now," his thumb brushed her cheek, "tell me why you are trying once again to leave me."

He didn't have to hold her to keep her immobile, his broad chest and wide shoulders were an indomitable wall keeping her close to the building. "You panicked again, didn't you?"

Lids flapping in uneasiness, her eyes dropped in slight guilt. "I, uh, it's just," green spheres flecked with gold rose up to see a rare, kind light in his dark eyes.

"This whole thing, being abducted, the reprehensible behavior of those sex-crazed people on the bus, the train, the dreadful Mr. de Vos, my granddad being so hurt," she sniffed back the tears that threatened.

"I've lived in virtual seclusion most of my life. This is all so…so…aberrant, so disturbing," her nose wrinkled, "so vile." Unsteady breath rippling with a sigh of uncertainty and despair, she said, "I- I'm scared, lost. I want to trust you, I do, and then," she shrugged sadly. "I get confused and frightened again."

Nodding his agreement, Déisi slipped her purse back in his suit coat pocket and moved the arm that blocked her to encircle her shoulders, subtly pulling her closer.

His long fingers gently netting her face, he said softly, "I know, Anyalia. I know you are frightened and panicking. I understand how difficult, how foreign all this… iniquity is to endure. Plus that shit with your boyfriend, Roger. And me," his grunt came with a bleak smile.

"I am not your run of the mill boy next door kind of guy. I have no illusions as to how menacing I look, how crude and violent I can be, what kind of man I am." He brushed her lips lightly with his and watched her eyes close when he did.

When she opened them, reacting to his mouth's caress, a befuddled haze blurred the green irises pushing aside the fear. She said absently, "His name is Raoul, not Roger, and he's not my boyfriend."

The alarming thought of what Déisi might have done to Raoul crunched the corners of her eyes. Recalling the blood on his knuckles, she cringed, what he could do to her, she turned her head away again, still held in his grasp.

Feeling her stiffen, withdrawing from him, Déisi growled, "I have told you again and again, Anyalia, I will not hurt you. I have promised you I would protect you and try the best I can to free your grandfather. The police will not be able to get to him. I am the only one that can help you. I swear, if he gets his hands on you and the key, de Vos will kill both you and your granddad."

His fingers gentle on her skin, he tipped her chin up again and stroked his tongue over her top lip. "Please try to trust me." His mouth settled more firmly on hers, his whisper against it liquid velvet, "Please, Anyalia."

His lips were hard and soft at the same time, his kiss equally gentle and rough. As she responded, his arms tightened and the kiss deepened, growing rougher, more aggressive as his body hardened and burned.

Anya's palms of their own volition coasted up his chest, her hands twined around his neck as she stood on her tiptoes to feel more of the steam of his kiss, melting the apprehensive pit in her belly, and igniting a sizzle between her legs.

Her fingers slid into his black hair, she dug them in grabbing hold of the thick locks.

Both oblivious to the world around them, Déisi's hand splayed on her back holding her soft body hard against him, wedging her breasts on his chest. A seething growl resonated from his chest. Slanting his head for a tighter fit, his tongue swept inside her mouth seeking hers until he found it and then sucked the hell out of it.

Anya tried to reciprocate the same actions with novice exploration. Her innocent strokes steeped the growl, deepening it to the timber of a hungry tiger, he burrowed his erection against her.

Liquid Velvet

His big hand dropped to her rounded bottom. Squeezing it, he tugged her, grinding her pelvis against the length of his rigid, distinctly enlarging shaft.

Anya could feel it. Fear of the unknown jumbled with excited curiosity electrified her senses. She knew she should stop, push him away, in the back of her mind niggled the thought that he was an assassin. No good for her.

But, his mouth slid languidly yet hungrily down her mouth to her jaw, lower to her neck where his lips and teeth bit and sucked her flesh with relish and ravenous moans. Her head fell back at the unique sensations generating from his mouth down her body lighting hot sparks at her core.

Just as she was becoming aware of her panties growing damp, her nipples straining against the granite warmth of his chest, his hand roughly clenching her butt so hard she wondered if she would have bruises tomorrow but didn't want him to stop-

Boisterous giggles, then loud hushing from observers followed by more giggles cooled her blood immediately. Her fingers untangled from his hair to drop to his chest. Keeping her head down she pushed at him.

But, he stroked his hand on her throat, cupping her jaw, lifting her head so his mouth could return to her lips. His tongue pillaging her mouth, his murmur came husky with desire, "Ignore them, *mi dragă,* kiss me." His other hand roamed up her back to keep her pressed hard against him.

But Anya pushed harder, turned her head, her cheeks flaming.

Three elderly women rattled past them, two still snickered. The third, her nose in the air snipped with a haughty scowl, "The indecent behavior of young people these days." With an appalled snort, "No morals, brazen hussy!" she hissed at Anya.

Anya pushed from Déisi's embrace, mortified at her behavior. The woman was right, she was brought up better than to make out in a public place, with a veritable stranger, one who kept her prisoner for heaven's sake, a hired killer.

Sickened, her stomach plummeted. Then, her ashamed gaze rose to Déisi.

His huge shoulders heaved with his intense ardor. Chest pumping heavy breaths, his hands still reached out for her. But his eyes, the cold, hard ruthless obsidian was melted chocolate, clouded with searing hunger. Dazed pupils dilated in limpid fervor blinked back at her.

Regardless of the judging old biddies, and whatever Déisi was, Anya's heart pattered insanely at the sight of his harshly handsome face flaming with his desire for her. Smiling, Anya set her palm against the side of his rugged cheek.

The haze clearing, he leaned into it, his smile slow, thoughtful. He set his hand over hers, then brought it down and kissed her knuckles. "Ah, *mi babia*, I lose my mind around you. I won't apologize. I must be honest, I enjoyed it too much, and I want more. Much more."

She said nothing, but her soft smile didn't alter.

"Okay, sweet, let's go to our room." He caught up her hand and brought her into the hotel and up to the fifth floor, then down the hall to their suite.

Unlocking the door, he held it open for her to go inside.

Eyes wide, she slowly twirled around. "Oh, Déisi, it's…magnificent, beautiful." She walked around the lavish room with beige carved columns.

Blue and ivory wallpaper separated by panels of mahogany, dusky blue furniture on thick white carpeting, sapphire drapes held back with silver tassels opened to a glassed balcony.

A dinette anchored between the living room and the separate bedroom. Hesitantly, she walked down the small hall to the bedroom and peered inside.

It was just as luxurious as the main room. Her brows rose at the two king-sized beds. She could feel him behind her. "We are to sleep in the same room?"

Déisi set his heavy palms on her shoulders. "*Da*."

She waited for an explanation, like he wanted her close to protect her, or guard her, keep her prisoner, but he made no further comment or explanation.

Feeling her stiffen under his hands, he said, "You have your own bed, Anyalia."

It was the most he would offer. He would never let her be out of sight in another suite, away from his protection. Truthfully, everything in him wanted to be cuddled up all night, for a week, a month, forever, with her in one of the beds.

When she made no reply, he cleared his throat. "I will, if you want me to, sleep on the couch in the other room."

Anya turned to face him. His hands, itching to tear off her clothes, dropped to his side. "You would? Really?"

Nodding with a shrug, he said, "*Da*. Of course. If it makes you feel more comfortable, *yah*, ah, yes." A couch would be heaven compared to the many places he's had to lay his head.

He could understand her anxiety. He was a letch anytime he was in arm's reach of her. Of course she would worry he would jump on her the second she climbed into bed.

If she really knew how he felt, the control he had to wield not to climb up all inside her every time he looked in her direction, hell, she would be running screaming down the hall.

He would do anything to waylay her fears, but he would be between her and the front door regardless of what she chose. Of course, he had no business touching her, if he told himself that enough times he might keep his hands to himself.

Déisi's gaze scrolled down her figure in the snug burgundy dress, and imperceptibly shook his head, *na*, not going to happen.

"Sweetheart," he said with a nod to the suitcase on a stand, "the steward brought up your case. Why don't we shower and change into something more comfortable?"

Earlier when he checked in, he had brought his own duffle bag up, last thing he needed was for an attendant to see the weapons he had stashed inside.

She pressed her palm on his face like she did earlier. Her smile unreadable, she said only, "Okay."

Déisi bent and gently kissed the top of her head. "All right. I'll shower after you then we can get something to eat. There's a neat patio grill that overlooks the beach I think you will like."

She headed for her case and he went towards the door to the living room.

Chapter Eighteen

After showering and changing into black jeans and a button-down shirt, Déisi found Anya out on the balcony.

Stepping outside, he breathed in the fresh air with pleasure.

"Ah, tis nice out here, eh?" He moved across the small space to where she was leaning over the railing and looking out over the enticing panorama.

The hotel was beachfront, waves crashed gently on the sandy shore. It was late afternoon and people were drifting away from the beach to go get ready for dinner. A few children still ran and shrieked chasing cawing gulls.

Moving beside her, Déisi resisted laying his arm across her shoulder like he wanted to. "Hey," he said quietly watching her fiery hair dance around her head in the breeze.

She wore pale blue jeans and a white blouse with a wavy collar and big cloth buttons he wanted to bite off with his teeth.

She turned to him with a smile. "Spring has finally come bringing unseasonably warmer weather with it. It is perfect here, isn't it? I wish we could stay, hide away from…everything," the smile dimmed. Looking up at him, she sighed. "But we can't."

Déisi cupped her face. "*Yah*, I wish as well, that we could shut ourselves away, and," he bent his forehead to touch hers, "get to know each other. I feel like I already know you, so well, Anyalia, and I like everything about you."

Liquid Velvet

He united their eyes. "Unfortunately, you only see me as this...hardcore mercenary, and," he broke off with a twist to the side of his mouth, dropped his hands, that was what he was. All that he was. It only reflected how different they were.

She was sweetness and purity, and he... Déisi looked down at his palms, he has blood on his hands. A lot of blood. The darkness of his eyes shaded further as he tilted them up to her. He had never cared for, or about, anyone, except his brothers. Until now.

Changing the subject, he asked, "You hungry?" At her nod he smiled. "Okay, let's go eat."

They sat at an outside patio grill listening to the surf, letting the gentle chatter float around them, the light clatter of utensils in the background.

They took their time eating blackened shrimp and scallops with linguini and antipasto salad. Enjoying relaxing to the music of the ocean, they chatted quietly.

Gesturing her head, Anya said with a sly grin, "And that one there, he looks like a bank robber and the girl with him looks like an accountant."

A laugh burst from Déisi. "*Yah*, you love this people watching thing you call it. I admit, I've never paid attention to people other than as a target or a-" his mouth pursed, he picked up his bottle of beer and swigged some.

Seeing his discomfort, Anya said, "Yes, well, you should try it, it's fun looking at people and trying to discern who and what they are, what they do for a living. You know," her head swiveled as she looked around, "it's nice this charming grill tucked in the back of such a grandiose hotel."

"I chose this hotel because I thought you would enjoy the view of the ocean. I wish we could go swimming, but as balmy as it is, tis still too cool to go in the water."

Anya stared at him, then stretched her hand across the table to him. He took it with a surprised smile.

She said, "You are so sweet, no," when he shook his head, she firmly stated, "you are. Hired assassin or whatever, but to me, you are thoughtful, caring, and sweet. Thank you."

Déisi blinked at her, he didn't know what to say. Those words had never been used before to describe him.

"Anyalia, you make it easy for me to want to do things for you, take care of you, want to protect you," he smiled at her smiling at him, and added, "want to fuck you."

"Ack-" Anyalia coughed out her soda. Slamming a napkin to her mouth, she sputtered, "Gosh, Déisi, that was so-"

"Vulgar, *da*, I'm sorry, it slipped out. I just lose my head around you, honey, I'm sorry. You know I mean that I want to make love to you. I am trying to work on my filthy mouth when I'm around you, forgive me, old habits, you know."

The sharp cheekbones on his hard face colored as he saw her embarrassment at his crassness. He had stopped denying he wanted her. He knew his desire for Anya burned in his eyes like ignited dynamite ready to explode.

Normally his face was blank of emotion, just a veneer of chilling confidence and promise of death, but when his gaze lights on this little fiery haired female, he can't hide his overpowering craving for her.

"I know." She sighed and looked out to the darkening ocean, watching the last of the gulls swoop and the curlews playing tag with the rolling surf. Facing him she said, "Déisi, I know this place costs a fortune. I promise, when I get back to work I'll-"

His head fell back, he looked to the heavens with a wail, "*Aii*, Anyalia." Lowering his head, his eyes narrowed at her. "I warned you about that. I told you there would be a penalty to pay if you mentioned money again, and I don't mean a financial penalty."

Her brows fixed in puzzlement. "What? What kind of penalty? What-"

Pushing his chair back, Déisi stood up. Taking out his wallet, he dropped some bills on the check and held his hand out to her, "You'll see. You remember I mean what I say. Come, little one, let's walk on the beach."

"But, you-" a wary smile lifted her apple round cheeks as she stood up. "Oh, okay, a walk sounds great."

He picked up a blanket off a chair that he'd brought with them from the room. They took off their shoes, then hand-in-hand they trotted on the soft sand still warm from the day's sun and sauntered down to the water.

The blue crystalline ocean lapped at their feet but the froth never quite reached their toes as they strolled along the shore while the sun started its descent.

After a while, Déisi led Anya up from the water to some sand dunes out of the direct, now cooling breeze. He laid the blanket out. "Go on, *babia*, sit. I thought it would be nice to watch the sunset."

They settled on the blanket, and listened to the surf and the rest of the night grow quiet as the flaming orange blur disappeared into the darkened horizon.

"This is nice, Déisi. I thought you said you weren't romantic?"

Déisi's arm swept around Anya, pulling her close. Several fingers curled around her jaw, he lifted her face up to his. "I did. I am not romantic. I know nothing about romance. I do know I've never been happier in my life than I am at this moment. You in my arms, on an exotic beach, the sun setting before our eyes, lighting your beautiful hair on fire. *Babia*, it doesn't get any better than this."

His fingers slid across her jaw into her hair, then combing them gently through the locks, he sighed at the silkiness tickling his skin.

"I hate to be the one to tell you this, Déisi," she giggled, "but that's what they call being romantic."

"Ah, I don't care about anything they say, whoever they are. I only care about this," his mouth lowered to take possession of hers. If she was a chew toy and he was a dog he'd be chewing the hell out of her.

He couldn't get enough of licking her skin, chasing her tongue, sucking her lips, nipping her flesh from her sensuous mouth down her long smooth neck to the pretty rounded collar.

Anya was drowning in the scorching sensations his mouth spawned over her every pore. Every single cell tingled where the lick of his tongue touched, every bite made her nipples hard. Every suck of her soft flesh made her core feel like the unbearable stinging of a million burning, prickling thistles.

She felt her panties becoming saturated. And he hadn't even really touched her yet. She splayed her fingers on the sides of his face, lightly holding on as his mouth roved all over her, reveling in the ride of his savoring every inch of her he could reach.

Déisi sprinkled butterfly kisses over her collarbone and down to the first button on her blouse. He didn't use his teeth as he had wanted to, he didn't want to tear the filmy material or make her think he was a marauding animal.

It took all his control to keep said animal under wraps. One glimpse of it and Anya would run away shrieking for help.

Anya's hands lowered to clutch his biceps. Déisi opened the top button of her blouse. His mouth followed his fingers, nipping and kissing across the swells of her scented cleavage. He smiled against her soft flesh at her tiny moans and the goose bumps that spread over her arms.

She was still relatively stiff under his experienced hands in her uncertain innocence, but she did not to try to stop him, and was receptive to his skillful, seductive stimulation, and that was all he needed to make her his.

He was being carried away himself, spinning mindless into flames that were igniting, burning up his body.

His mouth lowered with each button he opened. "Anyalia," Déisi groaned, his tongue lathing across the swell of a breast. "You taste like the richest cream, the sweetest honey, smell like wildflowers in the spring, I am so fucking lost in you."

He pushed the lapels of the blouse apart, his pupils enlarging at the sight of her breasts mounding over the silk bra trimmed in lace. She wore her own clothes, but she had on a crimson bra his brother had bought her. It had a front clasp, he silently blessed Kalo for once.

He stroked his hands up to her neck to cradle her jaw and kissed her, hot and deep, hard and hungry, then he lowered his head to drink in her breasts as his big fingers unclasped the delicate hooks of the bra.

"Déisi," gasping, Anya grasped his thick wrists as he undid the clasp and pushed the cups aside. He slipped his fingers under the straps at her shoulders then he slid them and her blouse off her shoulders.

Gazing at her finally unfettered bare breasts, his murmur dusted in besotted awe, "You are so beautiful, *mi babia.* I've never seen a creature more beautiful, more sensuous than you, you take my damn breath away."

Yet, hearing the ambivalence in her voice, feeling the hesitation in her hands gripping his wrists, he paused, giving her a moment to stop him if she wanted to.

Moans whispered in her throat, she held his wrists but didn't pull them away.

When she didn't move, he cupped her full breasts, bent his head and groaned as he clenched and kissed her satiny skin. His strong fingers wrapped tightly around the plump globes, burying his face between them. A disjointed hiss cracked out with his heavy breath, he licked across to a nipple and sucked it into his mouth.

"Oh, Déisi," her whimper part fear, part desire for more, her fingers tightened around his strong wrists. She went with his movements as he kneaded her breasts with feral groans and sucked on one, then the other nipple until it budded under his tongue and between his teeth.

Twilight descended. The darkened sky grew rife with twinkling diamond stars above them. The surf now soft as it rolled up, lightly crashing on the sandy shore, birds chirping as they flitted about finding a place to roost.

Déisi gripped her breasts, and moved his mouth up to ransack Anya's parted lips again until her whimpers were more passion and less uncertainty.

He moved his hands to spread across her back, and lowered her to recline on her back, positioning her hands to lie beside her head on the blanket. Still sitting, he stared down at her.

Anya lay on the soft blanket, her hair a fiery swirl around her head, beautiful face a pearly moon. Half lowered lids over eyes glazed with the sensations he was deliberately building in her body, his gaze lowered.

Blouse wide open, her lush creamy breasts like satin pillows topped with pink nipples as sweet as candy drops begged for his hands. His male hands, to grip hard and greedy. He struggled to keep from being too rough with her, he wanted Anya so badly Déisi thought he would burst with the craving of it.

Moving to kneel over her, he reached for her belt. Her arms still up by her head in a surrender pose, he bent and licked a nipple and unbuckled her belt.

"Déisi, no, wait," her protest whooshed out with lust and need, but she didn't move her hands.

"Anyalia, I have to touch you, I have to," voice harsh in rusted need, he undid the button and lowered the zipper.

"But," her gasp a panting ache, "we can't." Her bosom rising and lowering with a throbbing hungering she couldn't understand or explain.

"Shh," he spread her jeans apart and pushed them down far enough to fit his hand in them. He could feel the silk of her panties with his fingertips.

Swallowing the groan overtaking him, Déisi moved his hand down under the silk to cup her mound and growled, "Oh *mi Dios, babia*, you are wet, so fucking wet, for me, I can't stand it." His thick fingers dipped to feel more of her moistness.

Her hips jerked in surprise and desire. His fingers were creating a wildfire in her core, she moved her hands to stop his.

"Stop, please," her gasp sharp with want, flat stomach pulsating with uneven breaths.

When his hand continued moving lower, his cool fingers probing her woman's warm flesh, she grabbed at his wrists, this time trying to pull them back. "No, please stop, Déisi, please, we-we're outside, we can't-"

"Ah, sweet Anyalia." His fingers clinched over her sex with a sighed groan. "You are right." They could potentially be arrested.

Besides, he wanted her naked and he couldn't put her in that untenable position out here in the open. The warm air cushioning their skin, the dark sky shadowing their bodies, the rhythm of the gentle surf, if only they were on a private island they could- he shook his head, but they weren't.

He reluctantly fixed her pants. Then he rubbed his palms up and over her breasts then back down to squeeze and clench their rich plumpness. His head bent, hair ruffling over her skin, Déisi licked a nipple, sucked the other one, then slid his hands behind her back and lifted her to sit up.

"Déisi," her voice a hushed whisper.

Murmuring quiet affectionate words in his language, he pulled the bra cups over her breasts, clasped the bra, then drew the blouse closed and buttoned it.

"Tis okay *mi dragă*, it will be better upstairs where you are not so vulnerable." He rolled to his feet, bent and pulled her up.

Disoriented with the potent feelings he induced in her, Anya swayed.

"*Babia*, my precious." Déisi put on his boots and handed her shoes to her then swung her up in his arms and carried her across the sand to the hotel. He went to a side door and to the elevator at the end of a long hall.

Giggling, Anya's arms clung around his neck. "You can put me down, silly, I'm okay."

"*Na*." His lips enclosing on hers, he whispered, "I like carrying you, your mouth is easier to reach." He kissed her until they reached their room.

"Here," he gave her the key card to unlock the door and carried her inside.

Closing the door with his heel, he kicked off his boots and let her slide down his body to her feet, savoring every inch of her curves rubbing against his hardness.

His hands on her breasts, his voice hushed, he said, "I want you, *babia*, you know that. Do you want me? Tis okay if you say *na*, I will honor your wishes." *I'll try with everything I have...*

While waiting for her answer, he brushed her nipples with his thumbs, then lightly pinched them before cupping and kneading her fullness.

Anya looked down and watched his large, strong hands fondling her. Raising her eyes to his, she said, "You don't act like you'll take no for an answer."

A grin lifted his face, making a crooked full line through his five o'clock shadow. "I can't not touch you, Anyalia. Until you tell me *na*, I'm getting as much of you as I can."

While he continued massaging, squeezing her breasts over her blouse, she shyly caressed his face with both hands. On her toes, she pulled his head down and kissed him the same way he had stolen her lips and tongue.

Enjoying the kiss, Déisi pulled his head back, smoothed the hair from the side of her face, lifted the curls and set them off her shoulder to twirl down her back.

"Is that a *da*, ah, a yes, *babia*? You're going to need to be specific if tis not because I'm gonna take that as a yes. If it tis not, you better talk quick, I'm on a kind of cliff here and ready to go over."

Moving his hands to her shoulders, his gaze searching her face with hope, need, raw hunger, he saw her lips already swollen and red with his kisses, eyes dazed and glowing under low lids.

Her tongue slipped over her lips with her nod. "Yes, Déisi, I want you."

Watching her tongue sliding along her tiny plump lips, his thick fingers clenching her shoulders, his voice strong but tight, he asked, "You're sure, Anyalia, you want to make love? You are a virgin, you should wait for someone who is...nicer than me." *That's good fool, talk her out of it.*

Pretty smile curving her face, she said, "I'm sure, Déisi, I want you. Now." Her hands wove around his neck.

His fingers dug into her flesh, trying to hold back from jumping her like a savage rutting dog.

"The whole thing, *babia*, you want to do the whole thing? I'm talking about sex here, I want to be buried deep inside you. I need to know right now if you are in full acquiescence, because once we start, I'm telling you I won't be able to stop, and we can't undo it once tis done. You need to be sure."

He held his breath, his eyes flicking back and forth over hers, his fingers crushing her shoulders. It was all he could do to keep from going all wild ravaging animal on her. Another second and he would have passed beyond backing off if she said no-

Pressing her lips against his, she said, "Can you please stop talking and get moving?" Her smile an invitation, she stated, "Yes, I am sure. I want the whole thing, right now, right here. So stop talking."

He only unbuttoned the top button then impatiently grabbed the bottom of her blouse and drew it off her head, dropping it to the floor.

Groaning, "Ah, *mi babia*," his big hands on her hips, Déisi lifted her so her legs wrapped around his waist, and her arms flung around his neck.

Walking towards the bedroom, one arm under her butt, he unclasped the bra, dragged it down her arms and tossed it. Hugging her naked torso against his chest, he seized her mouth.

Chapter Nineteen

$\mathcal{T}$he drapes were partially closed in the bedroom making the room dimly lit by the hotel's outside lights.

Setting Anya on her feet, Déisi reached for a lamp but Anya put her hand shyly on his arm to stop him. "No, please."

Stroking his hand along her cheek, he said, "I want to see everything of you that I can, but you are bashful. Anything you want, sweetheart, whatever makes you comfortable."

Turning her slightly so she couldn't see him pull his gun out from the back of his pants, he set it on the end table.

Then, he bent and unbuckled her belt, undid the button, the zipper, same as on the beach but this time he pushed her jeans to the floor and helped her step out of them. His hands were actually trembling from trying to move slowly lest he frighten her away with his impatience.

She stood with hesitant modesty in a tiny swath of crimson.

His dark eyes heated. Staring at the bit of red silk over her sex, he moaned, "*Mi bréthaïdne,* ah," he dragged a palm over his hair. "My brother is trying to kill me." Kalo's choices of lingerie were extreme on tiny and over the top sexy.

Brows down, Anya self-consciously put her hands over her sex. "Why?" Her breasts bunched up between her arms.

Shaking his head with a chuckle, he said, "Never mind, *mi dragă.* Anyalia, come, don't be self-conscious with me. I've died to see your pure skin, every curve, hollow, soft peaks, all your sweet spots." He knelt in front of her and peeled the silk down and off.

"Déisi, um, I'm not sure..." her shyness was taking her over.

"Shh, *babia*, I will take care of everything. Don't hide your beauty from me." He reached up to skim his tough palms over her high full breasts before grasping them briefly, then he drew his palms down the curve of her waist to the inside of her thighs.

Nudging her legs apart, he gazed at her delicate sex. "Every damned part of you is soft and pretty," he murmured. One hand slipped around her back to clutch her bottom, the other slid between her legs to curl over her woman's mound. At her shiver, he smiled. Anyalia was made for loving, made for him.

Nudging her feet further apart, he palmed her core, stroking his hard fingers over her tender nether lips, his smile widened at the sizzled moan that escaped her. Drawing his fingers up her sensitive slit, he had to tighten his grip on her bottom from the quiver that rolled through her body.

"Déisi, *ah*," she groaned as he lightly rubbed circles over her swollen nub.

"What sweetheart, tell me," he encouraged her in a growly timber, "tell me what you feel." He stretched his fingers down to dip the tip of one just inside her to steal some of that luscious essence then brushed the dew on her bud with the pad of his fingertip.

Her hips moving with the motions of his fingers, she set her hands on his head then gripped his hair with a breathy whimper when he slipped more of his strong finger inside her.

"It's um," her hips wriggled, fingers tangling in his hair, "hot, heat. I feel wonderful tingly shimmers of heat." Gripping his locks, she lifted his head. Her voice tight and yearning, she urged, "Now, Déisi, please, put yourself inside me now."

Chuckling at her inexperienced words, he then moaned. "Hmmm, so fresh, tender, I've never felt anything as soft as you." He reached up to clutch a bobbing breast while continuing to roll his fingers over her clit, sliding them up and down her supple folds. Then he moved his finger deeper inside her. "*Na*, little sweet, you are not yet ready to take me."

Her lips pushed out in a sexy pout. "Ready? I am ready, please!" Her hips pushed at his hand trying to force his finger to go deeper. "I'm ready now, Déisi," her soft cry an ache of deprivation and the deep need to fulfill the culmination of what she was feeling.

His chuckle light, he denied her, "*Na*, you are tiny. Your passage is tiny and tight, if I take you now I will hurt you. Trust me." He leaned in and covered her entire sex with his mouth.

"Déisi!" she shrieked, her hips jolting with the striking pleasure of it. Her fingers clutched his hair pulling his face harder against her.

He licked her tender skin, sucked her pebbling nub into his mouth while inserting his middle finger slowly up as far as he could inside her before reaching her hymen.

Déisi licked and nibbled and moved his tongue faster while stroking his finger faster and deeper inside her, coming to a stop each time when he reached her maidenhead.

A faint wailing from her parted lips and the thrusting of her small hips told him she was on the edge. Kneeling, Déisi moved to look up at her.

The creamy breasts jiggled, her slender hips thrust against his man's thick finger. He saw a blush cover her chest and her breathing heaved rushing fast and shallow.

"Okay, Anyalia, listen to me." He paused his ministrations and waited.

A light film of perspiration made her face shiny. Her lashes fluttered on heated pink cheeks as she struggled to open her eyes and look at him.

The green eyes were deeply glazed, she licked her lips. "What Déisi, what did I do wrong? Don't you want me anymore?"

His fingers splayed over a perfectly rounded butt cheek and he squeezed it. "Always, *mi babia*, I will always want you. But there is a part now that I have to do that will hurt you. You need to be prepared. Do you know what I'm talking about?"

Trying to clear the buzzing fog from her brain, Anya blinked, blushed, then nodded. "Yes, I remember reading about…my uh, maidenhead. What will you do?"

"Ah," he stifled the grimace that the thought of harming her brought him. He didn't need her seeing his grim look and engendering second thoughts.

"I have to breech it, it will only hurt for a second, sweetheart, I promise." He moved his finger in and out, pressed his lips to suck her cleft then suddenly slapped her bottom hard at the same time he thrust through her hymen.

Anya cried out and forked forward. Her breasts pressed against his head with her whimpers. Her tiny belly blew in and out comprehending the dual pain.

Déisi paused. Her breathing harsh and rapid, tiny painful sounds emitting, punched his heart. Damn he hated hurting her.

She leaned back swatting his shoulder. "You spanked me. You hurt me down there, and you hit me." Her bottom lip protruded with her anger and confusion.

"*Da*, sweetheart, I diluted the pain of breaking your maidenhood so that it was not as painful as it would have been."

He gripped her bottom with both hands bringing her sex back where he licked her like she was melting ice cream. Moving his finger inside her, he carefully pushed it in deeper. "You will be all right in a minute, I promise."

Anya tried to pull back from him, but he held her, swirling his tongue over her bud and slit, while gently pumping his finger in her.

He said with a hint of a grin, "Besides, sweet, I owed you that spank. I warned you to stop talking about money, I said you would be punished." He laughed at her sputtering and kept his hand working her.

When she stopped fighting him and the faint moans gurgled up her throat, and her hips met each of his thrusts, he inserted a second digit stretching her. Curling his fingers inside, searching for her hot spots, he grinned when she groaned loud, without censure.

Stroking over her sensitive areas again and again, he plunged both fingers harder, faster. He felt her legs shaking, the quaking, huffing whimpers grew louder until her back arched and she wailed her release with a guttural cry.

Anya's body undulated with her gasping sobs. Déisi stayed with her, pumping his fingers in and out while she rode out her very first orgasm.

When the last of her breath went, and her legs buckled, she fell over his shoulders with a wriggle and a heavy exhalation. Déisi scooped her up and laid her on the bed then stood beside the bed looking down at her.

Her pale skin was blushed pink all over, chest heaving and pitching, spasms of shivers making her beautiful breasts bobble. Her eyes opened slowly to see him watching her. "Déisi," she murmured with a panted hush.

"*Yah*, sweet?" His gaze trailed up and down her nude body. There wasn't a more incredible sight than his nude Anyalia in the throes of an orgasm. Her first, and he was honored to have been the one she chose to give it to her.

"Um, I'm naked, and you, aren't." She smiled hazily at him.

"*Da*, if my pants were off, I would have quickly displeased you." He would not have been able to stop himself from impaling her as quickly as he could, virgin or not.

"Hmm. What about now?" The haze was clearing, her eyes danced up and down his body. She sat up.

"*Na*, Anyalia, lie down, let me get my fill of you." His fingers went to his buttons, but impatient as always, he reached behind his back and jerked the shirt off and dropped it.

Anya's eyes lit up as she studied his chest.

"You like what you see, sweetheart?" he asked with a lopsided grin.

Nodding, her eyes moving all over his broad shoulders, chest thick with slabs of muscles, biceps huge and rock-hard. A matting of masculine dark hair covered part of his strong chest. "You are beautiful Déisi," her sigh an admiring smile.

A palm spread over a pec, he laughed. "*Babia*, men are not beautiful, especially weathered soldiers." His body was covered with scars from knives, bullets, fights, near death experiences like when he had hurtled off a cliff and a myriad of other escapades.

Women had complimented his body before and weren't hesitant to say so. But, none of that meant anything to him, only his little Anyalia's opinion mattered to him.

Demanding, "The rest, Déisi, I want to see the rest of you," she lay back with her hair spread around the pillow. Her hands were back up beside her head, her knees bent, she pulled her legs up and modestly curled them to the side.

His eyes dark tunnels unwavering at hers, he removed a series of weapons stashed around his body then unbuckled his belt. Undoing his pants, he pushed them and the black briefs down to the floor pushing them aside.

He watched her eyes lower from his chest, following the trail of hair that tapered over his solid abs, and go round when she saw his manhood.

Hard and long and thick as a club it was waiting impatiently for Déisi to let them both get what they wanted. He waited, seeing the emotions flicker across her pretty face. Interest, desire, then fear.

Anya struggled to sit back up and move across the bed.

"Ah, *mi babia*, my baby." He sat on the edge of the bed, caught her delicate shoulders and pushed her gently to lie on her back.

"Déisi," the trepidation threaded through her small voice. Anya recalled the way Paulina's eyes had glittered when she'd gripped his manhood and had murmured, 'so big' with such relish. But why?

Her eyes narrowed at his shaft. It was huge, how could he fit that inside any woman, inside her? She said tightly, "I don't understand Paulina being so excited that you are so…big."

The corner of his mouth ticked up. "Mm, some women find it a…pleasure. *Babia*." He trickled his fingers down her thigh.

218

"*Yah*, you are small, but, I will go slow, you will expand to fit me. Tis nature's way, trust me. Okay?"

She said nothing, just stared at his throbbing cock. He got up and took his wallet out of his pants and fished out a condom.

Sitting back on the bed, he pushed her back down again as she moved to sit up and he skimmed his palm up the inside of her thigh until he cupped her sex with his large hand.

Her hips gave a little quiver. When he stroked her soft folds and then the sensitive slit, he felt her legs relax. Déisi rolled onto the bed to lie next to her on his side and palpated her sex until her eyes turned glassy again and her breaths quickened.

He slid one finger inside her, then a second, stretching her, feeling her natural silk lubricating his fingers. When her pelvis matched the thrusts of his fingers, he rolled the condom on and moved between her legs.

"Open for me, *babia*," he nudged her slender thighs wider apart. Fisting his shaft, he held it to the opening of her channel, rubbing it up her slit getting her silk slicking her and his shaft. He braced on his elbows on either side of her head and licked her top lip, then her bottom before sliding his tongue inside to find hers.

As he moved his tongue inside her mouth, he penetrated her opening, slowly.

His eyes open, Déisi watched Anya while kissing her. He had dreamed of this moment ever since his eyes had set on the picture of her.

When he held her in his arms as he abducted her, he knew at that moment he wanted to keep them around her and never let her go.

Slowly, he inched his breadth in her tender channel, letting her silk coat them both. Allowing her virgin's body to adapt to him filling her.

Déisi cupped a breast and lowered his mouth to it, sucked red spots over the soft mound while kneading it, then looked down to watch his length feeding into her lushly beautiful, pure body as he pushed deeper and deeper inside her.

Little sexy mews trickled up her throat as she accepted his thick girth that was so hard he could pound nails. Pinching a nipple with his teeth, he quickly lathed it at her whimper.

Releasing her breast, seeing slight pain crimping her brow, he cradled her face, brushing his thumb over her pale skin. "You all right, *mi dragă?*"

"Mm," she nodded briefly with a murmur. "You, uh," she groaned as he finally reached the end of her, was fully buried deep inside her sheath.

He paused to let her get used to him. "I what, sweetheart?"

Her hips wriggled as she squirmed to adjust to him. Chubby breasts rubbed against his chest enticing him to lower his torso so they were closer.

"It…hurts. I feel so stretched, but," her sigh sultry. "I can feel you throbbing, inside, against me."

"*Yah?*" His cock pulsed. Feeling the sudden surge, she squeaked and her pussy constricted squeezing his shaft.

His breath sucked in. Almost losing it, he cursed, "Damn, Anyalia."

At her giggle, he kissed her and said, "So that's how it tis, eh?" and started slowly withdrawing then carefully moving back inside her until she more easily accepted his breadth.

Seeing the pain ease from her face, he moved a bit faster.

"Now? How does it feel now, *mi babia?*" *Dios*, he had to make her like it, because now that he's finally had her, he wasn't letting her go. Literally.

He was going to fuck her every day for the rest of their lives and it will be a thousand times better if she loves it, wants it as badly as he does.

Her spine arched, and her graceful body stretched into a sensuous sinuous curl like a cat, her hips thrust up to meet his next plunge. "More," she murmured, raising her hips faster.

"Ah, my little minx, you tease me." With a chuckle, he set a rhythm, the speed of his deep thrusts with bursts of shorter ones. She tried to make him move faster, but he was controlling their pace. The feel of his tight balls slapping against her sweet body was driving him wild.

"More," her whine pretty and soft, hips lifting to his.

His deep delighted chuckle against her neck was teasing as he licked, tasting then sucking her flesh. Then, Déisi drove into her so hard he pushed a grunt from her with a gasping moan. His rhythm increased, he rocked harder, deeper into her silken channel.

He shoved his palm under her butt lifting her to meet his thrusts. Hearing her rapid breaths, plump breasts bouncing against his chest, her cheeks spun red, he pumped faster until the little walls inside her trembled around his cock. A beautiful flush rose on her chest, and wails etched up her throat.

Tiny squeaks eked out as she tried to meet his punishing thrusts, but he now pistoned so fast she couldn't keep up. Her fingers gripped his arms, she could only just hold on as he shunted grunt after grunt from her, pounding in her so hard, he wrapped an arm around her shoulders to keep her from getting shoved up the bed.

Anya's gasps hitched in her chest, her back started lifting off the mattress as her fingers dug into his skin.

"*Babia*," his growl dark, low, "look at me," he commanded.

"Anyalia," he kissed her, tugging hard at her lips, insisting, "look at me, open your eyes, see me." He kept pumping, faster, she struggled to lift her heavy lids.

The strain of him holding back was in the sweat at his temples, the vein beating insanely at the scar, his mouth grit tight.

When their gazes met, connected, Déisi hammered so fast and hard Anya's body jolted, breasts bounced, and a thin scream started at the back of her throat.

He reached down between them to pinch and purl her clit while encouraging her, "Keep looking at me, *babia*, I want to watch you come. I want you to see the man who is claiming you."

Déisi pounded like a jackhammer until her eyes glazed over, her spine arched, her body bubbled and her shoulders came up off the bed with a scream.

"*Déisi-*" she wailed as her body undulated roughly against his. Her eyes rolled back with a crushing wince, neck arching, her head dropped back.

Watching her climax take hold of her, her little body vibrating under and around his, as he felt her channel clamping him, squeezing, Déisi let go. His head dropped forward, black hair brushed her face.

Wrapping his arms around Anya, holding her savagely tight, Déisi pounded harder, harder, until the fire cramped in his balls like a fist before exploding up his cock with his seed.

Her name a harsh groan from numb lips, he paused deep inside her, held taut as he felt his seed leaving his body undulating out, into the condom, which he wished to *Dios* was into her.

He dared to dream of his seed taking root, creating a child that would bind her to him forever. He pummeled into her again and again until with a growling groan, he collapsed.

Shifting slightly to the side, Déisi tried not to crush her, but the feel of Anya's soft dainty body under him, his manhood deep inside her, was something he didn't want to move away from. Ever.

Her heart beat at his. His heavy panting pressed his chest hard against her firm breasts. They lay entwined without moving, just catching their breath, slowing their pulses, enjoying the throbbing heat that welded them together.

After a moment, Déisi turned onto his back bringing her with him, his arms holding her close.

Anya lay with her head on his chest listening to his heart still beating like crazy. She sat up, he growled trying to pull her back down.

Eluding his hands, she saw the condom and pulled it off, he was still semi-hard. "I'll take care of this," she said, squirming to the edge of the bed with the condom top clutched tightly in her hand. "I'll be right back."

His eyes closed, Déisi threw his hand out to catch her. "*Na*, stay here with me."

Giggling, Anya slid to her feet and padded into the bathroom.

She cleaned herself, then wetted a cloth with warm water and went back to the bed.

Déisi lay with his forearm over his eyes, his big chest still billowing with his heavy breaths.

The mattress barely dipped with her slight weight as she climbed back on.

His other hand reached for her. His voice a deep raspy rumble, "Come, lie down with me, *babia*, don't leave me."

"In a minute." Anya put the warm cloth on his penis and patted and wiped until he smiled.

"You keep doing that and I will be right back on top of you." His heart warmed with the cloth, no one had ever taken care of him like this before.

When she cleaned him, she dropped the cloth with her virgin's blood on the floor and dried him with a fluffy towel. As she patted and rubbed, his manhood hardened.

His tone roughly sultry, he said, "I'm warning you, sweet, you keep doing that and I will be inside you in a flash. And, you are too tender for us to do it again so quickly, we have to wait." His eyes still closed, he snaked his hand out, snagging her wrist and pulling her grasp from his erection.

"Fine," she chuckled and sat cross-legged to peruse his body.

"Lie down with me, *babia*, I want to hold you," he murmured. Never one to snuggle after the deed was done, he wanted nothing now but to lay there with her in his arms, praying it would be forever.

"No, I want to look at you." While she spoke, she leaned over to set her palms on his chest. At his rumbling moan at her touch, she sifted her fingers through the matting of black hair, rubbing her palms over the hard muscles of his pecs, down over his taut abs.

"You are so hard, Déisi, so strong, you have the manliest chest," her voice soft with wonder as she explored the feel of his broad shoulders, thick biceps that flexed when he moved his arms.

Her exploration took her lower. Anya stared at his manhood for a moment. She drifted her fingertips over his thighs, smiling at his groan and saw his penis twitch.

She wrapped her small hand around his shaft, it hardened more.

"Anyalia," he warned with a growl. "I said you need to wait."

"Uh huh." She wrapped her other hand around it as well. As one hand fisted around the top soft head, the other stroked down tentatively to cup his balls.

"Aw fuck, Anyalia." He gripped both her hands and pulled her back down to lie on his chest. "I love your hands on me, but I can't control the need. I will have to fuck you if you keep touching me. It will hurt you if we do it again so soon, so," he sighed, wrapping his arms around her, "we wait a bit."

She giggled at the growl in his muscular chest. Settling against him, she said, "Déisi?"

"Hmm?" His fingers stroked her hair. When he was sure she was recovering okay, he would let her touch him all she wanted.

Her small hand cupping his balls about drove him around the bend. It was something that had permeating his dreams since he'd met her. Her plump lips on his dick while looking up shyly at him through her long lashes would be even better. Later.

"Was I okay? I know I could never be as good as Paulina and your other women, but was I still okay?"

"Oh for fucks sake," he ground, and wound his arms more tightly around her. "*Babia*, first of all, I have never been with, nor do I ever want to be with Paulina." He shuddered at the thought.

"Second, do not bring other women, other people, into our bed." He slid his hand under her chin to lift her head so their eyes could connect.

His thumb stroking her silken skin, he told her, "Since I met you, other women have ceased to exist for me. You were a million times better than okay, Anyalia. This is our beautiful moment together, no one can ever take this from us, ever. Tis ours. Just leave us alone together in this bed, okay?" He lowered his head to give her a gentle kiss.

Anya moved her head back to lie on his chest and laid an arm across him. "Okay." She was contemplative for a few minutes.

Then, "After the uh, mission is over, will you return to your other women? Will another guard help Granddad and me to get out of Mr. de Vos' house and back home?"

The thought of Anya being in another man's arms made his stomach tighten and his balls hurt. His mouth ground into a harsh grimace, he said to the top of her head, "Is that what you want? Do you want never to see me again once this is done?"

She stirred against him. "Is that what you want?"

With a groan, he gripped her shoulders and brought them both to sit up. "*Na*, I want you by my side, in my life, my bed, every day. We've been together for over ten days, never apart. I have no desire to change that once the mission is done."

He studied the unreadable thoughts traipsing across her face as she pondered his words. When she didn't reply, he kept his voice steel, stilling the anxious feeling that she would say that wasn't what she wanted. That when the mission was done, so were they.

"Do you want to never see me again, Anyalia, when this is over?" Of course he could fully understand it if she said yes. He'd abducted her, molested her, threatened her. Shit. What woman would want to stay with a thug like him?

She studied the harsh face, the scar over his temple beating with the vein under it, full mouth hard, firm. His jaw worked, but his dark eyes were completely blank. It made her think of the beginning when he took her on the bus and gazed so coldly at her.

"I..." her palm set on his chest then skimmed down and off. "I don't know."

His held breath was killing him, he let it out. At least she hadn't said yes. His fingers webbed the back of her head tilting her mouth up to his where he descended on it. Like a lit match, heat blazed through him at the touch of her lips detonating a torrential firestorm.

It took all he had to break off the kiss. Breathing hard, he moved his hand to cup her jaw, his fingertips brushing the soft underside of it. Twin green lanterns, glazed with passion rose up to him.

He stifled his smile, if he could turn her on that quickly with just a quick kiss then there was definitely hope for him, for them.

"*Babia*, let's enjoy our time together for now, let you think about things. No pressure. Just," two fingers under her jaw held her for him to capture her mouth again, briefly, "know clearly, that I want you. Permanently. Forever.

"I know I'm in no conceivable way good enough for you and I should back off, step away, but I can't. I've already tried. Now that we've made love," he lowered his head and shook it, the black hair flopped, cinder-blackened eyes lifted under an ebony lock, boring into hers. "I could never let you go."

Her lashes flit up and down in confusion. "But you said for me to think about it, us. if I say…no? Then what…are you saying?"

He kissed her again. "Just think about us, *babi*a, think about giving us a chance. Now, I believe that you have become very dirty and need a shower. I need to get these hands all lathered up, get them real soapy and foamy, and wash every single square inch of you until I decide you are clean. What do you say about that?" His brows wiggled at her.

"Hmm." She cocked her head, gaze sweeping his hard body. "I think," in one move she rolled off the bed and ran, "last one in is a rotten egg!"

His laugh barked as he jumped off the bed and darted after her.

Chapter Twenty

They played for a bit soaping each other, then Déisi pushed her face first up against the tile wall.

Pinning her hands above her head, he fondled her well-washed bottom, squeezing her perfect roundness with relish then skimmed his lathered hands up her ribs to her soapy breasts.

Kneading them harder than he meant to, he would never get enough of them, he moved to her pussy playing with it until she was writhing in his arms, rubbing her back all over his torso.

He turned her and lifted her to wrap her legs around him, and jammed her down on top of his raging cock. Again and again, he had no rhythm, just brute strength and speed until the steamy glass was thick as fog and the chamber was filled with their groans and gasping cries.

As soon as he felt Anya fly over the moon, Déisi released and went with her. He pumped into her until she was like a mewling rag doll, barely able to cling to his neck.

Still holding her wrapped around him, Déisi leaned her back against the wall for support as they came down from the fireworks, sucking deep bolts of calming air, letting their temperatures ease down. Then they showered again and went back to the bed.

Déisi called room service, asked for champagne, some fruit and cheese and a variety of cakes to be brought to them.

They made love all night, taking little snoozes, then waking up and doing it again. Sometimes fast and reckless, sometimes languidly. Once, he just reached for her as she slept, pulled her to him and slipped inside and climaxed before her eyes completely opened.

He had paid the bellhop well to go out and buy him a box of condoms without Anya knowing to save her the embarrassment she would have felt at the man being aware of what they were doing.

Not that no one would clue into their tryst, the couple spent the night and day together in the hotel room, it was unlikely they were just playing cards.

In the afternoon, as Anya dressed in the bedroom, Déisi went to the living room to check the weapons he kept on his body, ensuring the guns were loaded and the knives placed strategically.

He didn't want her to see him arming himself. She hadn't told him she wanted to stay with him, and seeing him hiding weapons on his person would not endear her any to his tough side. He was rolling his long sleeves up as she came into the room.

"Hey," she said softly, cheeks rosy with their love-making and laughter.

Déisi went right to her and enfolded her in his arms. He held her, just to enjoy her curves pressing against him, and happy knowing she was willingly in his arms.

He cupped her jaw, his thumb under her chin lifting it. Smiling into her sparkling eyes, he asked, "*Babia*, you okay?"

Returning his affectionate smile, Anya nodded. "Yes. I'm ready to get to the bank, retrieve the formula and go get my granddad."

His lips lowered to cover hers. He said against her mouth, "I meant with us, sweetheart, with what we did." He kissed her with placid sweetness, he didn't need to get aroused just as they were heading out the door. "Do you have any regrets?"

Blushing as always, damn he loved the way her cheeks pinked with her shy embarrassment, it was so at odds with the surprising wildcat way she reacted, and reciprocated sexually with him.

He hadn't even had to make a suggestion of what he would like, yet at one point she had dropped to her knees, said she wanted to do everything to him that she had so enjoyed that he'd done to her.

His own face flooded with color at the remembrance of her small hands encircling his manhood as she tentatively tasted him, licked his phallus lightly as she got used to the feeling and taste of him. When she cupped his balls with those little feminine fingers then kissed them, he about- ah, he needed to shelve those memories for the time being.

And now, the way she moved her lips sensuously over his and inserted her tongue in his mouth chasing right after his tongue, told him more than words could say.

The kiss grew heated too fast, Déisi gripped her shoulders to hold her back. "You keep doing that, *babia*, and we won't leave this room and we need to get on the road."

With a sharp nod, she stepped from him and went to get her purse.

She left him so abruptly, a wave of bereft emptiness washed painfully over Déisi taking his breath. His hand landed hard on the sofa back to steady himself. By the time he got a grip and gathered their baggage she returned with her purse and shoes.

Shocked at the intensity of his feelings, Déisi knew he looked a little pale, so he kept his head turned from her. "You carrying a purse? You have nothing but the key to put in it."

Walking over to him, she said, "Oh, but now I have my passport, a brush, lip gloss, a tissue and a mirror to put in it."

The day she had been abducted she had left her purse in her trunk not wanting to bring it into work at the museum with her. She would have had to leave it on a different floor in a locker and didn't see any point to that when she kept her keys in her pocket.

Those keys were long gone with the clothes he'd burned and buried. She'd been too poor to have a phone.

They left the hotel and drove straight to the bank. A woman was just opening the doors as they arrived. She greeted them with a warm smile.

The couple was taken straight to the safety deposit box. Inside, there were bond notes, some jewelry, Dauphine's will and a few other papers and forms. Anya found the formula right away.

She took that and some of the other papers, then had the customer service rep come and retrieve the box.

Soon, they were back in the rented Jag and headed to the airport.

They reversed their trip back to the country that was far east of India where de Vos was holed up in.

Déisi rented a four-wheel drive truck to make the trek to de Vos' compound.

When they were a mile away, he turned off a side road then off again to a dirt road that led into a forested area. Down about a half a mile, they came upon another truck that was parked on the side of the road.

Déisi said, "Wait here," and he got out at the same time as Kalo exited the other truck.

Anya sat watching the brothers. This was it, she thought, they would either bring her granddad home, or...she didn't want to think of any other outcome.

Kalo handed Déisi a duffle bag and some boxes that Déisi put in the silver toolbox carrier that was bolted over the bed of the truck along the back window.

Kalo gave Anya a cheerful wave, she nervously waved back, and he hopped back in the other truck.

Déisi climbed back in with Anya and drove out to the main road. Kalo followed them until they reached the asphalt and he went in the opposite direction.

"Kalo isn't coming with us?" Her nerves so constricted her throat the words barely scraped out. She was finally starting to trust Déisi, yet strangely she had easily accepted Kalo, and had been comfortable right off the bat with the powerful man with a twinkle of mischief in his dark blue eyes.

Déisi glanced at her white face, her fingers strangling themselves and patted her leg. "Not to worry, honey, he'll be around, you just won't see him."

He drove close to the compound but parked in front of some row-houses on a street a few miles away. He hopped out and went to the passenger door and opened it. "Come on," he held his hand to her.

Her frown curious, she let him pull her out and help her down from the high step.

"Why are we here? Aren't we going to Mr. de Vos' estate?"

Holding her hand, Déisi brought her up a short walk to a house that was connected to other houses in a row that tracked up a hill.

Before he could knock, the door swung open. A man Anya had never seen before nodded with a short, serious smile at Déisi. His eyes flicked to Anya but went back to Déisi. He stood aside indicating for them to go inside.

"Anyalia, this is Bair, a...friend of mine. You will be staying here with him while I get your grandfather." He and Bair shared a brief nod then he went to the door.

"Huh? What? No, wait," stunned, Anya started after him.

The man, Bair, who looked like a bear with his big, broad, barrel-chest, appeared to be in his thirties. With brown hair and hooded eyes that hid his thoughts, he grasped her arm, halting her.

Aghast, Anya's mouth dropped as she jerked at his arm. "Let go of me! Déisi!" she cried out to him. "What are you doing?"

When the man didn't release her, she wrenched harder at her arm, so hard she winced in pain.

Déisi threw Bair a frown with a slight nod.

Bair wound both arms around Anya holding her back against his chest. He held her painlessly but immovable.

"Déisi!" she cried out, struggling in the big man's arms.

Déisi moved to her. He gently stroked her cheek. With a small smile, he said, "You are staying here. I can't do what I need to if you are with me. I won't allow you to be in that danger. You will be safe here with Bair. As soon as I have your grandfather, I will return. Please, trust me."

He leaned in, kissed her tenderly then turned and made straight for the door. Without looking back, he opened it, stepped out and closed it to her shrieking his name.

It wasn't easy for Déisi to close the door to her cries. It wrung his heart to not be able to comfort her, and to leave her under another man's protection.

But, he couldn't fight freely if he needed to, and worry about keeping her safe at the same time. And, he sure as hell didn't want her with him if things went asses over cartwheels.

He had known Bair for years, they had done many missions together and he trusted the man with his life. With Anya's life.

Déisi strode quickly to his truck and drove off before he changed his mind.

Chapter Twenty-One

Déisi parked the truck in the woods near the compound, then sat in it and waited until night fell. He had the windows open, but he still didn't hear the night arrive.

Usually there was a rustle of wind dying down, birds chattering as they roosted, leaves bustling, the sound of cars in the distance. Tonight all was deathly still and eerily silent.

He did though, feel the change in the air. Suddenly, a soft whirring, an almost silent roar sounded. Budding leaves and blades of grass swished and flattened, and a stampede of wings flapped as birds abruptly flew out of their roosts.

Exiting the truck, he grabbed a backpack, shrugged it over his shoulders and ran to the chopper.

Climbing in the helicopter, Déisi nodded at Kalo's grinning salute. They didn't speak as Kalo maneuvered the bird straight up through the copse of tree and out over the treetops towards the compound.

The back portion of the compound was surrounded by a deep ravine of water, somewhat like a moat around an ancient castle. Except this moat was home to several crocodiles. De Vos thought it would save on having his soldiers patrolling the vast area.

The elite sleuth chopper barely made a whisper as it soared across the land. The pack on his back, Déisi pulled on a vest that had loops on a harness that he slid his legs into. He unlatched then unrolled a wire rope and hooked the end to the harness.

It wasn't long before the copter whirred its silent way to hover over the compound. Kalo held it steady as Déisi opened the door, gave his brother a grim smile, and climbed out of the bird letting the wire rope lower him to the roof.

His hair and clothes flapped from the wind of the chopper as he descended. When his feet were on the cement, he unlatched the wire and vest. He signaled Kalo who was controlling the descent of the wire, and everything rewound back up into the chopper.

An instant later the helicopter was gone.

Déisi took his time striding across the roof to a door, the others needed to get into place. The steel door was locked. Dropping to his knees, he removed the backpack and opened it, took out a miniature blowtorch.

In seconds, he pushed the door open and stepped into the dark. Steep iron steps led from the roof down to the next level

Using inside information, Déisi had memorized the schematics of the building.

Kalo had taken one for the team by sleeping with de Vos' secretary, Fabiana to obtain information. She told him Dauphine had not been moved from where he and Anya had seen him.

Creeping down the stairs, Déisi reached another door, this one was locked as well. He made fast work of it and was striding silently down a carpeted hall. He heard voices coming from the opposite end of where he was heading.

It was doubtful de Vos would have too many guards on the unconscious Dauphine. He was strapped in with metal restraints, and de Vos would be alerted that someone was coming for the scientist before they could get to him.

Because a person would have to go through the first level and through de Vos' soldiers to get to the second story where Märtin Dauphine was being held. Assault from the roof hadn't been considered.

Déisi reached the room. The door was, as expected, locked. But it was a wooden door and Déisi wore steel boots. One vicious kick and the door flung open. Good, it was sudden and loud and unexpected, the two guards inside were momentarily stunned.

Before they could even gather their wits and put up a fight, Déisi was already upon them.

He slammed the side of his hand into the first man's throat, instantly mangling him and cutting off his air. The man clutched at his throat with wide eyes and mouth gaping with no sounds coming out, he buckled to his knees and gagged.

The other soldier was pulling out his gun, Déisi kicked it out of his hands then dropped him dead with a punch to the temple. He went to the first man, crouched and broke his neck.

Quickly, he moved to Märtin Dauphine and pulled off his backpack setting it on the floor. He put two fingers to feel the elder man's pulse, it was weak, faint, but there. The man's face was still battered black and blue.

Déisi knelt and opened his pack. Removing bolt cutters, he made fast work of the restraints.

As soon as Dauphine was free, Déisi very carefully lifted him and slung him in a fireman's carry over his shoulder, then headed straight for the door. He stood beside it, waiting.

It was not long before a ruckus sounded. Shouts, gunfire, screams, it was his signal to go.

Carrying Anya's grandfather, Déisi crept out of the room and hurried down the hall.

Downstairs, Kalo and Luc were initiating a full frontal attack. The plan was for them to make a clear path for Déisi to get through.

Déisi hurried down the back staircase, the sounds of fighting were muffled. When he opened the stairwell door and stepped out, his blood froze.

De Vos was standing there holding a gun aimed straight at his head, with a sneering Fabiana standing behind him.

Chapter Twenty-Two

Anya was furious. How dare Déisi treat her like a helpless woman!

She paced back and forth in front of Bair. Of course, she admitted, she was a helpless woman, but that was ending here and now. She peeked a quick glance at Bair.

The huge man was sitting beside the door reading a newspaper ignoring her fuming pacing.

The front door was her only escape. She'd checked out the bedrooms, the bathroom and the kitchen. All the windows had been boarded up, there was no way she could get out any of them.

Under her long lashes, she surreptitiously perused her guard. Her cries, pleas, begging, anger, had made zero impact on the bear of a man. He was well trained, and well prepped by Déisi. Her threats and histrionics had no effect on him.

She strolled towards the kitchen. Bair only glanced briefly over the top of the newspaper at her. He knew she couldn't get out of the kitchen, he went back to his reading.

The kitchen was a horseshoe shape, open-ended on the sides with a wall in the middle. Anya casually made her way inside.

Moving around, she rattled pans, ran water, and took a knife out of a drawer. She made a small slash across her arm, just enough to draw blood.

Smearing the blood around her leg, she put some on her forehead. Then, she pulled a stool near a counter, picked it up and slammed it to the ground with a terrifying scream, then she dropped to the floor crying.

Bair was in the room in a flash. To his horror, he saw Anya lying on the floor crying, blood all over her leg, her head. He exclaimed, "Miss Anya, *mi Dios*! Are you all right?"

Anya cried louder, "I'm hurt, I'm bleeding! I need bandages, hurry!"

Freaked, he yelped, "*Da, yah*, okay, right! I be back-" and he ran out of the room to go to the bathroom to get first aid equipment.

As soon as he was gone, Anya jumped up and ran to the coffee table where Bair had foolishly left his wallet. Taking out some bills, she grabbed her purse, and ran to the door, unlocked it and raced out.

Out in the street, she fled down several streets so Bair couldn't find her and flagged down a taxi.

She didn't know the address so she gave directions, praying she could remember the way. When Déisi had driven from the compound, Anya had studied the area, trying to memorize the way in case she had to return alone. She knew if she made it to the main expressway she could find the rest of the way there.

Thank goodness the driver knew enough broken English to understand her directions. Of course she used a lot of pointing and waving to further enhance his comprehension.

Alone, without Déisi, a shiver of fear rippled through her. Girding her strength, she sucked in a deep breath and bucked up. She needed to be there for Granddad.

Anya was half relieved, half afraid, when the taxi pulled up near the compound and let her out. She didn't dare go directly to the front of the building and be seen.

A shiver rolled across her shoulders when she recalled that the back of the structure was blocked by a moat crawling with crocs.

Feeling like some kind of ninja, Anya crept through part of the surrounding woods and made her way darting behind trees while zig-zagging across the lawn to a side entrance.

A man was standing guard at the door. Anya saw him before he saw her. She jumped around a corner of the estate then strolled out like she had just left the front of the building.

Muttering loudly, "Oh darn," with a frown, she clicked her fingers like she'd just remembered something.

The guard immediately lifted his weapon. Seeing the gorgeous young woman in snug powder blue jeans and yellow blouse with frilly collar, he lowered his weapon, but scowled at her.

Anya sauntered up to him batting her lashes. "Hello honey, you won't believe what an airhead I am." Giggling, she twirled a lock of hair around a finger and tipped her shoulder up coyly.

She watched his gaze roll down the front of her then back up to settle on her breasts. Sexy, dumb blondes hurtled over the language barrier every time.

"I just left the building. Anton said he had a meeting to attend. But," she rolled her eyes, "you won't believe what a goose I am. I left my keys in his office." Her yellow brows drew down, she looked at her heels.

"My feet are sooo sore, I just hate to think of having to walk all the way around again to the front. Do you think maybe you could just let me," she pushed her arms together to deepen her cleavage and watched his Adam's apple bounce with his heavy swallow.

Clearing his throat he rasped in a thick accent, "Uh, Miss, I-I can't. You know no one is allowed in any other entrance but the front." When she discreetly jiggled her chest, he gulped again harder, eyes widening.

"Oh, but," she set a few fingers on his arm, blinking harmlessly up at him. "Anton and I well, you know, we just left his," she blushed, lowering her eyes. "You know, his bedroom. I'm sure he would thank you for saving me some pain...you know?" She moved closer.

The color in his face turned dark red. "Um, yes, well, uh, I guess it'd be okay." He unlocked the door and watched her ass swing as she walked inside.

"Thank you ever so much. I will tell Anton what a gentleman you were!" Wriggling her fingers at him, she strolled off like she belonged there. The poor man never thought to call de Vos and check.

Anya scurried inside and down a hall. Suddenly she heard shouting and gunfire- her heart clenched- was Déisi being shot at? The thought made her hurry.

She darted from doorway to doorway. The sound of Déisi's voice made her heart weep with joy, he was alive, and angry. She crept around the corner, and her breath caught in her throat.

Déisi was standing just inside the open room with her granddad slung over his back, and that wretched man, de Vos, was holding a gun aimed at him.

De Vos' snide, arrogant voice carried over the marble tiles.

The woman who had thrown herself at Déisi was standing next to de Vos with a smug face.

De Vos thought it was the fear of the gun held on him that made the color drain from his jαύdraç's face, but it was the sight of Anya coming up behind de Vos that brought the terror to Déisi's black eyes.

Stalling for time, "Fabiana," Déisi said coolly, "you betrayed us. Why?"

One of her solid shoulders rose slightly. "Scorn, hon. You've heard there's no hell like a woman scorned? You push me aside but fuck that skinny bitch?"

Her entire face a resentful sneer, she said, "While your brother Kalo was sticking it to me, he nonchalantly asked about her grandfather's location, where there might be maps of the compound, and he talked about my letting him in a door from the garage that is kept locked from the outside.

"He said he wanted the maps so he could hide when I let him in, and we could spend some more time privately together. After

I let him in, I thought about it. And, it came to me," she tapped a finger against her brunette head.

"That the two of you were playing me." She put her hands behind her back and clasped her fingers, making her breasts jut out more. "You could have had me, Jαύδρας, but you scraped me off like I was gum on your shoe. So," her shoulder rose again, "now you will pay. I only wish that infant bitch was here too and I could make my due with her."

"Shut the fuck up, Fabi," de Vos snarled. Waving the gun at Déisi, he said, "Put the scientist down. I want that fucking formula, and the girl. Did you think to bring it? If not, I will start by shooting a foot, then a leg, a hand, and so on until you tell me where you stashed it and the bitch."

Carefully, Déisi laid the unconscious man on the floor. His head down, he peered up at Anya, and imperceptivity shook his head. She had found a lamp and now was slinking up behind de Vos with it raised.

Ignoring him, Anya moved more quickly. Just as she swung the lamp, Fabiana turned, and screamed, causing de Vos to turn, and Anya only caught a glancing blow off his head.

But it was enough. Déisi launched himself at de Vos and took him down. Fabiana ran off with a shriek.

In a blind rampage of fury, Déisi pummeled de Vos so fast, so hard, the man never got in a swing. Déisi beat him and beat him, Anya didn't even try to stop him. If he let the man live, or get away, they would all remain in danger.

When there was nothing left of Anton de Vos but a bloody pulpy mess, on his knees, Déisi stared at the man who was going to kill Märtin Dauphine.

Plus the hideous man planned to build a horrifically dangerous weapon, and keep Anya as his personal sex-pet. Déisi got to his feet with zero remorse.

His hands dripping blood, black hair sopping wet with sweat hanging over his livid eyes, he advanced on Anya. "What the fuck are you doing here? Where the fuck is Bair?" Face a mass of fury, fists clenched, he stood shaking in rage in front of her.

Taking a step back from him, Anya said, "Um well, don't you think we should get Granddad and get out of here?"

"You-" his hands raised to her, but she was already kneeling down beside her grandfather. "Motherfucker," he cursed a blue streak in several languages.

Before he could get to her, more armed men showed up. Their weapons aimed at Déisi, one man stepped forward.

"McDaniels," Déisi snarled, "what the fuck do you want?" He started towards Anya to block her from the men with his body, but the other man raised his pistol and released the safety.

"Stop, *na čelu vlad*" he said with a snort of disdain. "Death Comes, aye, I know what they call you." He spat on the floor. "But to me you are just de Vos' *jaύdraç* just an enforcer that has gotten too big for his boots."

Malicious blue eyes gleamed below dark auburn hair, the hook nose grew sharper with the coarse smile he aimed at Anya.

"No-" he commanded Déisi as he moved to shield her. "You take another step and I will kill her then take what I want." He said to the man next to him, "She wouldn't have come without the formula to trade for her grandfather's life, she carries it, take her purse."

The soldier nodded and stalked over to Anya. He grabbed her arm, jerking her to her feet.

Déisi's growl only made McDaniels' smirk nastier. The soldier snatched the purse that strung over her shoulder from her and handed it to Corporal Nate McDaniels.

McDaniels immediately opened it and took out a handful of folded papers that Anya had removed from the safety deposit box. He unfolded a few, glancing at them. The thin lips bent up in a blade of a smile.

"Ah, this is what that bastard de Vos was after." He shot a contemptuous glance at what was left of de Vos on the floor. Then back to Déisi.

The big man's harsh dark eyes glittered at McDaniels with promised death.

Then McDaniel's gaze flit to Anya, and every muscle in Déisi's powerful body turned rigid.

"Don't even think it, McDaniels, I will slaughter you."

"Ha!" The corporal sneered, "De Vos wanted this little bitch bad, I can see why. Too bad he underestimated you. That's not a mistake I'm making. Okay, woman," he said to Anya, "consider yourself the spoils of war, you're coming with me."

As he reached for Anya, his men closed in, keeping their weapons aimed straight at Déisi.

McDaniels grabbed Anya's arm and turned to cross the marble floor towards the staircase. He was yet another big muscular man with a grip of steel.

When Anya balked, pulling her along, he said, "Honey, you stop walking or drop down to the floor and I will just drag you by your ankle, which," he chuckled, "you are not going to like when we go up those hard stairs."

His voice quiet, calm, Déisi said, "Go with him, Anyalia, do not fight him." He needed her to get out of the line of fire.

"See?" McDaniels laughed, pulling her across the room to the stairs. "He knows when to give up, when he's lost the battle. He ain't coming for ya, honey, you belong to me now."

When he reached the top of the stairs with her, he paused, then ordered, "Take him out, boys," and strode quickly down the hall with Anya.

The sounds of gunfire gripped Anya's heart. "No!" she screamed and kicked out. The suddenness of her kick took the corporal by surprise and she took the opportunity to run.

She tried for the stairs, to see if she could somehow help Déisi if he wasn't already dead. With a sharp inhale to hold back the tears, she realized with the sound of all the gunfire there was no chance he could survive.

But, McDaniels, hunched over holding his leg where she'd kicked him was blocking the way to the stairs. So Anya swung around and ran down the hall.

She tried every door. They were all locked.

Panic was already choking her when she heard his boots stomping rapidly down the hall after her. One of the doorknobs turned. Shoving the door open, she darted inside.

Quickly slamming the door shut, the blood drained out of her body when she saw there was no lock on the door. Anya glanced around the room frantic to find something to block the door when it burst open.

The door flew into the wall and banged right back out. McDaniels blocked it with his arm and slammed it closed. Fury turned his face beet red, his teeth grit.

Glowering at Anya, he stomped into the room towards her. "You little bitch, I was gonna be nice to you. Just fuck you some, but now you're gonna be bloody and broken when I do. Come here," he demanded as he kept moving to her.

Frantically searching the room for a weapon, Anya backed away from him, but he continued stalking straight at her.

Spotting a marble figurine on a table she grabbed it up. Holding it like a bat, she threatened, "Don't come any closer!" She knew it was ridiculous that she thought she could take on the man as big and furious as a raging buffalo, but she wasn't just going to stand there and let him do what he wanted to her.

The door suddenly burst opened drawing both their attention.

A man filled the doorway.

McDaniels cursed at him, "Get the fuck out of here, the bitch is mine, you ain't gettin' a piece of her."

Anya quailed, her limbs quaked and her mind buzzed with fear. She would have no chance against two huge men. Her only chance was if they fought each other and she could run while they were distracted.

As it was, both men stood between her and the only door in the room that was either a den or a study.

The new man grinned. "*Na,*" his accent was thick and unusual, yet familiar. He said, "I'm thinking not." His hands on his hips, he shook his head. "*Mi bréthaïdne* would have *mi* head if I let any harm befall the *svini Engleză.*"

Anya's eyes rounded at the big man with chocolate dark hair and matching eyes. He had the same hardness to his face and body as Déisi. Forehead furrowing, she said, "Not another brother?"

He nodded, still grinning. His grin had a lethal edge to it like Déisi's, not mischievous like Kalo's. "*Da*. I am the oldest. May I introduce myself." He bowed. "Marshall Zukov at your service."

Spurting, "Oh fuck me, come on," McDaniels' anger escalated by the moment. "I have no time for this shit. Either get out or," he pulled out his pistol and aimed it at Déisi's brother. "I put some extra holes in your obnoxious head. Now," he waved the gun, "get out, asshole."

He turned from Anya to threaten Marshall with his weapon. The way he lifted it and cocked it, it was obvious he planned on killing Marshall whatever his decision was.

Anya swung the figurine with all her might bashing it into the back of McDaniels' head. As short as she was, it was only enough to briefly shock him, not enough to knock him out, yet it was enough time for Marshall to leap across the room and tackle him. Anya jumped out of the way as the two men battled.

"Always causing trouble, *mi babia*," a deep voice rumbled with humor from the door.

Her eyes wide, mouth open, Anya cried out, "Déisi! You're alive!" and she ran to him.

He grabbed her up in his arms, sweeping her right off her feet and hugged her tight to him.

She pulled back and said, "You need to help your brother!" Punches, grunts and groans filled the room.

Déisi smiled, setting her on her feet. "*Na*, Marshall never needs help. I will let him have his fun." As he said that, Marshall punched McDaniels so hard the man crashed against the window and through it- he tumbled out so quickly he was but a blur of color gone in a heartbeat.

"*Na!*" Déisi rushed forward. "The formula! He has the formula!" It was too late.

The three of them ran to the window, leaned out it and looked down.

McDaniels' screams traveled clear up to them as he thrashed, trying to fight off the marauding crocodiles.

As soon as blood pooled in the water and the screams ended, Anya turned away, her stomach queasy. He was a nasty man, but still, to die by being eaten, yuk.

Déisi rolled his arm around her, pulling her against his chest. They all moved away from the window.

"So," Déisi said, "you've met *mi bréthaïdne.*" He and Marshall shared an identical grin.

Rolling her eyes, Anya said, "Yes, just when I thought it couldn't happen again, yet another Zukov brother has jumped out at me."

Smiling and holding her close, Déisi said to his brother, "This is Anyalia Marvaux."

His head bowed slightly, Marshall said, "*Da*, I figured. Kalo described her, special features-" he broke off at Déisi's frown. "Ah, anyway, a pleasure to meet you, Miss Marvaux."

"Yes, you as well. Your timing is as impeccable as your brothers', all of them." Anya leaned back to rest her head against Déisi as he strung his big arms across the front of her.

Turning slightly to look up at him, she said, "How on earth did you get away from those men downstairs with the guns? There were so many, I," she heaved in a frightened breath. "I was so scared that you couldn't survive."

Snuggling her, Déisi kissed the side of her head. "Ah, sweetheart, I can't believe you doubt my skills. A dozen men with weapons, jeesh," he and his brother shared another grin. "Like taking candy from a baby. Bunch 'a babies."

"Sure. Can we please go and help my grandfather?"

"You bet, *babia.*"

The three of them started for the door when Anya reached in her pocket and pulled out some papers.

"By the way," she said casually. "I expected there might be trouble so I kept the papers on me. The documents in my purse were copies of Granddad's will and his mother's recipes for several dishes, but they were all in French. Seeing the numerical measurements, Mr. McDaniels assumed they were the formula as he obviously can't read French."

"You minx," Déisi said proudly, then sobered. "However, it might probably be for the best if the formula had been destroyed. Tis too dangerous to get in the hands of someone like de Vos or McDaniels."

"I know," Anya said as Déisi took her hand. "But I know Granddad needs the information because he wanted to create an antidote just in case someone else came up with the same formula."

They made their way down the stairs.

Halfway down, Anya saw her grandfather sitting with his back against the wall and she started to go to him, but Déisi held her back.

"*Na*, you will stay with me. No more of this running off. Which, reminds me," he squeezed her hand, "we're going to have a long talk about you eluding Bair and coming here, especially after I specifically told you to stay with him, that I didn't want you here in danger."

"Sure, big bad enforcer," she mocked. "But if I hadn't come, Mr. de Vos would have killed you."

The brothers wore smirks. Marshall said behind her, "You do not give *mi bréthaïdne* enough credit, *svini Engleză*. A roomful of armed men cannot stop him, you think one man could?"

"First of all," Anya said with a scowl, "stop calling me small. Second, I am not English, and third," she stopped to give Déisi a quick kiss. "You Zukov brothers are the most arrogant men I have ever met in my life!"

The brothers were still laughing when they reached the bottom of the stairs.

Anya blanched. Scattered all over the marble floor were dead men. Some were bloody messes, some were lying unnaturally, twisted.

Déisi tucked her under his arm to hide her view from as much of the carnage as he could as he brought her to Märtin Dauphine.

The professor was awake and sitting up, propped against the wall.

"Granddad!" Anya broke from Déisi's hold and ran to her grandfather. She sank down beside him and they hugged.

Tears poured down her face as her frail grandfather weakly stroked her hair with a shaky hand, "*Mon chère petite-fille*, my dear granddaughter, you are well, I have been wracked with worry."

"No, Granddad, it is I that feared for you." Her tears wetting his bloody shirt, she sniffed and took out the papers to show him. "I remembered and understood your words about the painting at the hotel. I got the key and the papers from the deposit box.

"You were afraid eventually de Vos would discover the box and get at the formula. You knew I'd keep it safe, or destroy it. Do what I needed to, to keep it out of his hands."

"Ah, my precious girl." He kissed her cheek with a small chuckle. "I have always known how smart you are."

"Anyalia, we need to get out of here," Déisi said as Kalo and Luc swaggered into the room, covered in blood, proud smiles bursting from their bruised and cut faces.

Déisi explained, "They fought off the guards, the soldiers, while I got to your grandfather, that was the first volley of gunfire you heard."

Murmuring, "Hmm," she smiled at them. "They are as bulletproof as you are."

"Anya, tell me who your friends are," her grandfather bade her.

At that, Déisi bent and took Anya's hand pulling her to her feet, then he and Marshall helped Märtin to stand on his shaking legs.

Anya made all the introductions as they made their way out of the compound and to the hidden chopper.

The brothers helped Märtin into the chopper and Luc climbed in the pilot's seat. With promises that Anya would see her grandfather in the hospital, the helicopter took off and disappeared over the trees.

The rest of them made their way to where Marshall had left his truck. As they prepared to get inside the vehicle, with a sly smirk, Marshall said, "Oh, I forgot, my part of the mission."

He reached behind his back and pulled a folder out that he had folded in half and tucked under his belt. He handed the folder to Déisi. "Breaking into de Vos' safe was a piece of cake, bro."

His fingers gripping the file, Déisi looked at his brother. His eyes blurred. "This…is it?"

"*Da*," Marshall nodded, his expression dead serious.

Kalo moved close. "Ah, finally, *bréthaïdne,* tis over." The two brothers watched somberly while Déisi opened the file, his hands shaking.

Seeing him so disturbed, Anya asked quietly, "What is it?"

Déisi didn't answer her, he was reading.

Marshall patted Anya's shoulder and explained, "They are the papers that he was forced to sign as a child to keep our baby brother with us, and for them to allow all of us brothers to stay together. He sold his soul to them. He couldn't ever get out of the contract, the agreement, or he would be thrown in jail for the rest of his life for breaking it. But," he took a breath and Kalo filled in.

"Now that he has the actual, original contract, no one can enforce it. And with de Vos dead, no one would even know about it. He is finally," Kalo's words broke off in a choke. "Ah," emotion deepened his cracking voice, "he is free. He is finally free."

The brothers hugged, and for the first time in his life, Déisi allowed them to hug him.

Anya stood to the side. It was amazing to see these hardcore assassins, tough mercenaries all choked up with tears in their eyes.

After a minute, Marshall, said, "Ahem," clearing his throat. "Let's get the hell out of here, eh?"

The others agreed, climbed in the truck and headed back to the safe house where Déisi had left Anya with Bair.

Chapter Twenty-Three

Back at the safe house, the men flopped around the living room.

After Anya went first, then the rest took turns taking showers. Her own personal shampoo, soap and deodorant products they had stopped on the way to purchase were set on a window ledge.

Anya was dressing in one of the bedrooms when Déisi came in.

Closing the door behind him, he strode right to her, cradled her face, and held her stock-still while he gave her the wickedest, most scorching, toe-curling kiss, even the walls around them seemed to burn.

Heatedly gripping her breasts over her blouse, he kneaded them with gusting lust. Their mouths glued together, his arousal escalating in rapid degrees, Déisi roughly crushed her breasts in his hard hands.

He walked her backwards to the bed while working on opening the buttons on her blouse and trying to wrench it over her head at the same time.

Anya pushed from him, panting, "Wait." She drew several sharp inhalations to catch her breath.

"Uh huh," he mumbled, pulling her blouse open, dusky eyes devouring the soft globes mounding out of the bra.

She put her hands up pressing her palms against his chest. "No, Déisi, stop-"

His mouth locked on hers cutting off her protest. His kiss domineering, forceful, ensnaring her tongue. Grabbing at her belt, he kept propelling her backwards until her legs bumped into the bed.

Pushing hard at him and turning her head, Anya gasped, "Stop, Déisi, stop!"

He moved his hands to spread over her back, trying to pull her close again. His mouth seeking hers, licking the corners of her lips, he fought to slow his frenzied stupor of lust.

His growl husky, he rasped, "Anyalia, I was terrified out of my mind when I saw you show up in the compound, and now I am so furious with you for not doing as I said, to stay safe with Bair, putting yourself at risk."

He grasped her chin, fingers clutching tightly, his wrathful eyes flit back and forth at hers. "The fear and rage, produced crazy intense adrenalin. You are here in my arms, but I have this horrible residual feeling of you in such dire danger, Anyalia. I have the overwhelming need to constrain you, dominate you, fuck you, hard. I know tis that alpha shit, but I can't help it. I need to fight or fuck to release the energy. To *feel* you are safe."

She recoiled from his embrace. "No, Déisi, stop!"

"I need you under me, to be inside you, *mi dragă*." He stroked his hands down her arms. "To feel you are alive."

"No," she pushed so hard he let her go. "Your brothers are right outside, they'll know. I feel…cheap. I can't."

Murmuring a harsh whisper, "Anyalia," he squeezed her wrists.

With a shake of her head, she said quietly, "No."

His released breath coarse with frustration, he let go of her. "All right. But," his flingers slid under her jaw. "I can hardly think for the want of you. Later, we have a date, *yah*?"

Her smile relieved at his acquiescence, he could easily overpower her if he chose to. "Yes, a date."

"Hmm," he kissed her lightly. "We will then take care of your punishment also for disobeying me."

Her lids flapped in surprise. "My what?"

"*Da*, you disobeying me could have cost you your life. I have the experience to know better, to handle those situations."

"But- I saved your life! Mr. de Vos had a gun on you, you had nowhere to run!"

His hands dropped to his hips, his head shook in slight chastisement. "You heard *mi bréthaïdnee*, I do this for a living. I would have had that gun pressed to his own temple within a blink of an eye. You were the one in danger, and I need to teach you to obey me. *Yah*? I can't go through that terror again of seeing you in such frightful peril."

Stunned at his ridiculous words, she could only stare at him with her mouth open.

"I will leave you now, Anyalia, to get settled. When you are ready, come out and join us." He spun and left the room so quickly Anya couldn't get a word out.

Fuming at his heavy-handedness, and his very thought that he could control her, tell her what to do- the nerve of the man! In a snit, she threw her shampoo and other toiletries in her bag.

The more she thought about what he said, the madder she got. Anya stormed out the door and down the hall, she could hear the men talking in the kitchen.

Déisi was speaking. Slight sarcasm clung to his words, "*Yah*, you know she is nothing of my type. Too delicate, too sweet, too ladylike. I have to watch my strength when I touch her, my language when I'm near her. The girl is so goddamned reckless, *da*, and so fucking stubborn, *iiaa*."

His brothers laughed. Kalo said, "*Da*, we never thought you would ever have anything to do with someone like her. I figured you had to have an ulterior motive-"

Bair's rumble was unintelligible.

Anya slapped her hands over her mouth to stifle her cry. He hates her. He was telling the truth when he said skinny little girls

255

didn't make him hard. And she thought his brothers liked her, especially Kalo.

Her heart leaking pain like a stabbed sieve, in a blind panic, Anya ran and grabbed her purse and fled out the front door.

She raced down the street, her broken heart screaming in agony. Her limbs numb with grief, stumbling past people, she ran a long way over cobblestone and brick walks.

Anya wanted to be far away, she didn't need Déisi to come out and catch her. His ulterior motive, it had to be the formula. The money he could get for selling it.

Tears streaming down her face, she wished she could take the damned formula and tear it into a million pieces, it's cost nothing but pain and trouble. But she couldn't, she promised herself she would help her grandfather come up with an antidote before destroying it.

She ran until she just couldn't go any further. Standing on the side of the road, her hand to her cramped side, chest heaving and panting, what to do? She still had money she'd taken from Bair.

Within the wad of cash she'd accidentally pilfered a credit card. She never intended to use it, and she had planned to pay him back for the cash she'd used. She flagged down a taxi and took it to the hospital.

Her grandfather had been admitted and given a private room, all on Déisi's dime. Huh, she snorted, he probably thought he'd get all the money he'd spent on her and Granddad back in the sale of the formula.

He would come after her, try to convince her he cared for her when he really wanted to get his hands on the formula. She needed to hide. Déisi would know she would go to the hospital, she'd have to be wary.

The taxi pulled up in front of the hospital complex. Anya wiped at her eyes, sucked in a bunch of gulping breaths to gain her composure. She paid the taxi driver and hurried into the hospital.

Noticing the visitor's desk as soon as she entered, she asked the elderly woman who greeted her amiably where her grandfather was.

Anya made her way quickly to his room. Opening the door slowly, she peeked in.

He was awake and sitting up.

"Granddad!" She rushed in and to his side.

"Anyalia!" He threw his arms weakly around her. They hugged, both in tears.

"Dear Granddaughter, I feared so much for you."

Anya sat on the edge of the mattress, her hand placed tenderly on his face.

"Granddad, it was you that was in desperate straits. Except for these bruises, though, you seem so much better."

Märtin nodded. "Yes, after I fell unconscious from the...uh, beatings, they never touched me again after that, there wasn't any point of course."

He looked around her to the door. "Where is your young man? The big, hard looking bruiser that rescued me?"

When she didn't answer and her eyes welled with tears, he patted her hand then held it. "Darling, trust your old grandpa, tell me everything."

Wiping her eyes with the backs of her hands, Anya pulled her legs up to sit cross-legged on the bed. It took her a few minutes to clear her throat, staunch the tears.

In a stiff voice, she told him everything. The abduction, Déisi's protection as well as his ill behavior to her, on the plane, the train. How he took her to de Vos, not letting the evil man near her, then when they went to the hotel and found the key.

She told him about Darryl Dassey grabbing her and tossing her in the car. Her eyes widened as she recalled Déisi throwing himself on the hood of the car and taking out each of the men.

Her face was bright pink when she told him everything, including that they had made love. Her face crunched into a scowl, sex, that's all it was. Sex. He slept with her to make her think he cared, so she wouldn't be suspicious that he really wanted the formula.

When she told him it all, she lapsed into miserable silence.

Märtin kept quiet until she was done.

"Darling," he patted her knee. "Are you sure about his motives? I mean, he's by far the scariest looking man I've ever seen, but, the way he looked at you-"

"It was an act, Granddad, all an act." She lowered her head as the tears welled again.

Shaking his head, he said, "I don't know, honey. When you obtained the formula from the bank he obviously could have forcefully taken it from you at any time. Even after you had the formula, he risked his life to get me out of there. Don't let your broken heart create incorrect notions in your mind. You only heard a snippet of their conversation."

"Granddad," she murmured morosely, her head down, she blinked by tears. Plucking at his blanket, she said, "I heard his words, there was no mistaking him saying I wasn't his type. That I'm too- too soft for him. Even his brother said he had ulterior motives for being with me."

"I'm sorry, honey."

"Yeah, see, just like I told you in the beginning. I'm done with men. They all have selfish, shady agendas."

"Well," he said quietly, "the good news is, I can be discharged tomorrow. We can go home as soon as we can get a flight out."

Anya stared blankly, her lips grim. Home. The last place she wanted to be. Yet, there was nowhere else for her to go. She had no money, she'd have to use Bair's credit card to get her and her granddad plane tickets.

How on earth will they get him on a plane? He has no ID. But nonetheless, Déisi had pulled connections when she hadn't had identification.

Her granddad had high security clearance, maybe that would help. Her body slumped. Tomorrow, she'd worry about it tomorrow.

She wouldn't be allowed to stay in her grandfather's room, and she didn't dare go to a hotel, she would have to use Bair's card and Déisi would be able to trace it as soon as she used it.

After seeing her grandfather comfortably settled, Anya wandered around until she found a waiting room that was empty and the lights off. She slept there.

Well, not exactly slept, she lay all night thinking of Déisi. The way his simmering obsidian eyes glowed molten when he looked at her body, the feel of his hands, his lips, he could almost make her come just from his kisses alone.

Feeling her face heat and her body flame at the remembrance of his tongue on her most tender parts, she tried to think of something else. School, work, her lungs emptied in a heavy sigh, nothing sparked her interest. Nothing.

Nothing but that big, hard, so terribly masculine, horrible man. *Gah*, it was going to be a long night.

In the morning, she grabbed a donut in the cafeteria and went to find her grandfather. She was surprised to see him up and dressed. He moved slowly, wincing sometimes, but he was on the mend.

"Granddad, you're ready to go?"

"Yes, Anyalia, the doctor has signed my release papers, we can leave right away."

"Okay, good," she muttered listlessly. They had to wait for a wheelchair to fetch Märtin.

The attendant arrived right away with a cheerful smile and a wheelchair. Märtin waved him off when he tried to assist the elderly man onto the chair.

The attendant good naturedly adjusted the foot pedals and soon the three were roaming down the tiled corridor.

When they moved onto the elevator, Märtin said, "He was here, you know."

Anya's blood curdled, she slowed. "Who?"

"Darling, you know who. Zukov. He had a brother with him, Kevin, Karl, no, Kalo. They both looked very upset."

"Huh, sure," she grunted as the door opened and they moved out across the lobby. "We need to go out a side door, he might be waiting out front. I've arranged for a car to pick us up at the east corner."

The porter pushed the chair as they detoured past several exits towards a far side of the hospital.

"You should talk to him, *mon chère, petite-fille.* I told him why you left."

"Oh Granddad," she scowled. "You shouldn't have even talked with him. He won't care why, only that I left with the formula."

"Ah," his head cocked to look up at her as the attendant pushed the chair. "I think he was quite devastated when I told him you heard what he said."

"Huh," a very unladylike grunt came with her pouted lips and frown.

"Really, honey. I could see the pain in his eyes, his shoulders drooping. Even his brother looked sad. He said you misunderstood, that you didn't hear the entire conversation, that what he-"

"Never mind, Granddad, they're all lies. It's done. Over. Let's go home."

They met with an official at the airport. Märtin Dauphine was highly regarded in the military, and he had top level clearance. A Colonel came personally to clear the way for them to board the aircraft.

Their trip was thankfully, uneventful. No abductions, car chases, frisking, orgies, beatings.

When they reached Washington, they took a taxi home to Wildhaven.

The taxi parked in the driveway that led to the cottage behind Anya's parents' house. They had no luggage so the taxi left right away.

"I can't believe it," Anya said in awe.

"What?" Märtin walked slowly, gingerly.

"He fixed it, Granddad, he fixed your door like he said he would."

She looked down at the threshold in astonishment. "He even had the blood washed away."

The door was unlocked, they went inside. She was even more surprised.

There had been damage from Märtin's abduction. Tables overturned, lamps broken, it was all cleaned up.

They went into the kitchen to make some tea, and when Anya opened the refrigerator door, she groaned.

"What?" Märtin asked, hobbling up beside her. "Oh!" Astonished at the fully stocked fridge, he grinned at her as he started down the hall. "And you think the man doesn't care?"

"It's part of his game," she sighed sadly. "Make me think he cares by doing such thoughtful things." Tears threatened, she hurried and filled the teakettle.

"Darling," Märtin put his hand on her shoulder. "He has nothing to prove. The formula is safely locked away with the proper authorities. Besides, my colonel friend said Zukov is stinking wealthy. That he has more money than God. The boy doesn't need the money from the sale of the formula."

When she kept her head down fidgeting with the teabags, he patted her shoulder and wandered out of the room. Seconds later he called out.

"Hey, Granddaughter, come see this!"

Turning the burner on, Anya hurried to see what he was all excited about. She found him in the lab. "Oh, Granddad," she uttered in wonderment.

The lab had been all torn and broken up when de Vos' men took him and searched for the formula. Now, it not only was all cleaned and fixed up, there was all new equipment; beakers, fridges, micros, compounds, everything was gleaming ready and waiting to be used.

"This ain't nothin' girl." Märtin's smile contained fond mirth. "Go check out the guest room, where you're going to stay."

Yellow brows down in puzzlement, Anya left him glorying over his new lab and went to the second small bedroom in the cottage.

Eyes wide in stunned bafflement, she took in the racks and racks of clothes, shoes, purses. "What on earth?" She wandered in gazing in all directions.

Touching this soft silk and that luxuriant faux fur, she didn't understand. On the bed was the sundress she had worn that first day they'd gone to see de Vos.

Just as her heart started to warm, Anya's lips firmed with a shake of her head. No, he was not going to buy her. It was all trickery to get the formula.

Out loud though, she wondered, "But, why are the clothes on racks and not in the closet?"

Chapter Twenty-Four

"Because, *mi dulce dragă,*" his deep voice rumbled from the doorway.

Anya turned slowly. Her heart beat faster, stomach tightened, heat and moisture pooled between her legs.

Déisi stood in the doorway, his shoulder leaning against the doorframe, arms crossed. A lock of raven hair flopped over one midnight eye in his ruffian hard face.

He was so big, so strong, so brutishly handsome, against her will, her nipples pebbled and peaked right along with the dampness that oozed from her sex.

She tried to fight it. Lips a hard line, brows blunt over bitter green eyes glowered hurt and anger at him.

Stepping into the room, his gaze lowered from her fierce eyes to her nipples poking hard against her blouse. He made no effort to conceal her effect on his swelling manhood. The long, thick rod straining against his jeans was clearly outlined.

When she took a step back, the corner of his mouth twisted up in a curl of glib humor. "Because, you are not staying here *mi babia*," he moved closer.

Backing away, she said, "No? Why not?" Putting a hand up to ward him off, she said, "Do not come any closer." She worried he would either beat her, or seduce her to do his will and she wasn't having it.

Seeing the flicker of fear in her eyes, he frowned, then let his desire for her flare in his dark eyes. "Ah, Anyalia, after all we've been through, you still fear me, don't trust me."

Another step closer, he said, "The clothes are not in closet because they are going with you, and you, are coming with me."

"No, stop Déisi, you can't make me. You only want the stupid formula and it's now with the authorities. You can't just take me this time, my granddad will have already called the police to come for you."

His lips pushed out, Déisi said with a forlorn smile, "*Mi babia*, you would have me arrested?"

Her silence and the dip of her lashes covering her eyes betrayed her feelings. No matter how hurt, how angry she was with him, Anya would never want him incarcerated.

His smile broadened, he took another step closer. "Ah, you do have feelings for me, Anyalia, that's all I needed to know."

Both hands up in defense, she snapped, "Stop. I will never allow you or anyone to make a fortune from that dreaded formula."

With a sigh, Déisi pulled a paper from his jean's pocket, unfolded it and handed it out to her.

She regarded it with distrust, her eyes rose to his. "What is that?"

"'Tis my bank account, Anyalia, well, one of them anyway. You will see that I have more than enough money I could ever hope to spend in a lifetime, take it, look at it."

Shaking her head, the fiery hair swept back and forth across her slender back. "No. It could easily be falsified."

"Enough, *petite-fille,*" Märtin said entering the room. He and Déisi shared a look and a nod.

Lower lip thrust out, Anya eyed the two men. They acted like they were comrades, friends. "What is going on, *Grand-père?*" she asked with suspicion and a hint of rebuke.

"Everything he has told you is true, Anyalia," Märtin said gently, firmly. "We both are close with General Garrison. After Mr. Zukov spoke with me in the hospital, I phoned Garrison and he confirmed that he knows Zukov." His brown eyes shifted from Anya to Déisi whose face remained impassive, his gaze intent on Anya.

Back to Anya, Märtin said, "He may be a...sort of an enforcer, but," he glanced back at Déisi with a smile, "Garrison says his integrity, his honor, is impeccable, without question, and his net worth is very real."

Her mouth hanging open, Anya looked from a relatively smug Déisi to her smiling grandfather. "But, Granddad, he abducted me! He kidnaps people, women, basically selling them. He sold *me* to that horrible man de Vos! How can that be honorable?"

"Anyalia," scowling, Déisi started, but Märtin spoke over him. "Granddaughter, his reputation is actually well known in the circles of military personnel I deal with. He doesn't kidnap or put any women or children in harm's way.

"He chose the task of taking you because he feared for your wellbeing if Anton de Vos or any of his disreputable men got their hands on you. As you see, the results are exactly as Déisi planned. You are safe and sound with the additional upturn of my being rescued as well as the safe keeping of the formula."

"But-"

"No," Märtin glared at Anya to hush her. "Enough. The man lo- uh cares for you. Everything he has said to you has been the truth. Like I said before, if he wanted the formula he could have just taken it from you anytime he wanted. He is not after the formula, he is after you.

"He came back halfway around the world for you. Now," smiling as he trod to the door, he said, "if you don't want him as a man, tell him straight and true. But, do not let your doubts of his honor or," he grinned at Déisi, "his wealth, have any reflection on your feelings. You either want him, or you don't." With a swift nod at Déisi, he left them alone.

Anya's head whirled with her grandfather's words, what she had believed to be true, her devastation at overhearing Déisi's true feelings for her, that she was too...delicate for his tastes. The pain of leaving him, darn, tears welled. Anya just didn't know, her head lowered.

"Ah, *babia*," his voice soft, he went to her and lightly grasped her arm gently before she could move away from him.

Curling a finger under her chin he raised it. "Anyalia, I hope you will give us a chance. You said before you would. I swear," tipping her head up so her wet eyes were leveled at his, "everything I've ever told you is true. Except for when I said I didn't desire you."

"You-"

He cut her off, "Everything your granddad said was 100% true. I care about you, I want to spend the rest of my life with you."

Resisting the passion his presence alone stirred in her, Anya said quietly, "I heard you, Déisi, with your brothers. You said," she bit the inside of her mouth to keep the tears from falling, "that I wasn't like the women you like. I'm not tough, you have to watch your strength, your language around me. I," she took a beleaguered breath, "why would I want to be with a man who has no desire for me?"

Blinking in consternation, her brow wrinkled, she asked, "Why are you saying you want to be with me anyway? It makes no sense if you don't find me attractive. What's your- your agenda? I don't see you as the pitying kind of guy."

Rolling his eyes, he gripped both her upper arms. "Anyalia, you didn't hear the whole conversation. My brothers were teasing me about my insane feelings for you. I was being sarcastic when I was saying you weren't like the other women.

"What I was saying was that those things about you are the very things I love about you. Attributes that I prefer over other women I've been with."

Squeezing her arms, he said with a soft smile, "I love that you are so petite, slender, yet have the lushest curves." He kept his eyes on hers as he spoke.

"And *babia*, you are so feminine and graceful, so ladylike but on fire in the bedroom," he smiled at her embarrassed flush.

Cupping her face, he said, "*Yah*, you're small and delicate. I watch my strength because the last thing in the world I would ever want would be to hurt you. Sure, I said I watch my language in front of you, because I *want* to. Because I respect you and I know my cursing makes you uncomfortable so I'm working at keeping it to a minimum."

His thumbs brushing the hollows under her cheeks, he said, "And, *mi babia*, you've got to be kidding if you think I have no desire for you. That day you left Bair's place, if you recall, I was trying to strip you and fu- uh, make love to you because I couldn't stand not being with you, touching you, holding you, being inside your sweet pussy." Her face turned so red he thought she was going to pop.

"I…" her gaze traveled his face, seeing his harshly full mouth, strong jaw, dark eyes glowing with hunger for her, Anya didn't know what to say.

Déisi let go with one hand, reached for her wrist and pressed her hand on his hard-on. "Honey, a man can't pretend, he can't just make himself be hard. I'm hard, for you. I want you. You can't believe all that fun and loving we shared in the hotel was fake."

He bent and lightly kissed her, then licked her lips, then slanted his mouth harder over hers and claimed her tenderness, capturing her tongue. When she responded, his hands dropped to cover her breasts.

She pulled back slightly, breathing fast. "Déisi -"

Against her lips, he said, "I've told you, *babia*, I cannot resist your beautiful tits. If you're near me, I'm going to have my hands on them." He kneaded them gently, long fingers stroking, squeezing, fondling until he elicited a breathy moan from her.

She grasped his wrists to stop him. Face flaming, she said, "Déisi, my granddad, it's the same as having your brothers in the other room."

Laughing, Déisi dropped his hands to her waist. "Then, come with me where we can have privacy, as much as we want for as long as we want. I can have someone come and pack your clothes and stuff. I left the sundress out because I'm hoping you'll wear it when we go to-"

"To where, Déisi? A hotel?" She made to move from him but he held her.

She stammered, "I…I mean we were in that hotel together because there wasn't really anything else we could have gone to at the time. But, I mean, I wasn't exactly brought up to hop into hotel rooms with men."

His hand slid to cradle the back of her head. Lifting it, he said, "*Na*, sweetheart. I have several houses; in Salzburg, France, other places, we can go wherever you want. We can stay in Venice while we have a house built if that's what you want."

He bit her bottom lip then lathed it. "I plan to make an honest woman out of you so you won't feel shame to…be…with me, eh? What do you say?"

Melting under his caresses, she stopped resisting him. Anya's smile burgeoning on sheer happiness, she asked, "Is that a proposal?"

He kissed her then lowered to one knee. Taking her hand, he said, "*Yah, mi* beautiful Anyalia. I love you more than life itself. Please, marry me. Will you marry me?"

Her hand fluttered at her throat as the tears gathered. "Déisi, I…don't know what to say."

"Ah, *babia*." He got to his feet and netted the back of her head linking their eyes so she could see the love in his gaze. "Say yes, just say yes," and he kissed her sweetly.

Her hands stroked up that thick masculine chest to twine behind his neck. Fingers tangling in the back of his hair, her body swelling and tingling against his, responding heat for heat.

Anya kissed him, crying softly, "Yes, Déisi, I'll marry you. I have been horridly miserable without you."

"*Mi Dios*, you make me the happiest man on the planet!" He lifted her, swinging her around before crushing her lips with his.

Epilogue

Her granddad and some of his friends, her father, a few friends of Anya's, and many of Déisi's associates, and of course his brothers were at the wedding.

Maisa wasn't invited.

Anya wore a silk and lace white wedding gown that Déisi thought about the entire ceremony peeling off her. He had to be patient. Their friends and family were so joyful at their union he had to be the cordial groom accepting best wishes, claps on the back, hugs and all that shit.

After the wedding service, they danced and ate and drank until the wee hours.

Déisi thought he would go insane watching every damned male, including his lecherous brothers, dance with his bride.

Finally, he just swooped her up and carried her out the door to hoots and hollers.

They had a reservation to spend their wedding night in a local hotel, but they left the reception too late and they had an early plane to catch to they headed straight for the airport.

At the airport, Anya slipped out of the gown and into slacks and a blouse.

It had been a long day and it was late. In First Class, Déisi tucked a cozy blanket around a drowsy Anya. Kissing her affectionately on the forehead, he murmured, "Sleep well, my wife."

Settling into the seat beside her, Déisi reached over and grasped her limp hand.

They snoozed in their captain chairs, holding hands.

When the plane landed, Anya nipped into the bathroom to change her clothes.

Déisi was standing at their seats waiting for her. "Son-of-a bitch," he groaned when she returned to him.

"Uh huh, sure, so much for trying to curb your cussing," she reproached with an affectionate smile.

His eyes ravishing her head to toe, pupils swollen a rich onyx and glittering fire-hot, he groaned, "Sweet, I can't be responsible for my behavior when you are wearing that fuck- uh, amazing sundress. You know damned well I'm going to go nuts being with you and not untying those strings."

Laughing, Anya bent to pick up her purse. "Hmm, I'm sure you'll be fine," and squealed when he smacked her on the butt.

"Déisi!" she scolded with a slap to his broad shoulder. "You need to behave while we're in public."

"*Da*, you should know better than to bend over in front of me. You're lucky that's all I did. I'm having visual memories of when I carried you onto the jet over my shoulder that first night. Damn, girl, I wanted so damned bad to crush your ass in my hands that day. It took all my will power to not- well..."

His grin mischievous, he said, "And now," he reached and gave her skirt a quick flip, pulling back before she slapped his hand.

"I'm doing my best not to haul you over my shoulder, shove that skirt up, pull those panties down just enough to spank that rear like I did the other night for your punishment in disobeying me and putting your life at risk. But then," he shrugged watching her face turn red, said with a grin. "I wouldn't be able to keep from playing with your pussy and sticking my fingers up-"

"Déisi! Stop!" She covered her flaming cheeks with her hands.

Chuckling at her discomfort, he said, "Come, let's go *mi* little temptress before I shove you into one of those teeny bathrooms and take you up against the door."

He set his hand on her lower back ushering her off the plane.

They had a limo waiting.

The limo hauled off down the highway.

In the back, "Déisi," Anya admonished after pushing his hand out from under her skirt for the fifth time. "The chauffer," she whispered, pushing at his other hand that was grabbing a breast.

"*Da, da*, I know, tis your fault, sweet wife, wearing that dress. You know how it turns me on. Damn," his groan sighed out, "you are going to regret teasing me when we get to the hotel."

Leaning into him with a flirtatious grin, pressing her bosom against his hard chest, Anya tickled his chin with a giggle. "Are you sure that I'm going to regret it? I don't think so."

"Minx." He swept her onto his lap, kissing her, trying to feel her up.

The chauffer struggled to keep his eyes off the rearview mirror.

The limo finally pulled into the hotel.

Déisi helped Anya out while the driver took care of the luggage.

The bellhop opened the door and handed Déisi two keys.

Before she could walk in, Déisi swept her up in his arms.

Announcing loudly, "Over the threshold, my bride, Mrs. Zukov." His lips sucked hers as he carried her in.

As soon as he set her on her feet, he said, "Now," eyes gleaming, he reached for a string at her shoulder.

There was a knock at the door. "Motherfu-" Déisi growled fiercely snatching the door open.

It was the driver with their luggage.

Anya stood to the side biting back her grin at a fuming Déisi as he waited impatiently for the driver, who was taking his time, putting their cases up.

When the chauffer moved to open the cases saying, "I will put your belongings up-"

"*Na!*" Déisi barked shoving bills in the driver's hand. "We're fine, thank you. Thank you, now," he opened the door and rudely pushed him out.

"Déisi!" Smothering her giggle, Anya scolded him, "Don't be so rude!"

"Come here, Mrs. Zukov, I have something for my bride." His grin lascivious, Déisi closed the door with his foot and reached again for the first string of her dress.

He couldn't help licking his lips as the string fell, and he untied the second. The bodice of the dress tumbled and Anya's bare breasts were exposed.

Groaning, "Ah, *babia, mi Dios*," he clutched her breasts, winding his thick fingers around them, his thumbs rubbing her nipples. Pinching them, he pulled on the rosy beads until they hardened into little peaks.

He licked his way down her neck to suck a nipple into his mouth. His hands moved to her waist and he pushed the rest of the dress down to the floor.

Standing back, smoldering eyes glazing, he murmured, "Ah, I am the luckiest man in the universe. I am married to the most beautiful, the sweetest woman in all the lands. I can't wait to sink inside your hot liquid velvet, Wife."

Anya stood in a tiny swath of white silk. She said with a coy wink, "That's what I used to call your sexy shivery voice." Her eyes filled with tender desire, she whispered, "I love you, Mr. Zukov."

"Ah, *mi babia*, what did I tell you about that, calling me by my last name? Come, I owe you several punishments now." He slid the white silk panties off leaving her nude and then lifted her into his arms.

He strode to the bedroom and gently laid her down on the thick mattress.

Never taking his glowing eyes off her, Déisi stripped off his shirt and stepped out of his trousers.

As he climbed on the bed, nudging her legs apart, his hand on her thigh working his fingers up to her sex, Anya giggled, "What about the condom, Husband?"

Smiling his love for her radiating from every pore, he replied, "Ah, we are married, Wife, they are no longer needed. I want a babe growing in your flat little belly as soon as possible. Do you agree, *yah*?"

"*Yah,*" she laughed, mimicking him. Holding her arms up to him, her words filled with love, she said, "I want to build a family with you, Déisi Zukov, my husband, my love."

Her arms encircled him as he lowered his body over hers and claimed his beloved wife.

The End

Dear Reader, thank you for acquiring <u>Liquid Velvet!</u>

I know you could have picked any number of books to read, but you picked this book and for that I am extremely grateful.

I hope you enjoyed this novel, and if you did, **please leave a review where you purchased it**, *and look for other exciting titles in my name!*

About the Author

Louise Furley loves writing romance with a huge helping of suspense. She finds it exciting to study new lands and learn everything she can about the area and the natives that call it home.

Sunny Florida is home where Louise is a graduate of St. Thomas University with a master's degree in Mental Health.

Louise is the author of numerous published novels. When not researching or writing, she is dreaming of unique plots, and discovering fresh ventures she hasn't yet experienced in the world.

Ride along with her as she travels new and thrilling journeys!

If you loved this adventurous romance, please check out the first chapter of <u>Shawn's Prisoner</u>!

Shawn's Prisoner

Chapter One

The five male prisoners were already secured and sitting one to a seat on the prison transport bus. Three officers in their olive green uniforms were scattered around safeguarding them.

Behind the wheel the driver worked the day's crossword puzzle, and the chief deputy stood in the open doorway. Another officer waited just outside the bus door.

All eyes focused on the last prisoner being led up the walk. The female prisoner's hands were cuffed behind her back and two female officers on either side of her held her arms.

One of the males on the bus whistled a long low note, muttered under his breath, "Boy, am I gonna dream about that tonight with my fist in my pants."

Prisoner Beau Dyce leaned his red head forward to whisper in the ear of the prisoner in front of him, Shawn Darkonn. "There weren't supposed to be any females on this bus, looks like we got three coming."

Shawn nodded, his eyes narrowed on the approaching women.

Beau shook his head and said, "That is not good, Shawn, but check that girl's hair. Hell, like all the colors of a sunflower, bro. Can't be real, tis like a big wavy cloud around her shoulders and curls spiraling down her back."

Shawn turned slightly in his seat to Dyce, a sarcastic brow rose. "Are you through? You gonna write a damned sonnet about the lass, Beau? Put your *bluidy* eyes back in your head."

1

Smirking at his friend and fellow prisoner, Beau Dyce leaned back and replied, "She's a bonny *bure*, lad. Aye, maybe I will write a song at that."

The men watched the officers bringing the girl to the bus. Walking awkwardly with her hands bound behind her, she wore a red dress that fit snugly over her slender yet softly curvaceous figure. The short skirt flipped just below her thighs as the shapely legs propelled her slowly towards the bus.

Dwarfed by the larger females, her blue eyes radiated such vivid panic her terror could be seen a mile away. If she hadn't been supported, she likely would have swooned from sheer fright.

The prisoner in front of Shawn, Daf Jamieson, dreads tied back in a ponytail, rested an arm the color of shiny mahogany on the back of the seat. The huge bicep bulging under the orange jumpsuit would make Hercules jealous.

Military tattoos on his upper arm stretched when his muscles flexed. His gaze also on the girl, he twisted his head slightly to say to Shawn behind him, "Looks like jailbait."

One of the corrections officers, Tomas Trent, informed him, "Can't be, she's being extradited to a woman's prison in Montana, has to be at least 18."

When the women reached the bus, the female officers hesitated, apparently trying to figure out how to get the prisoner with her hands shackled behind her back facing several very high steps, up and into the bus.

The last male deputy, the oldest at 50, Ritchie Marx, was still outside the bus combing his curly salt and pepper hair. He tucked the comb in his back pocket, wrapped his chunky hands around the girl's waist, lifted the petite young woman up all the steps in one move and handed her to the chief deputy, Vance Malone.

Appearing quite pleased to have custody of the girl, a leering grin split the forty-something Malone's thick face. He rolled a hefty arm around her waist, high up, just under her breasts and held her taut against him.

Her hands bound behind her, she struggled, twisting, trying to pull away. He laughed at her efforts like he was plucking the wings off a helpless pinned fly.

Malone maneuvered her into the front seat and sat down next to her. He unlocked her manacles, brought her hands around in front of her and then cuffed both wrists high up to a bar next to the window.

The door swung closed after the last three boarded.

The two female officers, Leena Shipley and Bella Calla, stood halfway down the aisle chatting while everyone got settled. Leena had a gun holstered on her hip, as a corrections officer, Bella did not.

Sitting back casually, Shawn Darkonn observed the occupants of the bus through lowered lids. He watched the girl prisoner trapped next to Malone struggling to get away from him. The husky deputy chuckled and whispered in her ear.

Judging by the way her pale face flushed with color, he wasn't talking about going to church on Sunday. She turned her head and the rest of her cornered body to the window, writhing away from him.

From his seat, Shawn could see shame, abject fear, and the glint of tears in her big eyes.

The girl was the only one cuffed the way she was, as if the deputy had deliberately put her on display, and to keep her suspended so she couldn't fight him off. She was utterly vulnerable to the letch sitting beside her.

The male prisoners had only one wrist comfortably shackled low to a horizontal metal bar along the armrest.

3

His voice like the low sound of an animal's rumbled warning, Shawn growled, "*Miss*."

Leena Shipley, in her late thirties, a tall, slightly overweight brunette turned hazel eyes back at him. He jerked his head once, motioning towards the front of the bus.

Leena followed his line of indication and saw Vance Malone with his arm around the female prisoner, pressing his barrel-chested body against her. Rolling her eyes, Leena huffed, "*Shit*." Her long legs striding swiftly up the aisle, she poked the chief deputy in the shoulder. "Malone."

The girl had her legs tightly crossed. Her cuffed hands were above her shoulders locked against the metal pole by the window, tears streamed down her face.

Malone's big meaty paw was high up her thigh, trying to shove between her legs. Glaring annoyed at Leena, he snapped, "What?"

Leena set her hand on the back of his seat, the other on her broad hip in the tight, olive green polyester pants. "Come on, Vance, you know the procedure. One of us has to be next to the female."

"Get lost," Malone sneered and turned back to the girl. "It's going to be a long trip and I have something here to keep me entertained, right honey?"

Grinning at the defenseless girl, he chucked her chin then slid his heavy hand around the back of her neck forcing her to face him. He leaned in like he was about to latch his fleshy lips on her small mouth.

Her voice slightly irked like she was talking to a child she was about to paddle, Leena snapped harshly, "Vance, you get up right now or I'll have the other officers help me get you up."

Exhaling a grating sigh, the irritated deputy released the girl and slid to the end of the seat. He shuffled to his feet with a beleaguered grunt.

Before leaving, he leaned down with his hand on the back of the seat. Combing brown hair straight back off his forehead with fat fingers, he drew one of those thick fingers down the girl's round cheek and said with a sly promise, "Remember, babydoll, we still have a party planned."

She tried to turn her head away from him. Cupping her chin, he roughly pulled her face up close to his and whispered in a guttural leer, "A party with just me," his hot breath steaming her skin, he smirked, "and you."

Although clearly terrified, the trapped girl labored to glare coldly at him, but the trembling plush lips and streaming tears negated the defiant glare.

Sitting behind them, his voice gruff with strength matching his powerful body, the skin of his dark face darkening further, Daf Jamieson said to the deputy, "Leave off the girl then, man."

None of the officers commented, but redheaded Beau joined in, "Yeah, bugger off, you asshole."

Not taking his eyes or hands off the girl, Malone sneered at the felons, "Fuck off, you Scotty dicks."

Still meanly pinching her jaw with his big hand, he said with a cringe worthy smile to the female prisoner, "It's okay, babydoll, I find those tears pouring out of those angry, frightened eyes a bitch of a turn on. Not that you need any other enhancements."

His lusty gaze showered so heatedly down her body she recoiled like he had physically groped her.

She jerked her chin out of his hand with anger, to his amusement; he liked a little fire in his conquests. It was more fun when they fought him. The lust turned into a snarky

5

smirk, he gave her an insolent wink, a promise of things later to come.

Patting the side of her face with a thick hand, he left her and flopped down on another seat, propping his feet up on a first aid kit on the floor in front of him.

Leena slid in and took his place next to the girl.

The bus finally started up and headed to the highway. His back against the corner of the window, Shawn slid down in his seat stretching his long legs under the seat in front of him. Crossing the arm not cuffed over his stomach he went to sleep.

Scratching his short-cropped beard as red as his curly hair, Beau Dyce asked the deputy in the seat across the aisle, "Jim, how long do you expect it to take for us to get from North Dakota to the prison in Montana?"

In a faint Hispanic accent Jim Vega replied, "We are going way up north, northwest, supposed to take 15 to 20 hours, maybe more. We will be passing the Kootenai National Forest, skirting the Cabinet Mountains Wilderness.

"The road we will be traveling on winds up and around some other mountains. Other than the high road up the mountain, there are no other roads or buildings in that part of the wilderness, so, I pray we do not break down or it will be a long damned walk out."

Crossing his bony legs, at 5'9 Jim Vega was the shortest of the officers. The only other person, other than two of the women that was shorter than him was prisoner Caleb Taylor.

At forty, Caleb was small and wiry and losing his hair which was also wiry. A quiet, nervous man constantly straightening his glasses like an uncontrollable tic, Caleb had been an accountant and had gotten caught embezzling from a huge corporation. He had five years to serve.

6

Beau said to Officer Vega, "Doesn't your wife miss you on these long trips?"

Vega chuckled with a swagger in the way he smoothed his short dark hair back with his palms. "Naw, but my girlfriends do. The wife is busy carpooling our daughters."

Beau nodded with an unreadable expression then laid his head against the window and did as Shawn had, closed his eyes and nodded off.

Altogether, there were 14 people on the bus; the driver, 5 male corrections officers counting Chief Deputy Malone, 5 male prisoners, 1 female prisoner, and 2 female officers.

The driver drove for four hours before stopping for their first break at a rest area.

Deputy Malone stood up first, stretching and yawning like a donkey after chomping a dry dinner of musty hay. He dragged a hand across his damp mouth then wiped the hand on his uniform and said to the driver, "You getting off, Stan?"

Shaking his head in the negative, settling back in the worn cushioned seat, the grey haired driver crossed his arms and closed his eyes planning a quick catnap while the rest took breaks.

Shifting down lower in his seat, he replied, "Nope. We got an unlucky number on this bus, 13. I ain't going nowhere until we get to the prison."

Chuckling, Malone shook his head. "That makes no sense, Stan. There are 14 of us altogether."

His eyes closed, the driver muttered, "I don't count me, I'm an extra, you all are the passengers."

Leena Shipley and Bella Calla unchained the female prisoner and took her off the bus first.

Deputy Malone's hungry eyes followed the red dress swinging up the walk to the building's restrooms. For

7

security, the men were taken to the restrooms one at a time after the women returned.

Shawn was last off. The big strapping black-haired man was handcuffed to the shorter, thinner Jim Vega.

Standing outside the bus with the female prisoner, drawing on a cigarette, Leena squinted at Shawn through a stream of smoke as he was returning with Vega.

Next to her, Bella chuckled. "You're liking what you see, girl?"

Leena's eyes traced the tall prisoner coming down the walk. "Oh yeah, hon." Her gaze straight at Shawn's broad shoulders. "I'm loving Shawn Darkonn's husky Scottish accent, his wavy black hair, and those midnight eyes."

Drawing in a long drag, squinting, she blew it out with her words, "Those black eyes look like they hold treacherous secrets deep inside, very hot."

"Huh." Bella turned ready to help the female prisoner up the steps. "What about those scars, Leena? Find them hot too?"

Her lips sucking on the end of her cigarette, Leena mused, "They hardly mar that handsome face, only give him a dangerous, violent edge. I bet he's rough and aggressive as hell in bed."

Her hazel eyes darted to Bella and back to Shawn who was nearing. "We've had a few talks. Even that deep quiet voice makes my panties wet." The female prisoner winced and blushed.

"Geez Leena, TMI," Bella moaned. "But I have to agree, we lucked out on this trip male hunk wise. Shawn and that dreamy Black prisoner, Daf Jamieson, and the gigantic prisoner Zachary Stockton are the tallest in the group. All have wide muscled shoulders like boxers." She confided with a grin, "I like 'em big too. All over."

8

Nodding in agreement, Leena tossed her cigarette to the ground and pulled her pack out for another one. "Oh yeah, hon, love those hard, sculpted arms and chests that are nicely outlined in the short-sleeved orange jump suits. The only one I have concerns about is that humongous prisoner, the quiet one."

Bella was nudging the female prisoner to the door of the bus. "Yeah, Zachary, brute's on the scary side. Guy is like a blond goliath. He's even damned taller and stockier than the other two leaner men, Shawn and Daf. He's built like a freakin' fortress."

Leena lit her second cigarette. "I'd do them all at once, no prob. Got three holes, yeah? But Shawn is my fav."

The female prisoner's face turned beet red. She ducked her head trying to turn away from hearing any more of the pudgy officer's salacious declarations.

Bella laughed. "Okay, on that note, I'm getting the girl set on the bus before Vance can get his filthy hands on her again." She gave the prisoner a little push up the steps, and followed her inside.

As Shawn and Vega approached, Shawn's eyes went to Leena's cigarette. Her smile flirtatious, she said, "Want one, tall, dark, and sexy?"

A corner of Shawn's mouth pulled in denting a dimple in his cheek that instantly drew Leena's attention. "*Sea,* pardon me," he corrected, "yes, that would be great."

Leena gave him a cigarette. She held the lighter close to her chest so he would have to lean over to her to get it lit.

He cupped his hands around the cigarette and lighter, his eyes didn't dip down the front of her shirt like she'd hoped. Still, she all but shook her breasts in his face.

Jim Vega took out his smokes and the three stood quietly for a moment puffing.

9

Shawn asked Leena, "What's up with the lass? I thought this was a male only transport."

The tall brunette tucked her shirt in deeper, deliberately causing the polyester green uniform to tighten across her drooping breasts and plump belly. All of the officers only wore the bare minimum of weapons belts.

Their radios would be useless in the mountains, and the additional batons, Tasers, etc. would be uncomfortable sitting through the lengthy travel, so they were stored in a lockbox in the rear.

"Well, hotness," Leena sidled up close to Shawn, "it wasn't planned. Her extradition paperwork just came through. I think Malone had something to do with it."

Jim Vega finished his smoke, un-cuffed himself from Shawn and got back on the bus.

"Hmm." Through the window, Shawn could see Malone trying to talk Bella Calla, a solidly built, athletic Latina, into letting him sit next to the girl.

Bella was shaking her head, her dark brown hair in a tight knot barely moved.

"So," Shawn asked Leena, "what's up with the dress? Why isn't she in a prison uniform?"

Blowing out a funnel of smoke, Leena shrugged. Her brazen gaze checked out the prisoner from his strong shoulders down to the orange pants. Zeroing in on the zipper as if trying to see behind it, her gaze darted up to the scars on his impassive face, finally settling on the inscrutable black eyes.

"We only had sizes 2X to 4X. There're some big girls in the jail. The jumpsuits were so big they just slid right off her. The dress isn't even hers. When she was first brought into holding, some of the other girls wanted at her. They shredded her clothes before the deputies could get in and get the women off her."

Shawn's black brows rose to his hairline, then drew down sharply. "You're kidding."

Shaking her head, Leena sucked on her cigarette. "Nope. Like a pack of junkyard felines tearing at a kitten. Some of 'um don't care male or female. She's a beauty and young, the deputies should have known better than to put her in there with those hardcore heifer-bitches."

Exhaling audibly, she flicked the butt of the cigarette knocking the ashes off. Her eyes still on the prisoner's face she didn't notice the ashes float down and land on her shoe.

A flicker of anger crossing his stoic features, Shawn muttered in a low voice, "You need *tae* get that dress off her."

Leena snickered. "Yeah, you sound like everyone else."

He frowned in annoyance. "*Na*, no, not what I meant. I meant you need *tae* get pants, a belt and a looser shirt *tae* hide those curves on her. She's too accessible like that. Gonna cause nothing but trouble amongst the males."

"True that. The chief has been trying to bang her since he laid eyes on her." Clamping the cigarette between her teeth, one eye squinting with the effort, Leena pushed escaped strands of brown hair back up in her bun.

Loose flab on her upper arms wobbled in the short sleeves with her efforts. She clipped two fingers around the butt again taking it out of her mouth and crossed her arms.

Shawn glanced down at Leena, his forehead furrowed in question. She was tall but he had a lot of inches on her. She was at least ten years older than him, he was still a few years shy of thirty, but there were ages of hardness in his shuttered eyes.

Taking a puff, he held his cigarette between the pads of his fingertip and thumb and curled it back in his palm, exhaling the smoke like a slow drawl.

"Yeah." Leena told him, "She's only been in our custody for three days. She was being held in the county jail pending her trial. She was briefly in the prison so she could be transported per the extradition. Malone couldn't get near her in the women's side of cells, but he finally managed to get to her in the laundry room this morning.

"Like you said, the dress made it too easy. He had her on the floor and was pushing between her legs tearing off her panties, when a practice fire alarm happened to go off and another deputy found 'em and wrestled him off her. The slob keeps trying to feel her up every time he gets near her."

"Why the hell wasn't he reported?" The dark brows now slashed straight down, his nostrils flared fiercely. He looked so angry Leena was taken aback. Shawn inhaled deeply and held the smoke in before harshly blowing it out.

She lifted one shoulder in a slight shrug. "It's prison, honey, no one much cares. If he wasn't so blatant he could get away with more. Mark my words, that sly horndog will have that girl pregnant before we get her to the prison camp."

"What's she being extradited for?"

She smiled cagey and amused. "Murder," she replied.

His eyes shot up to the young woman cowering in the blue vinyl bus seat. "Her? You serious?"

Taking a last puff, Leena nodded. "Yeah. To be honest, I don't believe it myself. I read the report, sounds fishy, like some guy is trying to railroad her into being with him. You'd need to read it to understand." She tossed her cigarette. "Let's go."

They climbed back on board and the bus took off.

If you would like to read about Shawn and Cheri's story, please go to your favorite book site and purchase it!

And, remember, all author's live for their reviews.

If you enjoy Shawn and Cheri's dangerous adventure and HEA, please leave a review!

Thank you!

Don't forget to check out other books in my name.